BE
THE
GIRL

BE
THE
GIRL

ALSO BY K. A. TUCKER

A Fate of Wrath & Flame

A Curse of Blood & Stone

A Queen of Thieves & Chaos

BE
THE
GIRL

K.A. TUCKER

ISBN 978-0-9916860-8-7 (ebook)

ISBN 978-1-9990154-0-4 (Ingram paperback)

ISBN 978-0-9916860-7-0 (KDP paperback)

Editing by Jennifer Sommersby

Cover design by Hang Le

To Lia,
All of my greatest hopes for you.
And many of my worst fears.
Don't let anyone take away your smile.

CHAPTER
ONE

AUGUST 25, 2018

Dear Julia,

I'm writing this because I promised Mom I'd start keeping a journal. A diary, I guess I should call it. Dr. C. said it would be a good way to channel my deepest thoughts and feelings, so I don't bottle things up again. Between you and me, I think Dr. C. smokes a lot of weed. I'd rather keep my deepest thoughts safely locked inside my head where they belong. But I've put Mom through hell these past months. I've seen her cry way too much. So ... here we are. I have no idea where we are, actually. Somewhere near Brandon, Manitoba, I think the sign back there said. I knew a Brandon once. In second grade, someone dared him to drink a bottle of red paint during art class. It was nontoxic, but he had to be closely monitored in art class after that.

What do people write about in diaries, anyway? Dr. C. said to start with the basics—how I feel about our big move across the country and beginning at a new high school, where I don't know a soul. You know, easy things. As long as I'm *being honest, she said, because the only person I'll be lying to in here is myself. I'd prefer to call it denial.*

She also said that if "journaling" feels weird or pointless, pretend I'm writing a letter to someone. Even an imaginary someone. So ... hey, Julia. I'll try not to bore you. Mom promised that my diary would be off-limits to her snooping, but I don't believe that for a hot second, so expect a lot of mind-numbing entries about grade eleven English and my mother, until I can find a good hiding place for this at Uncle Merv's.

Until next time,

Aria Jones

P.S. I've written my new last name at least a thousand times on this drive so far. If I still screw it up, I'm a lost cause.

MOM CASTS a nervous smile at me as we wait for the front door to open.

"Do you think he fell asleep?" Light flashes through the gauzy curtains of the small, white house's bay window, and a buzz of voices carries. A TV is on somewhere inside.

"I hope not. But it *is* late." Her forehead wrinkles, checking her watch. "He's usually in bed by seven."

It's after eleven now. And Uncle Merv is eighty years old.

"Maybe he can't hear over the TV?" I roll my shoulders to loosen them. Three twelve-hour days in the CR-V and motel sleeping has left me stiff and aching for my bed.

Too bad Mom sold it.

It would've been too big for my new bedroom at Uncle

Merv's, she promised, as I watched two men march out the door with the plush queen-sized mattress in their hands and triumphant grins on their faces. They scored a great deal. *Everyone* who came through our house during the rushed "everything must go" contents sale Mom threw together scored big, leaving us with just enough to fill our car and a small U-Haul cargo trailer. It was a hasty departure—a decision she made only a month ago, solidified after a phone call to an uncle I've never met and an I-quit-my-lawyer-job-today-let's-start-over-somewhere-new dinner conversation over cold Hawaiian pizza.

The hinges on the metal storm door screech as she pulls it open to knock on the wooden door again, this time harder.

Still no answer.

"What do we do now?" I take in our surroundings. The remnants of a plant sit by my feet, brown and shriveled within its forest-green ceramic pot. Next to it is a worn wooden bench on a porch that has lost half its white paint to peeling. To my left, a hedge of leggy bushes runs along the property line, hiding whatever's beyond. The gardens are overgrown, the bushes threaded with long grass.

Even in the dark of night, it's clear that Uncle Merv's modest two-story home is the most neglected of the four houses in this cul-du-sac, surrounded by farmers' fields, on the outskirts of Eastmonte, Ontario.

Mom tests the door handle and finds it unlocked. "I guess we go in. This *is* our home now, too." She shrugs and pushes the door open. "Hello?"

My nose crinkles with disgust.

The air inside the house smells *rotten*, though I can't be more specific. Mom smells it, too; I can tell by the way her nostrils flare. That's the first thing I notice when I trail her through the cramped doorway. The second thing I notice is that we've stepped back in time. To which decade, I can't be sure, but it involves tacky rose-patterned wallpaper, lace curtains, and wood *everything*.

"Hello? Uncle Merv?" Mom calls out again.

"Debra? Is that you?" A gruff voice calls from our left. A hefty, white-haired man struggles to haul himself out of the salmon-pink wingback chair that faces a TV, no more than four feet from the screen. "I'm sorry, my hearing isn't the greatest anymore."

Mom's tired face splits with a wide smile as she traipses across the living room of mismatched furniture and floral wallpaper to embrace him. "You had us worried for a minute."

"Worried about what? That I finally kicked the bucket?" He chuckles, returning her hug, his rotund belly making her slight frame seem all the more slender. "Likely soon, but not yet. How was the drive?"

"Oh, fine." She waves it off, as if a thirty-six-hour road trip through flat lands and remote forest with everything you own is nothing. "I'm so sorry we're late. There was a terrible accident near Elliot Lake this morning and the road was closed for hours. A car ... a moose ..." She grimaces. "Anyway, we're glad to finally be here. Uncle Merv, *this* is my daughter, Aria." She gestures toward me and I step forward, feeling my uncle's clouded eyes settle on me.

He clears his throat and offers me a curt nod, his sagging jowls jiggling with the gesture. "You're the spitting image of your mother when she was your age."

I smile politely as I tuck strands of my long, sable-brown hair behind my ear. "Yeah, that's what everyone says."

He opens his mouth, but then hesitates as if reconsidering his words. "You know, Debra used to spend two weeks

4

here every summer with us. Until you were how old—thirteen, was it?" He peers at my mom.

Her face pinches with thought. "Fourteen. I stopped coming the summer before high school."

"That's right. You were busy with summer jobs after that." He shakes his head. "Connie always looked forward to those visits. She'd spend the whole month before cleaning this place top to bottom until it sparkled."

It's far from that now, I note, eying the layer of dust that coats the nearby lamp and the stacks of hastily folded newspapers on the floor. A sizable cobweb dangles from the ceiling in the corner.

"And what about *you*? You didn't look forward to my visits?" Mom teases, reaching out to squeeze Uncle Merv's forearm—her signature move for offering comfort. I imagine the wound from losing Aunt Connie to a massive stroke five months ago, after sixty-one years of marriage, is still fresh.

"I looked forward to the free garden labor." He runs his thumbs along the underside of his red suspenders as he chuckles. No doubt they're all that's holding up his pants.

Mom laughs. "Well, now you have free labor times two. How is the garden this year?"

He grunts. "Wild. The apple trees are ready to split in half and there're too many damn tomato plants. I told Iris not to plant so many but she didn't listen. Now I don't know what to do with them all. I've got tomatoes coming out my a—"

"Aria and I will be happy to pick and can them for you. If I can remember how, it's been so long. Right, Aria?"

"Uh ... sure." *Can them? What does that mean?*

"Well, that'd be much appreciated." Uncle Merv has the kind of gruff voice that makes me think he'll need to cough to clear the phlegm from it any moment now.

"There's a tuna casserole in the fridge if you're hungry. Iris's not as good a cook as Connie but it's not half bad."

Who is Iris?

"That sounds great." Mom gives him her best fake smile and I purse my lips to stifle my grin. She likes tuna *anything* as much as I do—not at all.

Uncle Merv more waddles than walks toward the narrow staircase ahead of us. I can't tell if it's on account of age or his excessive weight. Probably both. "Also, Iris tidied upstairs. Haven't been up there in years but I'm assuming it's in order. She always was the fussiest of Connie's friends."

Ah, mystery solved.

"She didn't have to do that, and I'm sure it's fine."

"Well, then ..." He smooths his hands over his belly. "It's past my bedtime. You know me, I like to get up with the birds. 'Course, you guys are still probably adjusting to the time zone. I'll try not to make too much noise in the morning." He stops near the open door and scowls at the driveway. "I thought you weren't bringing anything with you!" It sounds accusatory.

"*Barely* anything. A TV and coffee maker, stuff like that," my mom placates in a soothing tone, catching my eye as she pats Uncle Merv's shoulder. She warned that he might have a hard time adjusting to this new arrangement, despite his willingness. He *is* eighty, after all, and he tends to fret when his routine is interrupted. I'd say taking in his forty-five-year-old niece and her *almost* sixteen-year-old daughter for the foreseeable future hasn't just interrupted his routine; it's about to wreak havoc on it.

He makes a sound that might be acceptance. "I suppose you'll be needing help unloading. The kids from next door should be able to help. Emmett's a big, strong boy."

"There's nothing in there that Aria and I can't manage. Don't you worry about it, Uncle Merv." In an airy tone, she says, "Aria, why don't you head upstairs to check out your room. It's on the left."

I can tell that's code for "I need a moment alone with Uncle Merv to talk about you."

The narrow, steep steps offer a noisy creak as I climb them and venture into my new bedroom—a narrow space with steeply slanted ceilings painted Easter yellow. A window sits centered on the far side, draped with thin, gauzy curtains that do little to block out the street lights. It's framed by bookshelves and a small bench. My mom was right—there's no way my furniture would have fit in here. It's already cramped with a twin bed as it is. I don't even have a closet. It smells freshly cleaned, at least; the scent of lemon Pledge and fabric softener battling to mask the rotten odor wafting from downstairs.

"You haven't told Iris *anything*, right?" I hear my mom whisper. I pause to listen from inside the doorway.

"That old gossip? Hell, I'm no fool. All she knows is that you and Howie divorced and he's got a new family. I had to give her something and I figured you wouldn't care if they knew that much."

"No, that's fine. I don't care if the town knows my ex-husband is a cheating bastard who knocked up his paralegal." There's no shortage of bitterness in her voice. "But I want to make sure Aria gets a fresh start and she can't do that if anyone finds out about what happened."

I feel my cheeks burn with a mixture of embarrassment and shame.

"They won't hear it from me." There's a pause. "How's she doing?"

"I think she's okay. Seems to be, anyway." The way my

mother says that, it doesn't sound convincing. "Listen, thanks again for taking us in. I know we're turning your life upside down—"

"No, no, I'm happy to have you. Truth is, it'll be nice to talk to someone besides myself. And I can use the help around here. I've been relying on Iris too much and I'm afraid she's getting the wrong idea. In case you haven't noticed, I'm not quite as fit as I once was."

"Yeah, Cheez Whiz sandwiches and whiskey will do that." Mom's musical laughter carries up the stairs. "Good night, Uncle Merv. We'll catch up more in the morning."

The stairs creak and I venture farther into my bedroom so I don't look guilty of eavesdropping. I'm at the window when Mom leans against the door frame, a wistful smile on her lips. "This used to be my room when I stayed here." Her eyes dart from corner to corner before settling on the bed, adorned with a green leaf comforter. "I slept in that."

"It's small." Almost too small to be called twin-sized.

"Let me know how the mattress is. We might have to invest in a new one. Nothing's been updated here in decades." She wanders over to gingerly sit on the window bench, as if testing it. "Uncle Merv built this for me when I was eight. I'd sit here and read for hours." She smooths a hand over a bookcase. "They could use a new coat of paint."

"Everything in here could," I mumble.

"That's a good idea! Let's go to the paint store tomorrow morning and pick out a color. You know, freshen this place up a bit. What do you think?"

"Indigo blue?" I raise a questioning eyebrow.

Mom's nose crinkles. "What about something more bright and cheery?"

I shrug. "I like dark and moody." My gaze drifts over the

slanted ceiling. "I think it'd look good. Kind of like a night-time sky."

Mom's eyes trail mine, as if reconsidering her objection. "Yeah, okay. We could get those glow-in-the-dark stickers you like."

I bite my tongue against the urge to remind her that I'm not five anymore.

Mom rises and wanders back slowly, opening the desk drawers on her way past. "This will work for your home-work, right?"

"I don't do homework at a desk."

"What? Of course you do! You had that little purple lamp that we'd shine on the wall at night. Remember, shadow puppets?" She uses her hands to mime the shape for a dog.

"That was when I was, like, eight." I've been doing my homework at the kitchen island or sitting cross-legged on my bed for years now. Mom's never been around to notice though, too busy at the law firm or buried under a stack of legal paperwork in her home office.

"Right." Her head bows, and the guilt radiates from her. "Things are going to change, Aria. You have a new school; you'll have new friends. I can't write the Ontario bar exam until March so I'll be around *all the time* for the next seven months. So much, you'll be sick of me." She laughs. "And even when I go back to work, I'll make sure I'm only working part-time, so I'm more"—her throat bobs with a hard swallow—"involved in your life. Things are going to change. For both of us. I promise."

I could say things now—namely, that none of what happened was her fault, that it was all mine—my thoughts, my feelings, my choices. But, just like her, I am ready to put the past behind me.

"They kind of already have?" I hold my hands out to gesture at my new room in this sad little white hovel, a far cry from the sizable house we left outside Calgary. But here, three provinces away, I'm not that same girl. My name's not even the same, now that I've legally changed it to take my mother's maiden name. My dad didn't bat an eye when we set the paperwork and a pen in front of him. That's when I knew he'd already all but disowned me.

"You're right, they have. And we have a lot to do around here to get this place back in shape." She sighs, catching a cobweb that dangles from a corner with her finger. "I knew Uncle Merv was having a hard time adjusting to bachelor life but Aunt Connie must be rolling in her grave." She rubs a hand over her weary eyes. "Get some sleep. We have a busy day tomorrow." She drops her voice to a whisper. "God knows how long it will take to find the corpse of whatever died down there."

CHAPTER
TWO

It's after ten by the time I venture downstairs, my hair damp from a shower. Mom is in the kitchen on hands and knees scrubbing furiously, dressed in her yoga outfit and yellow rubber gloves. "'Morning."

"Oh, good morning, hon! Try Iris's carrot cake. It's delicious. And there's some coffee left in the pot for you. Mugs are in the cupboard above it." She sounds *way* too cheery.

I pause a moment to take in the kitchen for the first time. It's as old and derelict as the rest of the house, with golden oak wooden cupboards huddled into a small space and mismatched white-and-ivory-colored appliances. A four-person rectangular table sits tucked in against the wall. Half of it is covered with flyers and unopened mail. Along the brown laminate countertop are miscellaneous pots and pans—contents of the cupboard she's scrubbing, if I had to guess. The smell of bleach lingers in the air.

"Did you sleep well?" Mom asks as I fetch a coffee mug and pour coffee.

"Not really. The sun woke me up."

"I figured. That room faces east. We'll get you some blackout curtains when we go shopping today."

"It was hot, too."

"Doesn't the ceiling fan work?"

"Yeah, but it was making this weird rattling sound, like it was going to fall and, like, *chop my head off* or something." Worries that don't inspire a deep sleep. I spy Uncle Merv in the garden through the back door, plucking red tomatoes off the vine and tucking them in a basket. The tomatoes match the color of his suspenders, the same ones he was wearing last night. It's a decent-sized yard, I note, full of fruit trees, with neighboring farm fields stretching far beyond.

Uncle Merv shuffles slowly along, his mouth moving as if he's talking to someone, but I don't see anyone around. "He wasn't lying about getting up early." Four thirty, according to the clock on my nightstand. That's when I woke up to his first of *many* phlegmy coughing fits.

Mom chuckles. "Yeah. We'll have to buy earplugs."

I flop into a kitchen chair at the table, my fingers busy combing through my freshly washed hair. I cringe with disgust at the slick strands. "Oh my God, I still have shampoo in my hair!"

Mom glances over her shoulder once before returning to her task. "I noticed the water pressure is bad."

"*And* it suddenly turned scalding. I think I have third-degree burns on my back." My body stiffens, as if mention of the injury is enough to make the pain flare.

"That was my fault. I shouldn't have used the kitchen sink while you were showering. That's the thing about these old houses." She sighs. "Don't worry. Calling a plumber is at the top of my *very* long to-do list, along with getting cable run into our bedrooms and the internet upgraded. He's still on dial-up, can you believe that?"

"I don't even know what that means." I spy the pad of lined paper next to her coffee mug. She must have at least twenty things jotted down already. That's my mom—the queen of organization and order. Sure enough, the word "plumber" is scrawled on the first line, followed by "new toilet" and "fix water pressure?" in brackets beside it. Below that reads "cleaning lady."

I frown. "Why are you cleaning if you're going to pay someone to come in and clean?"

"Because I couldn't leave the moldy spoiled bag of onions that stunk up the house for that poor soul. But I think I've got it out. A few hours of fresh air and some candles, and maybe my stomach won't turn." She stands with a groan, peeling off the rubber gloves and brushing away a strand of her wavy, sable-brown hair from her sweaty forehead. Gray roots peek out from her ponytail, something my mom is normally on top of but let slip this past month. I scan her list again. Sure enough, "find a new hair salon" is on there—number four.

"How could he stand it?"

"Who, Uncle Merv?" She snorts. "He's always had a terrible sense of smell." She takes a large gulp of her coffee and checks her watch. "Come on, you'll have to eat that in the car. We have a million things to do."

"What about unpacking the U-Haul?"

She waves it off. "Later. Let's try to be home for lunch at one, after Uncle's had his nap. Preferably with something better to eat than what's in there." She points to the fridge in the corner, her nose crinkling with disgust.

"WHICH BOX NEXT?" I ask through pants, sweat coating the back of my neck. When we left Calgary, temperatures were dwindling, the cool nights needing heavy blankets. But summer shows no sign of leaving Eastmonte, Ontario, anytime soon.

Mom's hands sit perched on her hips as she stares into the U-Haul. "You know what? Let's leave the rest until after the house is cleaned and your room is finished. No point moving things twice and I don't have to return it until Monday."

"Okay. I guess I'll start painting?" I was fully expecting Mom to reconsider her agreement to my dark and moody indigo blue when we stood in the paint aisle of Home Depot, but she was the first to pull out the various paint chips for comparison.

"We have to prep first. Why don't you start by taping around the built-ins ..." Her voice trails as she watches a black sedan pull into the driveway next door.

"Are those the neighbors?" The ones she met at Aunt Connie's funeral earlier this year. She hasn't told me much about them, other than that they have two teenaged children and they've lived next door for years.

"The Hartfords, yes." We watch as a blonde lady in her forties steps out from the driver's side. She waves at us.

"That's Heather." Mom returns the greeting. "She's a portrait photographer. She took one of Uncle Merv and Aunt Connie for their sixtieth anniversary, the one sitting on the piano."

I watch another female climb out from the passenger side, this one much younger, with a short blonde bob and glasses.

"She's very nice. They're *all* very nice."

The girl seeks us out immediately. "Hi, guys!" she

hollers with familiarity, grinning, her hand waving wildly in the air. "You're our new neighbors! We're so happy you're here!"

I note the girl's slightly stilted and slower dialogue.

My mom grins and calls back, "Hi, Cassie! It's good to see you again!"

Heather begins walking this way.

"Wait!" Cassie suddenly sounds frantic. "The you-know-whats!"

"They're on the back seat. Get them and then come over. You can do it." Heather continues walking toward us. Meanwhile, Cassie rushes into the back seat, reappearing with a brown bag a moment later. She gallops more than runs after her mother, gripping the bag in both hands in front of her, as if it contains something of great value.

"Debra! It's so good to see you again." Heather takes my mom's hand in both of hers, a friendly gesture between two people who aren't acquainted enough to hug yet, her eyes crinkling with a smile. "Merv's been talking nonstop about you two moving here for the past month."

My mom chuckles. "Good things, I hope?"

"I haven't seen him this happy in a while."

"Hi. I'm Cassie," the girl next to her blurts out, thrusting the bag toward me. "We bought you cookies. The double chocolate are the best."

Heather gestures to her. "*This* is my daughter, Cassie. And you must be Aria?" She regards me with soft gray eyes. She is a pretty lady, and around my mother's age, though I note more fine lines marking her forehead.

"I am." I smile politely, sizing up the large cat graphic on Cassie's T-shirt. "Hi."

"You're going to my school!" Cassie announces, adjusting her red-rimmed glasses as she peers first at me, then at my mom, then at her mom. Her gaze doesn't seem to hold on anyone for too long. "Yeah, you're in grade eleven and I'm in grade ten. Emmett's in grade twelve. Do you know Emmett?"

"Uh ... no."

"Aria has never been to Eastmonte before. Remember we talked about that?" Heather reminds her daughter in a slow, articulate voice.

"Oh, yeah." Cassie grins sheepishly. "Emmett is my brother. You'll like him. He has *a lot* of friends."

"Cassie has been waiting anxiously for you. I think she's asked me *every day* for the past three weeks what day you'd be here," Heather says with a smile and a look of forced patience.

"Shh! *Mom!*" Cassie giggles, then turns to my mom. "I met you at Aunt Connie's funeral."

"You're right, you did."

"She's not really my aunt. We're not related. She's a friend-aunt," Cassie says, as if Connie is still alive and well.

My mom smiles. "A friend-aunt. I like that."

"Yeah. I miss her. I wish she didn't die." Cassie's grin is at odds with her words.

Mom frowns deeply. "I miss her, too."

"Yeah, do you want to come see my room, Aria?" Cassie asks me in her next breath.

"Uh ..." I look to my mom, feeling overwhelmed by the swirl of conversation.

"Maybe another day, Cassie. Aria is busy unpacking," Heather says evenly, as if she can read my hesitation.

"Okay." Cassie nods. "Maybe tomorrow?"

"*Maybe* tomorrow," Heather answers for me, then turns to my mom. "Do you still have a lot to unload? Because we can help."

"Actually, I think we're done unloading for now. I have to make room in the house first. But we have a few heavier boxes—books, mainly—that we might need strong arms for."

"If you can wait until Sunday, Emmett and Mark will be back. They left this morning to visit a college campus in Minnesota."

"*Wow*! College in the US!" my mom exclaims, and I can practically hear what she's thinking because I've heard her say it before. *Poor parents who have to pay that tuition!*

Heather's eyes widen with understanding. "I know."

"My brother plays hockey. He's *so* good," Cassie blurts out. "He has a scholarship."

"If he keeps his grades up," Heather says. "Okay. Well, we'll let you get back to it. And we want to have the three of you over for dinner, once you've settled."

"We would *love* that." My mom beams, sounding genuinely interested in the prospect of dinner with our new neighbors. I can't remember the last time she made a friend.

"It's nice to meet you, Aria." Heather hooks an arm through Cassie's. "Let's go."

"See you tomorrow." Cassie's eyes veer to the paper bag in my hand. "Those are *really* good cookies. They're fresh."

"Yeah?" I hold them up to my nose to inhale the chocolate scent. "Good, because I love cookies."

"Me too." She giggles. "Maybe I can have one?"

"You've already had *two*." Heather smiles apologetically to us and begins leading her daughter away, whispering, "Those are *a gift* for them."

"Okay."

"You can't give a gift and then ask to eat it!"

"Okay. I *know*!" Cassie's voice turns petulant.

I catch Heather's heavy sigh as they walk away.

"What other flavors are there?" Mom yanks the bag

from my grip and eyes its contents, finally pulling out an oatmeal raisin. She takes a bite. "Mmm ... She was right. These *are* good."

I help myself to the double chocolate. "So, Cassie's *different*."

"Yes, she has autism," Mom says, dusting crumbs off her shirt.

My eyes trail after the girl, who climbs the porch steps of their house with the caution of an elderly woman. "She seems so social though." There were a few kids with autism at my last school. I don't remember ever saying much to any of them. One boy named Michael spoke in a stilted voice and moved in slow motion and *never* made eye contact with anyone, but he won races on the school's swim team. Another boy named Robbie couldn't talk at all and had a service dog to keep him from running off school property.

And then there was that guy who showed up halfway through the year. I can't even remember his name. I overheard a teacher talking about how his parents were in denial, refusing to have him tested because they didn't want him labeled, even though there was definitely something off about him. He made people nervous with what he might blurt out. Apparently, one day in class, he wouldn't stop frowning and pointing out a giant zit on Sue Collins's forehead that she had tried in vain to cover with concealer. Finally, she ran out of the classroom in tears and he was suspended for bullying. And then there was the story about how he hated the sound of toilets flushing—like, pacing-screaming-hitting-himself-in-the-head hated. He'd tell anyone in the bathroom with him that they couldn't flush until after he'd left. Of course, that didn't go over well with a bunch of teenaged boys.

After a few weeks, he stopped coming to school.

"Yes, she's always been overly friendly, according to Aunt Connie. She used to spend a lot of time visiting. Almost every day, after school. It made Aunt Connie happy, having a little girl around to dote on again." Mom hands the cookies back to me and closes the trailer. "She seems like a lovely girl and I'm guessing she could use a friend. And *you* don't know anyone around here. It'd be great if you got to know her." Mom looks expectantly at me.

"I'm sure I will."

"Good." Mom throws her arm over my shoulder, pulling me into her as she smoothly snatches the bag of cookies from my grip again.

CHAPTER
THREE

Dear Julia,

I've survived the first few days living in Eastmonte. I finished painting my room last night and my new mattress was delivered this afternoon. Plus, Mom took me shopping for bedding and lights, and cushions for the window seat. My room's actually cozy. Still hot as hell, though. Uncle Merv promises I'll be complaining that it's too cold come winter. Can't wait.

Uncle Merv is okay, for an old guy. He says "damn" a lot, and groans even more than he says "damn." And I think he might have a drinking problem. Mom says it's because he's been so lonely. She's been rationing his whiskey and making him drink tea after dinner, which has made him grumpy. Grumpier. He complains a lot, too. He saw all the salad in the fridge and started mumbling about rabbit food. But he could stand to eat some rabbit food. His stomach is big enough to be carrying quadruplets. It can't be healthy.

Mom's had a parade of cleaning ladies and servicemen marching through here. The Bell guy tried to sell Uncle Merv a PVR. He told him to go to hell. That was kind of funny, in a *totally mortifying way. Still waiting on the plumber. The toilet in our bathroom doesn't work properly. We have to jiggle the chain to get the tank to fill so we can flush it.*

Let's see ... what else can I tell you about? Oh, I boiled and peeled, like, ten thousand tomatoes so Mom could can them for the winter, for sauce. And all that work for, like, FIVE jars. And then I had to help her put them in the cold cellar—a scary, spider-infested room in the basement that I'm never going back into. I don't even like tomatoes.

Cassie's been around a lot. She shows up in the morning and hangs out, following me around and blurting out whatever pops into her head. Usually it's something about a neighborhood dog or her brother or her brother's girlfriend, whose name is Holly—and is apparently really nice and really pretty and Cassie's best friend. That or she drills me with questions about dogs and brothers. She asked me if I had a brother. I lied and said no, because I don't feel like answering a thousand MORE questions about my dad's new family. Something tells me she'd have a hard time grasping the details of that mess.

It's Labor Day weekend. School starts in two days and I'm nervous. Cassie said I can go in with her and Emmett, whose plane is landing tonight at 6:32 p.m., by the way. She's kind of obsessed with her brother, in case you couldn't tell.

Anyway, that's about all that's going on. Told you this would be boring.

~Aria Jones still practicing

"THAT POT ROAST was damn near as good as Connie's." Uncle Merv leans back in the kitchen chair, rubbing his swollen belly.

I eye the chair's frail legs as it groans in protest under his weight. If it breaks and he goes down, I doubt my mother and I together could haul him off the floor.

"It was her recipe. I haven't made it in forever." Mom's lips curve in a small, tight smile. It's the one she gives when she's proud, but doesn't want to appear smug.

"You know, when your mother was here during the summers, she'd spend all day puttering around the kitchen with Connie," he muses.

"I didn't think she could cook." I scoop a second helping of mashed potatoes.

He sets my mother with an incredulous stare. "What on earth have you been feeding this girl all these years, Debra?"

"Howie did the cooking," Mom admits sheepishly through a sip of red wine. "But usually we ordered in."

Uncle Merv grunts his disapproval. "Connie always said you worked too hard. I guess that's a lawyer's life, though. Too bad. She would have liked having you visit once in a while."

Mom flinches but recovers quickly. "That's not our life. Not anymore. Right, Aria?" She reaches out to squeeze my hand.

Uncle Merv's droopy eyes flitter to the clock on the wall. "It's past my bedtime." He groans as he pulls himself out of the chair and hobbles over to the kitchen cupboard. He pulls out a bottle of pills.

The rattling sound sends a ripple of tension through my spine.

"Where did you get those?" Mom's panicked eyes flash to me.

"Huh? Oh, I asked Heather to pick them up for me. For all these aches and pains I didn't feel at night when someone wasn't hiding away my whiskey," he says, his tone thick with accusation.

There's a long pause and then Mom asks in a strained voice, "Aria, are you finished dinner?"

"Uh ... sure." I shovel the last two mouthfuls of potatoes in and begin collecting dirty dishes.

Her hand presses against mine, staying it. "I'll clean up. Why don't you finish unpacking those boxes in your room?" she says with a forced smile.

I duck out and ever so slowly climb the stairs, my ears perked.

"Merv! That's *aspirin!*" my mom whispers. "You can't be pulling that out in front of Aria like that!"

I can't hear whatever she whispers next, but I don't need to. I know the gist of the conversation.

There's a long moment of silence. "I wasn't thinking," Uncle Merv says in a low, grating voice. I doubt he could whisper if his life depended on it. "I'll hide it away."

With a resigned sigh, I climb the rest of the way and disappear into my bedroom.

My eyes are closed and rhythmic music pulsates through my earbuds when a knock sounds on my bedroom door.

"Come in!" I hit pause on my playlist.

The door eases open.

"Hey, your mom asked me to—bring these in."

I bolt upright in bed as a towering guy with wavy chestnut brown hair strolls in, his arms loaded with two cardboard boxes, his lips pressed together firmly as if trying not to laugh.

Cassie trails him, her mouth splitting wide with a grin when she sees me. "Your face is green!" she declares with a bark of laughter.

And burning red beneath this mud mask.

"Why is your face green?"

"It's just ... nothing," I mumble.

"Is it a face mask?" she presses.

"Yes."

"Where do you want these?" the guy asks, having the decency to avert his gaze.

"Over there?" I croak, pointing to the shelves by the window, desperate to tunnel beneath my sheets. As if the mask isn't bad enough, my hair is piled messily on top of my head and I'm wearing an old cotton T-shirt with my former high school's logo and boxer shorts that, while comfortable beyond compare, are far from cute.

"This is my brother, Emmett. He just got home from the United States," Cassie introduces proudly as he leans over to set the boxes on the floor, giving me a great view of his muscular arms and the shape of his broad back, straining beneath the weight. "This is Aria with a green face. She likes dogs, just like me, and she hates tomatoes, just like me." The introduction comes out in one long string of words, using her slightly offbeat inflections.

Emmett eases to his feet. "Hello, Aria with a green face who likes dogs and hates tomatoes." His smile is wide and broad, and shows off his perfect white teeth and two deep-set dimples in his cheeks. His eyes are a rich, dark brown and they complement his olive-toned skin. His nose is angular and in perfect proportion. His jawline is square and solid, any hint of boyishness gone.

Much like my ragged ensemble, this guy is far from cute.

He's *gorgeous*.

I swallow my embarrassment. "Yeah. Hey."

"Look what Emmett brought me!" Cassie holds up a stuffed animal in a burgundy jersey with a yellow "M" across the front. "His name is Goldy Gopher. He's a hockey mascot. I love mascots. Do you like mascots?"

"I don't know? Maybe?" What I do know is that I *really* don't want to carry on a conversation about mascots with my hot neighbor and his sister while I look like *this*.

"So, we'll ... uh ..." Emmett casts his thumb toward the door.

"Yeah. Good. I mean ..." I shake my head, cringing at myself.

"You have stars!" Cassie's wide eyes lock on the stickers above my bed.

"Yeah." More humiliation to add to tonight's collection. Mom "stumbled upon them" in the wallpaper section at Home Depot. Truthfully, I think she went looking for them. She's like that when she gets something in her head. I plastered on a fake smile instead of telling her I'm too old for glow-in-the-dark stars.

"I like your room. It looks different." Cassie's eyes drift, scanning the space as if memorizing it.

"See you around, Aria." Emmett ruffles Cassie's hair on his way past, and then hooks an arm around her shoulders and steers her toward the door. She stiffens. "Come on. Let's give green-faced Aria some privacy," he mock-whispers, earning her burst of childlike laughter.

He pulls my door shut, but not before turning back to offer one last devastatingly handsome look, his brown eyes twinkling with amusement.

And in that moment, beneath a cluster of tacky glow-in-the-dark stars, my face green with clay and red with embarrassment, I fall hopelessly in love with the boy next door.

As soon as the door clicks, I flop back into my bed with a groan.

MY MOM POKES her head into my bedroom at nine on Monday night to find me curled up on the window seat. She smiles. "I knew you'd like that spot."

I tuck my bookmark into my page. "Did you get hold of the electrician?" My new ceiling fan is sitting in a box in the corner.

"Not yet. It's a long weekend. But I did speak to the plumber and he's coming tomorrow afternoon. I'm hoping he can hook up the new washer right away, for the sake of my sanity, and so Uncle Merv can see that laundry machines *shouldn't* move halfway across the room when they're running." She bites her lip. "You ready for tomorrow?"

I nod toward the new jeans and red top I laid out over my desk chair, as if that's adequate armor for the first day at a new high school.

"Oh, that is a nice outfit." My mom smiles as if picturing me in it. "Cassie will come by around eight to get you. And, listen, I told Heather you'd be willing to walk Cassie home after school. Emmett apparently has hockey every day." She shakes her head, as if the idea of that is unimaginable. "It's less than fifteen minutes. You're good with that, right?"

"Sure. I guess." It's not like I have anything else to do.

She hesitates. "I was also thinking, Dr. Covey passed

along a name of a therapist, not too far from here. About a half hour, I think. I could call and—"

"No, Mom. I'm good. Seriously."

"But you should keep talking to—"

"No! That means a new doctor and going through it all again. Dr. C. helped me. She was good. I'm good. It's been more than a year. I want to move on."

Mom's brow furrows deeply, as if she wants to push but isn't sure if she should.

A chorus of shouts sound from outside. "What's going on out there?" She wanders over to peer out my window.

"Emmett and his dad are playing road hockey." I assume it's his dad, anyway. The man is about the same height and he has a similar stride as Emmett, and he's thrown his arm around Emmett's shoulders twice since they hauled an enormous hockey net from the garage and set it up under the street lights in the quiet cul-du-sac an hour ago.

"It sounds like he's the next big thing. Heather said he was scouted by that college a year ago. They only offer scholarships that early if the kid is going to be a star." Mom watches as Emmett deftly maneuvers around his dad and shoots the puck. It sails into the top left corner. "They're a nice family, aren't they?"

"Seems like it." I flip my book open again, pretending to read, though my eyes are still trained on the street. I've been staring at the same page for the past hour.

While Emmett's dad goes to fetch the puck from the net, Emmett stretches his arms over his head. His gaze wanders casually over the street.

It comes to rest on my window.

I duck my head. "Mom, you're *staring*!"

"Right. Sorry." There's a hint of humor in her voice as

she steps away, moving toward the door. "I have a good feeling about this year."

"Yeah, me too," I lie. Right now, I'm waffling between stomach-churning nerves and paralyzing fear of what tomorrow and beyond will bring. But for my mom, I'll front.

"I think I'm going to turn in early. I'm exhausted after these past few days."

"Okay. Good night.

"Good night. I love you."

"Love you, too."

Her eyes drift to the window, and a tiny, knowing smile touches her lips. "Don't stay up too late." She pulls my door shut softly.

I shift my attention back to the street in time to see a small red car pull into the Hartford driveway. That seems to be the man's signal to head inside, patting Emmett on the shoulder. He walks past the driver's side just as it opens and a girl wearing black shorts and pink tank top that show off her muscular legs and well-endowed chest steps out.

I groan. "And you *must* be Holly." I take in her thick mane of honey-blonde hair that hangs halfway down her back in stylish waves and swishes as she skips toward a waiting Emmett. I can't make out the details of her face from here, but I'm guessing she's beautiful. A guy like that wouldn't go for anything less.

I watch him coil his arms around her waist; she wraps her arms around his neck. She squeals as he lifts her up into a kiss.

And then I pull my curtains shut, an uncomfortable feeling churning in my belly.

I might as well slather on another mud mask because I am green-faced with envy.

CHAPTER
FOUR

"T<small>EXT ME SO</small> I <small>KNOW HOW IT'S GOING.</small>"

I hike my backpack over my shoulder. "I'm not allowed to use my phone during school hours." The rule is stated in bold on the first page of the student handbook I received at our visit last week.

"Just send me a quick message during your lunch break, from the bathroom. I'll be here and I'll answer right away." Mom wrings her hands. I think she's more nervous than I am. "And remember, *no* social media."

"That's easy with the parental control." I wave the new phone she bought me, reminding her. I can't load any apps without her blessing and she's not giving her blessing for Instagram or Facebook or "that evil" Twitter. Basically, the phone is a means for her to get hold of me and nothing more, complete with a GPS tracker.

"I'm not dumb. I know you can still go onto those websites."

"I don't *want* to," I remind her evenly.

"Right." But the frown on her face won't ease. "Don't

forget you have a guidance counselor appointment today, too. Her name is Ms. Moretti."

I nod.

"I talked to her over the phone. She sounded nice. Energetic ... like she actually enjoys her job. And she's the cross-country coach—"

I groan. "I told you, I don't think I want to do cross-country again."

"Of course you do! Remember how well you placed at provincials?"

"That was two years ago." Before we found out about Dad's secret family, before my parents divorced. Before my life fell apart.

A knock sounds, cutting our argument short.

Mom opens the door to find a grinning Cassie waiting. "Good morning, Cassie! Ready for your first day of school?" Mom asks with a broad smile. She seems to smile more when Cassie's around. So does Uncle Merv, and that's quite the feat because the old man wears a perpetual scowl on account of all his loose, sagging skin.

"Holly gave me this shirt," she says, as if we've met Holly. She looks down at her T-shirt of a sequined unicorn. It's paired with capri leggings and running shoes that are fastened with elastic band–like straps. "I like it."

"So do I! Aria is wearing new clothes today, too."

Cassie's gray-blue eyes coast over me as she nods vigorously. "Wow. She looks nice."

A car horn sounds.

"Oh, that's Emmett. We have to go." Cassie turns to ease down the steps.

"Remember. Text me," my mom calls after me, tacking on an "I love you!" for good measure.

I roll my eyes and throw a hand in the air as we make our way toward the navy-blue Hyundai Santa Fe.

"You can sit in the front if you want." Cassie doesn't wait for my answer before climbing into the back seat.

My stomach flutters as I open the passenger door. "Hey," I say as I slide in, trying not to stare at him or make it too obvious that I'm inhaling the delicious scent of soap that lingers in the air. Emmett's wearing dark jeans and a crisp white T-shirt. So simple and yet so hot. He's styled his wavy hair with product this morning, to make it full and stand on end.

"Hey." Emmett gives me a crooked smile before peering over his shoulder at his sister. "You gave up the front, Cass? I'm impressed."

"Yeah. Aria's my friend. And she doesn't have a green face anymore."

Emmett snorts with laughter as he cranks the engine.

My cheeks burn. "Thanks for reminding me."

"You're welcome," she chirps, then after a pause says, "Oh. You're joking."

"Yeah, Cass. She's joking." Emmett throws the car into drive.

"Wait! I'm not ready! This seat belt is tricky!" She sounds panicked.

"I'm *waiting*." His fingertips drum over the steering wheel as his brown eyes drift over the street. "Following the rules is very important to Cassie, in case you haven't noticed yet."

"I *heard* that," she mutters as a metal click sounds. "Okay, I'm ready."

He pulls out. "So, who do you have this semester?"

"Mr. Eason," Cassie answers.

He smirks. "I meant Aria."

"Um ..." I frown as I search my memory, meanwhile inside I'm buzzing with excitement over the fact that Emmett wants to talk to me. "Mr. Lewis for math."

"He's good, but his tests are brutal."

"Great. As if I didn't already hate math."

Emmett chuckles. "Yeah, same here. I've got Calculus this semester and I'm dreading it. Who else?"

I fish my course syllabus from my back pocket and unfold it. "Ms. Singh for Biology."

"Never had her."

"Lunch period four."

He cringes. "That's the late one. That sucks."

"Which one do you have?"

"Period three."

"Me too!" Cassie chirps.

My disappointment swells. The only two people I know in school and I'll be left to eat by myself. I continue scanning my agenda. "Mr. Kapp for English, last period."

"*Oh.* Him. He's ..." Emmett's eyes flash to the rearview mirror. "I'll warn you about *him* later," he says softly.

Because Cassie will repeat whatever she hears, I'm guessing.

"Okay." The thought of a secret conversation between us sends a thrill through my body. "And Ms. McNair for Social Studies."

He frowns. "Which period?"

"First."

"Hey, I'm in that class!"

"Really?" I get to spend my morning period with Emmett? Stealing glances at every opportunity?

I am *so* going to fail this class.

"Wait, what grade are you in again?"

"She's in grade eleven!" Cassie yells from behind, as if excited to be able to join the conversation.

"Eleven," I echo. "But I took a course that's identical to a prerequisite for this one, so..." I wave a hand, as if the rest is self-explanatory.

"Cool. I can walk with you. You're on your own after that."

A mixture of relief and trepidation swirls inside. "That's okay." I hold up a second sheet of paper. "I have a map."

DAUNTING.

That's a great word for Eastmonte Secondary.

I knew this last week, when Mom and I came by to finish registering and get acquainted. The principal, squinty-eyed Mr. Keen, announced that I would put their enrollment at sixteen hundred and sixty-six students. "Don't worry, that doesn't mean you're bad luck," he joked as he guided us out of his office.

Now that I'm standing in the parking lot watching the old building come alive with students—filtering through doors, lingering in groups, their eyes wandering, their laughter and shouts carrying—that number weighs heavily on me. It's more than double my previous high school.

"I'm nervous," Cassie announces, adjusting her backpack on her shoulders.

"You don't need to be nervous." Emmett reaches into the back seat to grab his backpack, the move stretching his white T-shirt across his curvy, hard chest. "You went here last year, remember? And you have the same teacher. You're in the same class, with most of the same kids. You'll be fine."

"Yeah." Cassie giggles. "I know."

We begin the slow walk toward the front doors, and I'm so thankful to have both Hartford kids right now. Otherwise, I'd be doing this alone.

"But imagine how nervous Aria must be," Emmett says, grinning playfully at me. "She doesn't know *anyone* here."

"She knows *me*," she says, not catching on to her brother's gentle ribbing.

"You're right. She does. And don't worry." He winks at me. "With Cassie around, you'll know half the school in no time."

"Hi, Mr. T!" Cassie waves at a tall, thin man with a hard face who hovers outside the gymnasium's double doors.

"Cassie Hartford!" His face lights up. "How was your summer?"

"Good. This is Aria." She jabs a finger toward me. "She lives with Uncle Merv now. She's my new neighbor."

Mr. T nods once to me. "Welcome to Eastmonte, Aria."

"Thanks." I smile politely, feeling my cheeks flush, as we keep moving.

"What's that now? Eight teachers?" Emmett asks, high-fiving a guy as he passes him in the hall.

"Nine. And two janitors," I correct, tugging at the collar of my suddenly uncomfortable shirt.

He chuckles. "See? They'll all know you soon enough. 'Kay, Cass, here's your classroom."

"And my locker." She opens the door of 971.

"That's last year's."

"No! This is mine this year, too!" she insists, unexpected frustration flaring in her voice as she pulls out a lock and loops it through the latch with a concerted effort.

He sighs heavily, and then leans into the room to wave at someone. "Hey, Mr. Eason, Cassie's here."

A middle-aged man with no hair on his head and too much on his face strolls out to meet us. "Hey, Emmett. Cassie! Good to see you again," he greets, his voice deep.

"Which locker is hers this year?" Emmett asks.

"Same one. Keeping it consistent."

"*See?* I *told* you, Emmett." She focuses on unpacking her backpack, that same petulance she used with her mother the other day creeping into her tone.

Emmett holds his hands up in surrender. "I should've known better. We'll see you later, Cassie. Remember, you're walking home with Aria after school. She'll meet you here."

"Oh, Mr. Eason! Have you met Aria?" Cassie asks, distracted from her locker for the moment.

"I haven't. But you told me about her last week when you came in to visit the classroom, remember?"

"Yeah. This is Aria." She points to me and says by rote, "She lives with Uncle Merv. She's my new neighbor."

Kind, green eyes shift to me. "Welcome, Aria. You have lucked out with the friendliest neighbor you'll ever meet in your life."

I laugh. "Yeah, I've picked up on that."

"Have a great first day at Eastmonte. Cassie, come inside when you're finished up here." With that, he ducks into his class.

"You good, Cassie?" Emmett asks.

"Yes." She nods to emphasize.

"Don't show anyone your code," he warns, pointing to the push button combination padlock.

"Okay, Emmett!"

"All right." He turns to walk down the hall. He's patient with his little sister's peculiarities and outbursts. I guess he's used to them.

"See you later, Cassie," I say.

"At three forty-six. Right here." She points at her locker.

"Yes." I guess I need to be more specific.

"Okay. Bye." She turns her attention back to her locker.

I rush to catch up with Emmett. "So, what's that class Cassie is taking?"

"It's a community class. They do life and social skills learning. Eason is amazing with her."

"Does she not take any regular classes?"

"She takes a couple that are special for kids like her, on the spectrum. Hey, man! How was your summer?" We stall as Emmett shares a few words with a shorter, stocky blond guy who steals several glances my way but never says hi. I'm sure if Cassie were here, I would have already received an introduction.

"Do you think she'll go to college after?"

He frowns. "Who, Cassie? No, she'll be here until she's twenty-one."

I cringe at the thought of being in high school for that long.

He nods in greeting to a passing guy, and laughs at another. Walking through the halls is probably not the best time to try to carry on a conversation—about anything —with him.

"This is me." I point at locker number 698.

"That was my buddy Zach's locker last year. I'm just down there." He points haphazardly and keeps going.

I split my time between unloading my lunch bag and blank notebooks from my backpack and watching Emmett stroll down the hall, his gait casual, returning smiles and greetings from at least a dozen people. It's obvious he's well known. And well liked.

He hooks his combination lock into his locker just as a blonde in a flirty black skirt and wedge heels barrels into him from behind, her arms looping around his waist. In the light of the hallway, I can see how perfect Holly truly is, with her sculpted cheekbones, expressive blue eyes, and wide, pouty lips.

I groan.

"You okay?"

I turn to find a round-faced girl with owlish eyes and an upturned nose at the locker next to me, and realize she's talking to me.

"I'm fine. Just ... life. It's *so* predictable."

"Tell me about it." She snorts, pushing her frizzy auburn hair off her freckled face. She's at least five inches taller than me and on the heavy side, with broad shoulders and a slightly hunched posture. The corners of her mouth are naturally curved downward, making it look like she wears a perpetual frown. "I'm Jen. Or Jenny, if you want. Just *not* Jennifer. You're Aria, right?"

"Uh ... yeah?"

"Mr. Keen assigned me to you," she explains, and that downturned mouth curves into a reassuring smile. "The buddy system?"

"Oh. *Right*. I forgot." He did mention something about a student being assigned to me, to help me adjust. And this student happens to be wearing a beige shirt with a yellow #2 pencil print.

"So, I have a locker beside you." She points at it. "Plus

we have first period and lunch together. I'm here to show you around, answer any questions you have, that sort of thing. Anything you need. I'm in my last year so I know the school pretty well."

"That's great. Thank you." At least now I know *three* people here, not including the teachers and janitorial staff Cassie introduced me to.

"Where are you from?"

"Out west. Calgary area."

"Cool. Why'd you move *here*?" She says that like there's something wrong with Eastmonte, and I guess maybe to some people, there is. It's a sleepy town surrounded by a lot of corn and hay. When Mom and I drove along the main street at night, I half expected a zombie to meander out, it was so dead. There's one Tim Hortons, two grocery stores, and a restored two-screen movie theater. As far as excitement goes, there's none.

But it's only an hour's drive to downtown Toronto, a city we haven't had a chance to venture into yet but I'm excited to see.

And so the questions begin. "My uncle is getting older and he lost his wife. My mom wanted to be closer to him." I practiced that line in the mirror last night, and it comes out smoothly now.

The first bell rings.

"Cool." Jen shuts her locker door with a slam. I can't tell if she was interested in knowing that or just being polite. "Our class is right here." She points to the open door across from us, where a short, plump teacher with a black bob stands, greeting students.

I steal a glance down the hall in time to see Emmett and Holly approaching, Holly burrowed against Emmett's side, his arm slung over her shoulder.

I feel a pull in my gut. I *hate* being envious of other people. But I'm human as Dr. C. liked to remind me, and feeling a range of emotions along a wide spectrum is normal. Envy is normal.

Right now, I am *sick* with envy and I haven't said two words to this girl yet.

"See?" Emmett winks at me. "Making friends already."

"Buddy assignment," I mumble, feeling Holly's blue eyes size me up.

"Right. Hey, Jen."

"Hey, Emmett." She hesitates a beat. "Hey, Holly." I could be wrong—I've known Jen for all of five minutes—but her tone shifts from genuinely happy to forced with that latter greeting.

"Hey Jenni*fer*," Holly says in a soft, sexy timbre. "Good summer?"

"It was great. Thanks for asking. I'll save you a seat inside, Aria." Jen speeds into the classroom.

"Holly, meet Aria, my new neighbor. Aria, my girl-friend, Holly." Emmett gestures between us.

"*Hey*." Holly's bright blue eyes practically sparkle and her smile grows even wider, if that's possible. "I've heard *so* much about you from Cassie. I feel like I already know you."

I laugh. "Yeah, I can imagine." Is there anyone in Cassie's world who doesn't know about me already?

"Right?" Her laugh is like a well-tuned flute. "Emmett tells me you're going to walk home with her after school? That's *so* nice of you."

"No big deal. I live next door." I shrug.

"But it makes me sad." She pouts. "I used to walk her home once a week. That was one of *my* favorite things to do."

Emmett frowns down at her. "You can still walk with them, if you want."

"I can't, given my tutoring job. I don't know how I would've managed. It's kind of worked out that Aria's here now."

"*Right*," he nods with the reminder.

"*But* I'm glad she has you. She deserves to have more friends." Holly's smile oozes warmth.

Ugh. Emmett's girlfriend is beautiful *and* nice. Not a surprise, I guess.

"Mr. Hartford, Ms. Webber, second bell's about to go." The teacher, Ms. McNair, I presume, calls out, her warning gaze drifting over me as well.

"Good thing we're all taking your class then." Emmett grins as he trails Holly in, leaving me to walk in last.

Jen waves to me from a two-person desk, front and center.

With a soft groan, I sink into my seat.

CHAPTER
FIVE

"Aria Jones." Ms. Moretti pushes the door to her office shut. "How's your first day at Eastmonte going so far?"

"So far, so good," I say, watching her strut around the desk in her four-inch heels, her muscular calves bulging from the strain. Other than that, she's a tiny woman, with an olive complexion and jet-black hair pulled into a sleek ponytail.

"Good. I'm glad to hear that." She settles into the leather office chair behind her desk. It's giant in comparison, and I can't figure out if it's because it's oversized or she's *that* small. "So, tell me something about yourself." She flashes a wide smile.

My eyes get caught on the gap between her two front teeth for a few seconds before I avert my gaze. "There's not much to tell."

"Oh, come on, of course there is. I'm at a loss, unfortunately." She holds her empty hands out in front of her. "Moving out of province is like moving countries as far as the school system goes. We don't get much in the way of information about the student."

Thankfully.

"So ...?" she prods, her perfect, symmetrical eyebrows arching with question. "You moved here last week, right?"

"Yeah. We're living with my uncle. My great-uncle."

"You and your mother, right?"

I nod.

"And is your dad back in Calgary?"

"Outside of Calgary. You know ... divorce."

"Do you speak to him often?"

I shake my head, studying the surface of her desk so she doesn't see the truth in my eyes—that I haven't talked to my father in months.

"How long ago did they separate?"

Do *all* guidance counselors prod for private information right out of the gate? "Two years ago? Yeah, almost two years ago." Halloween night, to be exact. My friend Denise and I decided to go trick-or-treating as a joke. We dressed up as zombie brides and went door to door in her neighborhood. It was hysterical, up until a pregnant, redheaded woman opened her door to hand us bags of chips and I spotted my father kicking back on the couch in the living room, beer in hand, a little girl I'd never met before perched on his knee.

The woman, Sonya, is a paralegal at the law firm where he works.

He didn't even bother denying the affair or that the coming baby was his.

Ms. Moretti nods and gives me one of those downcast sympathetic smiles. "I remember when my parents divorced. I was about your age and I thought it was the end of the world at the time. It turned my life upside down and

I didn't move across the country. This must be hard on you."

I shrug.

"I'm guessing you left some friends behind that you probably miss?"

"Sure, but they can text me."

If they had my new number.

If they were still my friends.

It's quiet for a moment as Ms. Moretti sizes me up. How much has my mother told her? Not too much, I'd imagine. The whole point of moving here was to have a fresh start, and I won't have that if Mom drags out our baggage and puts it on display.

Finally, Ms. Moretti shuffles some paperwork on her desk before sliding a page across the desk toward me. "One of the best and easiest ways to make new friends is through sports and clubs. I've taken the liberty of highlighting a few of the best ones."

I scan it quickly. Lo and behold, "cross-country" is highlighted in bright yellow. Twice.

"Your mother *may* have called me and *may* have mentioned that you placed second in provincials." She grins sheepishly. "I'm the coach. I'd love to see what you can do."

"I haven't been training. I doubt I'd be a good addition."

She waves it away. "I'll bet you'd surprise yourself. We practice three times a week, before school. More, as we get closer to regionals. Please consider it. We haven't had any luck placing in years. Even with Emmett Hartford on the team. Between you and me, we could really use a win."

My heart skips a beat. *"Emmett's* on the team?"

"Yeah. You've met him already, I take it?"

"He's my neighbor." My cheeks heat, and I hope she can't see it.

"*Well*, he's also quite the athlete, though his heart is tied up with hockey. I think he uses this for his morning workout." She leans in and whispers conspiratorially, "So come out and help us win a trophy for our display case!"

I can't help but smile. So far, Ms. Moretti is about as opposite to my last guidance counselor as you can get. Aside from the physical attributes—Mrs. Forester was gray-haired, had yellow teeth from smoking a pack of cigarettes a day, and her style consisted of shapeless dresses and UGGs—she didn't give a rat's ass what happened to me or anyone else, as long as she got to retire with her pension at the end of it all. She even said as much to me once.

Meanwhile, here's this youthful, compact woman across from me, wearing a flirty eggplant-colored dress and a smile, making a genuine effort to motivate me.

Little does she realize, she's dangled a gorgeous, dimple-cheeked carrot in the air that I can't ignore.

I hesitate. "So, when does training start?"

I ASSUMED all high school cafeterias were the same—dark, crowded, and comparable to the prison meal rooms you see on TV. And, before a renovation two years ago that saw a giant addition built onto the back of the school, the same probably could've been said for Eastmonte Secondary's cafeteria.

I inhale the smell of gravy-laden meat wafting from the lunch line as I take in the bright space—double-story ceilings and a full panel of glass that overlooks the sports field and track and allows in ample daylight; everything is in soft shades of gray and tan with a mixture of round and rectangular tables that seat anywhere from two to twenty people. They even have television screens mounted on the walls!

I spot Jen waving me over to a table by the window and relief swarms me. I duck my head, trying to ignore the glances. In a school of sixteen hundred and sixty-six students, being the new girl is still notable.

"How was the rest of your morning?" Jen asks around a mouthful of her ham-and-cheese sandwich. She's sitting beside a small Asian girl with a heavy bang cut just above her eyebrows; she peers up at me with a timid smile.

"Okay."

"This is Josie. Josie, this is Aria."

Josie nods at me, and while her mouth moves, I don't actually hear the hello that comes out.

"Hey." I dump my own lunch—an apple and cream-cheese bagel—out of my lunch bag, starved. Emmett was right—the late lunch sucks. "Math with Mr. Lewis."

Jen grimaces. "I had him last year. He's tough."

"So it seems." His thick gray mustache lifted with his easy smile as he strolled around the classroom handing out a three-page pop quiz full of equations for us to complete. It's meant to help him gauge what he's working with. A pop quiz, five minutes after sitting down. And I don't think I answered any of the questions right.

Next to that, Biology with Ms. Singh was a breeze.

"At least one more class and you've made it through your first day, right?"

"Right." And English has always been my favorite. I glance around at the sea of faces. I recognize one or two from my classes, but that's all.

A burst of laughter carries over the loud buzz of conversation. I glance over to see Holly strut down the stairs from the second floor with a tall, willowy brunette, turning heads as she strolls toward the lunch service line, her toned thighs flexing with each step on those wedge sandals. She waggles her painted fingers at a table nearby, nodding as they point to the vacant seats beside them, mouthing "Thank you!"

"Is she for real? Holly Webber, I mean."

Jen's blue-gray eyes flash to the blonde bombshell, where they sit a moment. "Why are you asking?"

"No reason. She just seems so perfect."

"She does, doesn't she?" Jen picks at the top of her bun, breaking off bits of bread to make it look like something has nibbled on it.

Josie doesn't say a word. I have a feeling we won't be having many conversations.

"So, when did she and Emmett hook up?" I ask casually.

"The start of last year. That's when she moved here. It didn't take long for that to happen." Jen's eyes widen with emphasis. "She looks like *that* and Emmett's like, Mr. Popular, in case you haven't figured that out yet."

"I took a wild guess." I join in, pulling my bagel into bite-sized chunks.

"Yeah, everyone's saying he's going to end up in the NHL." She shrugs. "I don't know. I don't like hockey. But he's nice. And smart. We were biology partners last year and he did his fair share of the work, and never made fun of people. Not like the other jock assholes who just want to get drunk and laid and be general jerks. Not that Emmett's lacking in the 'getting laid' department. If the rumors after every party are true, those two are doing it every chance they get," she says. "But at least he's nice."

My stomach squeezes. But of course they are. I would be, too. Even though I haven't actually done "it" with anyone yet. But if I were with Emmett, I doubt I'd be able to keep my hands off him.

I squash that flare of envy, needing to get my mind off the boy next door. "So, what do you know about Mr. Kapp?" Emmett alluded to there being something worth gossiping about.

Jen freezes, her sandwich halfway to her mouth, exchanging a wary expression with Josie.

"Aria."

My heart jumps at the sound of my name on Emmett's tongue. I spin around to find him hovering over me, backpack slung over his shoulder, his wavy hair tousled as if he ran his fingers through it—or someone ran *her* fingers through it. His phone is in his hand. "Hey."

"What's your number? I should have it, in case of an emergency."

I swallow against my suddenly dry mouth. "I don't remember it. It's new."

He grins. "Gimme your phone."

I dig it out of my side pocket and hand it to him, glancing around to make sure no teacher's watching.

"It's locked." He holds it out for me to unlock with my thumbprint.

"*Wow*. Black home screen. This *is* a new phone," he says, his thumbs flying over the key pad. "'Kay. I'm in there. And now"—he sends himself a text on my phone. A chirp sounds in his pocket with the incoming message—"I have yours." He hands me my phone, his fingertips skating across mine, sending an electric current through my entire body.

"See you later, AJ. Gotta run. Coach will kick my ass if I'm late."

"Yeah. See ya," I manage, staring at his retreating back.

"Well, girls ...?" Uncle Merv pauses trimming the bush by the front porch to watch us approach, his wide-brimmed straw hat shading most of his face. "How was the first day of school?"

"Good. There are two new kids in my class this year. Adnan and Ophelia. Adnan is fifteen and Ophelia is fourteen. She has a dog named Rusty. He's a mixed breed," Cassie declares. Details I've already heard during our walk home, along with the names of every pet on the street, the names of the dogs at the shelter where she volunteers, and her favorite chocolate brands. Which is *all* of them, just ranked.

Uncle Merv's eyes narrow. "And are these kids troublemakers?"

Cassie laughs. "No, Uncle Merv. I think *you're* a troublemaker."

He chuckles as he leans in to inspect a thorny branch. "You might be right."

"Whose truck is that?" She points to the red pickup in our driveway, parked behind Uncle Merv's silver Oldsmobile—that I haven't seen leave the driveway since we've been here.

"That's the plumber. He's been here for hours. Woke me up from my nap with all the *damn* noise."

Cassie giggles as she always does when he says "damn," but then her face goes blank as she seems to process this new information. "There's something wrong with your plumbing." It's a statement, not a question.

"*So I've been told,*" he grumbles.

"There is?" she corrects.

"Cassie!" Heather calls from her porch, waving her daughter home.

"Oh, I have to go. I have swimming tonight!" She rushes off, galloping across the grass toward her mother.

"Thank you for walking her home!" Heather smiles at me.

"No problem!" I sigh with the sudden peace. If Cassie's not prattling, she's asking question after question.

After question.

Two yard bags full of pulled weeds sit next to the freshly churned soil by the porch. "Mom was gardening?" I ask, though I know the answer. There's no way Uncle Merv managed that himself. He can barely reach his shoes. Most days he wears slippers that he can slide his feet into, even outside.

"That woman can't sit still, can she?" he mutters, his wrinkled fingers smoothing over a wilted leaf.

I sense it's a rhetorical question, but I answer anyway. "By the time she goes back to work, this house will be turned upside down."

He makes a sound, and I can't tell if it's a happy one or otherwise. "How was *your* first day, by the way?"

"Uneventful."

"Uneventful is good, from what I remember of high school." Fetching a spray bottle from the edge of the porch, he spritzes the leaves.

The storm door creaks open and Mom steps out, wiping her hands on a tea towel. "Aria, you're home! Come on." She nods, beckoning me inside.

The house smells of warm cinnamon. I inhale deeply. "What is that?"

"Muffins!" she exclaims, holding up a plate that's sitting on the kitchen table. A streak of flour coats her forehead, and the apron covering her capris and T-shirt is dusted with more. "There are *so* many apples on the trees in the backyard, I don't know what to do with them. I'm going to make a few batches of applesauce tomorrow."

Gardening, baking ... I stare at her with mock concern. "Who *are* you and what have you done to Debra Wiser? I mean, Jones," I quickly correct.

"Ha. Funny. I'm actually enjoying domestic life." She pulls a chair out. "Come, sit. Tell me three things that happened today."

I groan. "Mom, I'm tired."

"You heard Dr. C. We're doing this, Aria," she says in that firm voice that promises I'm not going to win this battle. I've often wondered if there was a course in law school on bending people to your will simply through tone of voice. She certainly didn't learn it being an involved parent. "If there's one thing I've realized, it's that we don't talk. So *talk*." She slides forward a plate with a muffin. "And eat. But talk."

"Fine." I slump into the chair, slowly peeling away at the paper cup. "Number one: I had my meeting with Ms. Moretti. She seemed nice. She wants me to try out for cross-country."

"That's good news! And you said you would, right?"

"Number two: I'm going to *think* about going to the first cross-country practice next week. But I have to train a bit first. I'm so out of shape, I'm not showing up there to embarrass myself." Especially not in front of a certain hot neighbor.

"You know, Heather mentioned that Emmett runs every morning," Mom murmurs through a sip of tea, as if plucking his name from my mind. "Maybe you can go with him?"

I shrug, feigning indifference. "Number three: Emmett's in my first-period class, so at least I know someone. Two people, actually. This girl named Jen is my 'buddy.'" I air quote that word.

"That's fantastic, Aria." Mom's shoulders seem to sag with relief.

"Mrs. Jones?" a male voice calls out, and the stairs creak.

"That's the plumber," Mom whispers, yanking off her apron and heading for the foyer, tucking her hair behind her ears and smoothing her shirt over her hips on the way. "It's *Ms.* And Debra. *Please,*" she says, smiling. She hates being called Mrs. *anything*, especially since Dad cheated on her with a woman ten years younger.

"Right. Sorry. I've been warned once already, haven't I?" the deep, smooth voice says with a chuckle, a moment before a lean man steps onto the landing and into my line of sight, his thumbs hooked on his tool belt.

I'd put him in his midforties, with crow's feet at the corners of his eyes and gray at his temples of otherwise light brown hair. "Something smells *good* in this house."

"Oh! Here!" She rushes over to collect a napkin and a muffin. "They're still warm from the oven."

"I couldn't," he says, in the way that means he *totally* could. His gaze drifts to me, his blue eyes crinkling with a smile.

"I insist." Mom thrusts a muffin into his hands. "Any news?"

"So, the washing machine and toilet are hooked up. I can change the shower faucet and valve upstairs to help with the temperature regulation, but that means cutting into the back bedroom closet to get to the pipes."

"That's fine. We can get someone in to patch it up. I was going to paint my room anyway."

"I can do that for you, no problem. I do more than just plumbing."

"That's *great!*" She grins up at him as if that's the best news she's heard all day. "And what about the water pressure?"

The man's cringe doesn't bode well. "This house was built in the 50s, so all your pipes are galvanized. There's decades of buildup. It's only gonna get worse. You need to think about repiping the whole house."

Mom groans. "I was afraid of that."

"Sorry, I wish I had better news for you. I'd be happy to give you a quote if that's something you want to look at doing. Going with PEX will save you a few thousand ..."

I tune them out, gathering my backpack and muffin and ducking past to head to my bedroom.

CHAPTER
SIX

DEAR JULIA,

So, I did it. I survived my first week at Eastmonte and it wasn't that bad. Though, if I'm being honest—that's what I'm supposed to be doing here, right?—it has more to do with Emmett. Between the ride to school and first period, my heartbeat doesn't settle down to a normal, healthy rate until Math.

McNair doesn't believe in assigned seating, but Jen and I sit together every day. I've managed to drag her away from the front of the class the last three days and we've sat behind Emmett. I'm beginning to think that's a bad idea. I tend to zone out and miss notes. I can't help it, though. He has a hot neck. I didn't think that was a thing, but it is definitely a thing.

Of course, this also means I'm stuck watching Holly twirl his hair and paw his thigh every morning, too. She can't seem to keep her hands off him. It's annoying. But if I had free rein to paw Emmett Hartford, I'd be just as bad.

And, again, full honesty here, right? No judgment? I'm insanely jealous of her. Like, prays-she-says-something-

dumb-hopes-she-bombs-a-test-crosses-my-fingers-that-she-accidentally-farts-in-front-of-everyone jealous. Something—anything—to make her a touch less perfect.

I know it's wrong to wish that kind of stuff upon someone. But it's how I feel. Don't worry—I won't tell anyone besides you.

At least she's nice. She says hi to me and Jen every morning (though she keeps calling her Jennifer, emphasizing the FER, even after I made a point of saying JEN, emphasizing the JEN, within Holly's earshot). Still, it would suck a hundred times over if she was a bitch.

Still ... it sucks.

Talk later,

~AJ (Emmett's been calling me that all week. I love it. I think I love him. Whoa! WAY too soon, right?)

"I LIKE to eat early and in a quiet environment. That way I have time to digest before bed." Uncle Merv hobbles up the path ahead of us, his usual green khaki pants swapped for black ones. Mom says he only has two pairs of pants that fit his waist, so she bought a few more and sent them to a seamstress to be tailored.

"Heather promised dinner for six." Mom juggles the wine bottles in her grasp to free up a hand so she can fix the foil cover of the apple pie I'm holding, still warm from the oven. "Emmett had hockey this afternoon so they couldn't do it earlier. And apparently, it's rare to have a Saturday night without a game, so they wanted to take advantage while he's available."

"That kid and hockey," he grumbles. "I guess it's going

to pay for his college, so there's that. You reminded Heather that I can't eat cauliflower, right? It gives me *terrible* gas."

"I mentioned it." Mom shares a look with me before turning away, pressing her lips together to keep from laughing.

Mark Hartford answers the door with a grin and dimples that match Emmett's. There's no doubt Emmett took after his father; they have the same brown eyes, olive skin, and chestnut brown hair—though Mark's is peppered with gray and beginning to thin on top.

"Wine for the hosts. One red, one white." Mom practically thrusts the bottles into his hands before collecting the dish from mine. "And a homemade apple pie that I hope isn't too runny, for dessert."

"Never met a pie I didn't like." He chuckles softly. "Thank you. And welcome. Come in, come in." He backs up, giving us room to enter. He grins at me. "It's nice to finally meet you, officially, Aria."

The Hartford house isn't much bigger than Uncle Merv's and it's similar in layout, but every room I see so far has been renovated. Rich, warm planks of wood run the length of the hall, all the way to the kitchen in the back, where new white cupboards hang. The walls throughout are painted a dove gray and *covered* in framed photographs. Everywhere I look are pictures of Emmett and Cassie at different ages.

"We're having schnitzel, Uncle Merv!" Cassie declares as I inhale the aroma permeating the air. "It's your favorite. That's why we're having it."

He frowns. "How do you know it's my favorite?"

"Aunt Connie told me. I came to your house because of the snowstorm, remember?"

"Snowstorm ..." His frown grows deeper. "That was *years* ago, wasn't it? You were tiny."

She shrugs. "That's when she told me."

"Good God, kid. What I'd give to have your memory."

"Yeah." She giggles. "You want to come see my room, Aria? I mean AJ?" She draws *AJ* out like she's in on a secret.

I do a quick glance around. Emmett's nowhere in sight, but I already knew that—his Santa Fe isn't in the driveway. "Sure."

We climb the stairs, my eyes on the collection of pictures hanging on the wall. I stall on the one with a much younger Emmett and Cassie—under ten, I'd guess—posing in front of a snowman, toques on their heads, their cheeks rosy from the cold. Emmett's face is thin, his form gangly. Cassie is wearing the biggest grin I've ever seen on a kid. The two of them are almost the same height.

"Cassie, did you clean up your room like I asked?" Heather calls from the kitchen.

"I *did*! It's clean!" She adds an "Ugh ... mothers" under her breath as she stomps the rest of the way up the stairs.

I press my lips together to stifle my laugh at the petulant streak that flares every once in a while and follow her into her room.

Into the bubblegum-pink cave of disaster—dresser drawers sitting open, dirty clothes scattered across the floor, an unmade bed heaped with piles of stuffed animals and more clothes, a box overflowing with naked dolls of various sizes and styles, dog and cat posters and a calendar that sits on January. It's not the room you'd expect of a girl turning sixteen in February, but the moment I see it, I'm not at all surprised that it's Cassie's.

She grins and then says, in that slightly stilted way of hers, "It's not that messy."

THE FRONT DOOR creaks open as I'm heaping a spoonful of mashed potatoes onto my plate.

My heart skips a beat and then thumps in my chest, my attention locking on the Hartfords' dining room threshold.

Waiting.

"Dining room, *now!*" Mark calls over his shoulder.

Heavy footfalls sound along the hallway and then Emmett appears, his hair still damp from a shower.

Nervous flutters stir in my stomach.

Mark gives his son a scolding look. "You're late."

"Coach wanted to have a team meeting after practice to go over a few things before tomorrow's game."

"If *only* there was some way you could communicate that to us."

"He could text," Cassie says, not picking up on the sarcasm in her father's tone.

Mark snaps his fingers. "You're right, Cassie! He could text. If *only* he had a phone—"

"All right. I'm sorry," Emmett mumbles, sliding into the empty chair beside Uncle Merv, across from me. "Hey, Merv. How's it going?"

"Still alive." His clouded eyes are focused on his dinner, clearly more interested in eating than carrying on a conversation. He likely won't utter a single word through the meal.

Emmett smirks, unfazed by the old man's response. I'm sure he's used to that acerbic personality. And then his beautiful brown eyes shift to me. "Hey."

"Hi." I'm staring, I realize, and so I duck my head, refocusing on my plate.

"So, Emmett says you guys have a class together, Aria?" Heather spoons a few carrots onto Cassie's plate.

"That's enough," Cassie declares, blocking the air above her plate with her hand.

She gets a warning look and two more spoonfuls in return, which earns a scowl at her plate.

"Social studies. Yeah."

"*And* they'll be on the cross-country team together soon, too. *Right?*" My mom looks at me expectantly.

"You're joining the team?" Emmett slaps a heaping serving spoon's worth of mashed potatoes next to the two large cutlets he grabbed. Is it just my wishful thinking or did I catch a hint of excitement in his tone?

"*If* I can get my time up before then." If my run last night after dinner is any indication, I won't be joining.

"I jog through Miller's Park on the off-mornings. It's not far from here. It's hilly but it's good training ground. You can come with me, if you want?"

Me, run with Emmett? Just the two of us? A thrill races through my chest. "Yeah. For sure."

"I want to come!" Cassie exclaims.

"You want to *run* three kilometers at seven in the morning, Cassie?" he says doubtfully.

"Yes!" She nods in emphasis.

"*All the way* around the pond, without stopping?"

She seems to consider that a moment. "No. Maybe not," she agrees.

He smirks. "AJ's gotta try to keep up with me."

"Don't be surprised if she gives you a good challenge," my mom chirps, and then takes a sip of wine. "She placed second in provincials."

"That was two years ago," I remind her quietly, my cheeks flushing.

"So! I'm still allowed to brag."

I bite my tongue against the urge to remind her that she's never even been to a race. We're both starting over, fresh.

"I wish I had a tenth of the energy these kids have." Heather's attention shifts between my mom and Cassie, who is gripping her butter knife awkwardly in her fist and sawing away at her meat with little success. Heather's hands reach out but then pull back, as if wanting to help Cassie but deciding against it.

"We're watching a movie in the basement, tonight," Cassie declares. "AJ, do you want to watch with us?" She nods, as if coaxing me into saying yes, her eyebrows arched with hope.

"Zach's having people over. You should come with me," Emmett throws out, taking a gulp of his milk. "You can meet a few people from school."

Did Emmett just invite me to a party?

"Are his parents going to be home?" Heather asks.

"Of course," Emmett says with his focus on his plate, in a way that doesn't sound at all convincing—at least not to me.

"I don't know ..." my mom begins, wariness in her voice.

"I want to go to Zach's, too!" Cassie bursts. "Can I go?"

Heather spears Emmett with a knowing glare.

He sighs heavily. "It's mostly the hockey team, plus the music will be too loud. You wouldn't have fun there."

"Yes, I would!" She insists with a determined set of her jaw. "Zach's my friend, too!"

Is he, though? Cassie calls *everyone* her friend.

"Hey! What about *our* night?" Mark jumps in, gesturing between himself and her. "I thought we were going to get banana splits at Dairy Queen?"

Cassie frowns deeply. "I didn't know that."

"I can't believe you forgot. Don't bail on me, kid."

Something tells me Cassie wouldn't forget something like a trip for ice cream. Something also tells me it's meant as a distraction and a bribe, a treat that Cassie won't pass up.

"Can AJ come?"

Mark shrugs, glancing at me. "Sure, if that's what—"

"She's coming to Zach's with me," Emmett cuts in.

"Hold on. I didn't approve that," Mom says.

"*Mom*." I stare at her, trying to convey with my eyes how badly I want to go. If I miss out on a night with Emmett, I will *never* forgive her.

"Maybe you should spend some time with Cassie tonight," she says softly.

"It's just a small group of kids from school, Mrs. Jones," Emmett offers in a cordial tone.

"Call me Debra, please." Her lips purse as she studies my pleading eyes. "Is this a gathering that would be suitable for my *fifteen*-year-old daughter?"

"*Almost six*teen," I clarify through gritted teeth, my cheeks burning.

"No drinking," Emmett promises.

She gives him a flat look. "I'm not naïve."

He holds his hands in the air. "I have a game tomorrow so I'm driving and coming home by midnight."

I can see the struggle within Mom's eyes.

"If there's one thing my son takes seriously, it's being well rested for his games," Heather adds, and I silently thank her for the motherly seal of approval.

Mom takes a deep breath. "Fine. As long as she's with you and you're home by eleven."

"Mom!"

"Eleven is fine." Emmett smirks. "I can use the extra sleep."

I let out a long, shaky breath, struggling to keep my excitement at bay.

That's when I notice Cassie is staring at her plate with a crestfallen face. Heather's hand is smoothing over her back in a comforting manner, her pained eyes flickering to Mark.

What must it be like for Cassie, to be told she can't go to a party, but meanwhile I'm going with her brother? I'm technically only three months older than she is. How many times has she been told no to going out like other teenagers do?

Guilt for choosing the party with Emmett over a movie with her overwhelms me.

I think fast. "Hey, Cassie, do you want to go to the movies tomorrow afternoon to see that one you mentioned?"

Her eyes widen and then light up, the party at Zach's temporarily forgotten. "*Teen Queen*? I really want to see that."

I know. She's only mentioned it every day this week. "Do you want to go with me?" I have no idea what it's about, but I saw the name on the marquee as Mom and I passed the theater today and I thought of Cassie.

She looks to Heather, a strange—almost terrified—expression on her face. "Can I go?" she whispers.

Heather's shoulders sag with relief. "Of course. That sounds like a great idea." She flashes an appreciative smile at me. "I can drop you two off."

"Alone? You mean, just AJ and me?"

"Yes."

Cassie, already beaming, lets out an excited squeal that earns Uncle Merv's grimace. "Oh Lord," he grumbles.

I can't help but laugh as I meet Emmett's gaze.

To find his soft smile as he regards me.

THE ENGINE of Emmett's SUV is already running when I rush across the lawn, five minutes late, adjusting the collar of the navy-blue boatneck shirt I threw on.

"Hurry up, before Cassie and my dad get home." His wary eyes are on the street as I slide into the passenger seat.

"I thought she was okay with this?" I fasten my seat belt, discreetly inhaling the clean scent of his cologne. Emmett has changed too, into a pair of dark-wash jeans and a charcoal-gray T-shirt that clings to his torso without being too tight.

"She is, but if she sees us leaving, she'll forget how excited she is about tomorrow and focus on what she's missing tonight. And then she'll cry that she's being left out and I'll feel like an asshole." His voice sounds heavy as he puts the car in drive. "That was nice of you, by the way, offering to take her to the movies."

I shrug. "I don't have any plans tomorrow."

His mouth curves with a secretive smile.

"What?"

"Nothing, just ... you've never watched a movie with Cassie before."

"Why? What happens?" I ask warily.

"Nothing bad." He laughs. "You'll see."

I'm distracted from pushing for more information by my mom's silhouette in my bedroom window, watching us drive away. My guess is she'll be hunting for my journal as soon as we've rounded the corner. I don't think she'll find it. I tucked it under a loose floorboard I found under the desk while I was dragging furniture around to paint the walls. It's a pain to fetch, but it was the best hiding spot I could find.

"Kind of surprised your mom didn't change her mind about letting you out." Emmett makes a right turn at the end of our street.

"Oh, she did. That's why I was late. I had to pry the shackles from my ankles. Thank God for that hacksaw Uncle Merv keeps by the door."

Emmett chuckles.

"Seriously though, he *keeps a hacksaw behind the front door*." Mom questioned him about it the other day. He said it's to trim all the damn branches.

"She seems a little overprotective."

"Yeah. It's the move," I lie. "And she has a lot more time on her hands to worry right now. I'm sure it'll change when she goes back to work. So how far away is Zach's house?" The street has led us out of town, where there are no street lights save for side road markers. I haven't ventured out this way yet.

"About ten minutes out."

"Who's going to be there?"

"Mostly guys from hockey."

"So does this Zach guy play with you?"

"Not anymore. We used to, but he wouldn't make my team now. He plays on the school team. You've seen him with me. He's the blond guy I hang out with."

I frown in thought. "I don't think so?" Though, I don't pay much attention to *anyone* else when Emmett's there.

"He's seen *you*, that's for sure."

A nervous twinge stirs in my stomach. "What does that mean?"

Emmett smiles, showing off that deep dimple. "Let's

just say he's happy I'm bringing my cute new neighbor tonight."

I look out my window at the dark fields as my face burns with Emmett's words. Is he simply relaying what his friend has said about me? Or echoing his own thoughts?

An awkward silence ensues.

Emmett dials the music up a notch. "It'll be fun. Holly and a few of her friends will be there, so you can get to know them, too."

Disappointment flares at the reminder that yes, Emmett has a girlfriend and yes, *of course* she's going to be there. "How long have you guys been together?" I ask casually, though I already know the answer. I'm more curious about how he'll answer it—does he like talking about his girl-friend? Or is he like other guys I've known who shrug off the topic?

"Almost a year. If you can find out the exact date for me, I'll owe you *big* time, because I forget. I know it was September. She was like you."

"*Like me?*"

"Yeah. The new girl in school."

"Oh. *Right.*" New and blonde and beautiful, with that honeyed voice and sweet smile. Not exactly me. "She's nice," I offer, because what else do I say?

He smiles softly. "Holly's great. Cassie introduced us. I can't remember how they met but the next thing I knew, we were at the fall fair together." He snaps his fingers. "That's when we hooked up. It was the last weekend of September, but I can't remember if it was the Friday or the Saturday."

"You have a few weeks to figure it out."

"Yeah." He pauses. "What are you supposed to get your girlfriend for your one-year anniversary, anyway?"

"I have *no* idea." I've only had two boyfriends, for a total of four weeks of "dating" experience. The first one treated me to a McDonald's burger, the other one got me high on weed. My guess is Holly wouldn't go for either of those gift ideas. "Jewelry, maybe? Like a charm bracelet or necklace?" That's what my friend Denise got from her boyfriend Dennis—worst name match ever—after they'd been going out for six months.

"Yeah. Maybe." Emmett bites his bottom lip in thought. "Like a little hockey puck or stick or something, to remind her of me."

I laugh. "Wow. You *really* like hockey."

His deep, shiver-inducing chuckle fills the car.

"FARMER ... WHAT'S UP!"

"Harty!" The tall blond guy who opened the front door claps hands with Emmett, then backs up to allow us into the impressive two-story brick house, surrounded by corn and hay fields. Apparently Zach's family owns, like, *half* the land around the outskirts of town. Some they've sold off to developers—and made a killing—while other plots are actively farmed.

Hence Zach's nickname.

His blue eyes lands on me, a twinkle of curiosity in it. "AJ, right?"

"Aria. But sure. Hey." I do recognize him from the hallways. He's hot—with a square jaw and playful grin, and pretty eyes framed by long lashes. He's the same height as Emmett and solid, though not nearly as fit. If not for my instant infatuation with Emmett, I'd probably be crushing on him.

"I'm Zach."

"I figured that out." I blush as I recall Emmett's cute-neighbor comment on the way here.

He holds up a bottle of beer. "Want one?"

"I'm good for now, thanks." My eyes flash to Emmett—he shrugs and tugs a can of Coke from the six-pack he brought with him. I guess he didn't lie to my mom. *He's* not drinking.

Where are Zach's parents, anyway?

Kicking the door shut with his heel, Zach leads us toward the back of the house with a leisurely stroll, the hum of music and laughter growing louder. "Did you hear that Gibby broke his leg?" he says to Emmett.

"Yeah. In like three places. He's out for most of the year. Sucks bad."

I tune out what I assume is hockey talk as we step into a double-story living room, my eyes furtively scanning the group of twenty or so teenagers. Most are faces I could pick out of the hallways at school.

Including Holly.

She's sitting on the far end of the couch, sandwiched between the girl she lunches with and another pretty blonde. The second her eyes land on Emmett, she's off the couch and skipping over, wasting no time wrapping her arms around his waist, molding her body to his.

"Hey, you. What took you so long?" She mock-pouts, lifting on tiptoes to press her lips against his.

I look away, unintentionally to Zach, who rolls his eyes but then grins.

She finally peels her mouth from his to flash a brilliant, white smile at me. "Hey, Aria! Glad you could make it."

"Thanks. Yeah. Me too."

"Now, if you don't mind, I have to *borrow* this guy for a

sec." She pushes Emmett, forcing him to step backward toward a hallway, a sly smirk curving her lips as she peers up at him.

Emmett's hands are in the air in surrender, as if he has no control, but he's grinning.

"I guess I'll see you later, bro." Zach shakes his head. Under his breath, I catch "like rabbits."

And I feel my body sink with disappointment that he's leaving me alone out here, that he would invite me out and then abandon me so quickly, with a bunch of people I don't know.

Zach sucks back a gulp of his beer, then nods toward the couch. "Come on, AJ. Let me introduce you to some people from school." He points to a guy with a shaved head and sunken cheeks. "Have you met Mower yet?"

CHAPTER
SEVEN

Dear Julia,

It's midnight and I can't sleep, so I figured I'd write to you.

Tonight was fun, even if I spent most of it watching Zach and Mower play PS4 hockey. I'm still not sure what his real name is, or why they call him Mower. I asked Zach and he shook his head and smiled secretively, which tells me I probably don't want to hear that story.

Which makes me want to hear that story.

If Zach does think I'm cute, either he changed his mind or he's shy. He didn't try anything on me, and let me tell you, that's a relief because I don't know if I would want him to. Sure, he's nice, and hot, and funny. But I just didn't feel that thing. You know that thing ... when you meet eyes with a guy you like, and then they smile at you, and you have to remind yourself to breathe?

Like when Emmett looks at me.

Speaking of Emmett, he and Holly were gone FOREVER. And when they came back, Holly's hair was messed up and Emmett seemed sleepy. It doesn't take a *genius to figure out what Holly was "borrowing" him for. I can see how those rumors Jen was talking about got started. It's because they're true.*

Still, when Emmett finally joined us, he sat down on the other side of me and the first thing he asked was if I was good, if I was having fun. And when everyone was razzing him for leaving so early, instead of telling them he had to get me home by my curfew, he took the fall and said he was tired.

He's so nice.

And so DAMN gorgeous (I think Uncle Merv is rubbing off on me).

I can't wait for our run on Monday morning.

~AJ

"How was the movie?" Heather asks as I slide into the back seat, her attention on Cassie.

"It was *so* good. I ate *a lot* of junk," Cassie announces proudly.

"Why am I not surprised." She waits for Cassie to fasten her seat belt, glancing over her shoulder at me. "Did you enjoy it, Aria?"

"It was *okay*." I study the two-screen, 1950s retro movie theater on Eastmonte's main street, wishing I had done a little more research about the movie before offering to go. At least now I know what Emmett was smiling about in the car. Cassie cannot stay quiet through a movie. Granted, it's to ask questions about what's going on, and then to ask follow-up questions on the explanations I gave her. But she also asks questions that make me stop to wonder how much she truly understands. Over and over, I had to reassure her that, yes, these are all actors; yes, the dog is a paid actor; no, he doesn't have any lines; yes, this is all fake; no, this isn't a real prom.

Thank God the theater was mostly empty and we were sitting far enough away from people that we didn't irritate anyone. Still, if it had been a movie I was interested in watching, I'd be annoyed.

Heather pulls out. "What was your favorite part of the movie?"

"The dog."

I laugh, because Cassie's so predictable.

She giggles too and says in that slightly stilted, exaggerated way of hers, "I know, *AJ*. I like *dogs*. And cats. I like animals."

Heather reaches out to pat her daughter's arm. "What about the parts that have nothing to do with animals?"

I can see the reflection of Cassie's face in the side view mirror. Her face is twisted up like she's giving this serious thought. "I liked it when the girl went to prom. Prom is a big dance. Have you heard of it?"

Heather smiles. "Yes. I know what prom is. My school had a prom."

"Does my school have a prom?"

"As far as I know. I think I heard Holly saying something about Emmett's prom."

"When is mine?"

"It'll be the same time, I guess? Spring of your senior year?"

Which will be when, exactly? Emmett said that Cassie would likely be in high school until she's twenty-one.

"Are *you* going, AJ?" Cassie asks, catching me off guard, though I should have expected that question.

"Maybe. It's too far away to plan."

"I think I'll go to prom," Cassie announces with certainty.

Heather's eyes leave the street long enough to offer her daughter a soft smile. "You want to get all dressed up?"

"Yeah." Cassie nods. "Except I'm *not* wearing high heels because I'll fall."

"You don't have to wear high heels," Heather assures her.

"Yeah ... and I'll have to find a date," she says matter-of-factly.

"Or not. You can go alone."

There's a long pause. "I don't want to go alone."

"Well, then, maybe you can go with Dillon."

I recognize that name. Cassie has talked about him on our walks home. He's a boy with autism in her class.

Cassie shrugs. "Dillon doesn't like music. I don't think he's going."

"Okay, well, maybe Emmett could take you."

Would Emmett do that? Come home from wherever he is in five years to take his little sister to a high school prom? Knowing him, probably.

"Yeah." I watch Cassie think about that for a moment. "Or Zach could take me."

That's a stretch. I know he's Emmett's friend, but is he that good of a friend? Would the tall, blond popular guy come back in five years to walk arm-in-arm with his friend's autistic sister? And what would she wear? I can't picture her in a short hem or a plunging neckline. Sure, she's developing like a woman but the more I get to know her—how innocent she still is—I can't see her in anything but a puffy pink Cinderella dress.

"Maybe." It could be this angle, but the smile on Heather's mouth wavers.

71

THE FIRST THING I notice when we pull into the Hartford driveway is that the Santa Fe is still gone.

"When is Emmett coming home?" Cassie practically plucks that question from my mind.

"He said five, I think. Cassie, can you take that bag by your feet into your father right away so he can finish dinner?" Heather points to a reusable grocery bag. "I'll be there in a second."

I sense that she wants to speak to me, so I linger outside the car, watching Cassie trudge away.

Heather offers me a warm smile. "Thank you for taking Cassie to the movies today."

I shrug. "It's no big deal. Really."

"No, it *is* a big deal." She sighs. "Cassie doesn't have a lot of friends. She *knows* a lot of people. Between neighbors and families we've gotten to know over the years through Emmett's hockey, she's surrounded by a lot of people who care and are great with her. But none of them are *her* friends. People who make time for her. Holly did for a while, but ..." Heather frowns. "It means a lot to Cassie to be able to go to a movie with you. We're grateful to you for suggesting that last night." Her voice has taken on a slightly husky tone.

I nod, unsure of how to respond. "I had fun." And I did, I realize, even with Cassie's prattling and the sense that I had to watch over her like a babysitter watches over her charge.

"Well, in case you haven't noticed, she idolizes you. She came home the other day and demanded that we repaint her bedroom to match yours."

"Really?" I laugh.

"Yes. Your mom gave me the color chip from your room. Mark is *very* excited about painting." Her laugh carries a derisive note. With that, she collects the rest of the groceries from the trunk.

I watch her disappear behind the front door, feeling a sudden lightness in my chest that hasn't been there in so long.

EMMETT IS WAITING for me at the end of his driveway, stretching his hamstrings, when I emerge on Monday morning at 7:00 a.m. His brown eyes roll over my black running shorts and my bare legs—that I thankfully remembered to shave last night, because the air is crisper than I expected and I have gooseflesh—before landing on my old high school shirt. His face splits into a wide grin. "Llamas?"

"Hey, *I* didn't pick my high school mascot." I grab an ankle and begin my warm-up stretches, stealing a covert glance at his form—long legs coated with dark hair and rippling with muscle; broad shoulders that lead into a shapely back. He's wearing a burgundy-and-gold Eastmonte Eagles T-shirt that's threadbare and clingy around his sinewy arms and powerful-looking chest.

His body is not that of a seventeen-year-old boy—at least not one I've ever met.

"At least llamas are more creative than eagles."

"Fair point." He grins, connecting his hands behind his back to stretch his chest, a move that shifts his collar, revealing a purplish-red bruise on his collarbone.

"What happened to your neck?" I blurt out without thinking.

"Nothing," he says, tugging at his T-shirt collar to cover it, his cheeks flushing.

"*Oh.*" It finally dawns on me—Emmett has a hickey? "*Really?*"

He groans. "Don't you start, too. I've already gotten enough chirping from my team yesterday."

"Sorry, I just haven't seen one in a while."

"Since you were twelve, right?" He grimaces. "Holly knew what she was doing, too. She thought it'd be funny."

"It kind of is." I press my lips together to keep from laughing.

"Yeah, to everyone else." He's annoyed but at least he's smiling now. He tucks his earbuds into his ears. Now I wish I'd brought mine. "Come on, Jones. Let's see what you've got."

"Jeez ..." A bead of sweat runs down the side of Emmett's face by the time we reach the end of our driveways. "I can't believe you kept up. Your mom wasn't kidding." His breathing is as ragged as mine.

I bite my tongue against the urge to taunt him, to remind him that I only just started training again. The truth is, I wouldn't have gone that hard had I not had the carrot of Emmett dangling there to push me. But my thighs and lungs burn, the three-kilometer route around Miller's Park—a hilly conservation area with a small pond in the center— equal parts peaceful and grueling. We were the only ones out this morning, save for a lady walking her black Lab.

Emmett uses the hem of his T-shirt to wipe his face, giving me a sublime view of his six-pack and the dark trail of hair disappearing into his shorts.

I have to turn away to hide my bulging eyes.

Seriously, he's only seventeen?

"Moretti's gonna have a lady boner when she sees you run." He checks his watch. "'Kay. We better grab a shower before school." He frowns, and points at both our houses. "I meant separately. As in, two showers. In our own bathrooms."

"Yeah, I figured." I laugh it off, though in my head, I'm suddenly wondering all kinds of things, namely, has Emmett ever showered with a girl before? And what does the rest of him look like in the shower? And did he think I'd take that to mean something different?

Can he tell I'm crushing on him?

My heart, already racing from the run, takes on a whole new tempo as my stomach flutters with nerves.

"See you in a bit." With one last grin, he jogs toward his house.

FORTY-FIVE MINUTES LATER, I'm waiting by the Santa Fe when Emmett walks out of the Hartfords' front door, a half-eaten banana in his grip. He's freshly showered and looking as hot as ever.

"Cassie, come on or we'll be late!" He hits the button on his key fob to unlock the doors for me and then strolls to the end of the driveway to toss the peel into the green bin.

Cassie rushes out about thirty seconds later and climbs

into the back seat. "I'm not ready!" she warns, as she does every morning.

He drums his fingers on the steering wheel, his lips pressed together tightly, as if he's struggling to keep his patience this morning. What's it like to have Cassie for a sister?

Her seat belt clicks. "'Kay, I'm ready."

He pulls out of the driveway.

"When is your next hockey game, Emmett?" she asks.

"Thursday night."

"Is it in Eastmonte?"

"Yup. Why?"

"AJ should come. Do you want to come with us to watch Emmett play, AJ?"

A rush of adrenaline courses through my body. Yes, I want to watch Emmett play. Now I have a valid excuse to go. "Uh ... yeah, sure. Maybe?"

"You don't have to," Emmett offers in an apologetic tone.

"No, it's cool. I've never been."

"You've never been to a hockey game?" Cassie asks with exaggerated shock.

I laugh. "No. It wasn't a thing for my family."

"I've been to a lot of games," she says. "How many games have I been to, Emmett?"

"I don't know. *Hundreds*. You're a rink rat."

"I'm *not* a rink rat. What's that thing on your neck?" she asks suddenly, changing topics without warning or pause.

I press my lips together to hide my smile as I steal a glance at the red bruise.

"It's nothing," he dismisses, his jaw tensing as he tugs at his shirt collar.

"There's a dark mark right there. On your neck. I see it.

What is it? Emmett?" A second later. "Emmett?" Another three seconds pass without answer. "Emmett."

"It's *nothing*, okay? A bruise, from hockey."

"Oh. Okay." There's a long pause, as if she's thinking about it, and then, "But don't you wear a neck guard?" There's a hint of skepticism in her voice.

"Of course you'd figure that out," he says under his breath.

"Is that really a bruise from hockey?" When he doesn't respond, she asks, "Is that really a bruise from hockey, AJ?"

Emmett shoots me a warning look.

I briefly consider keeping up his lie, but he's not lying to protect her. He's doing it to save himself from embarrassment. He *should* be embarrassed. "No. It's a hickey."

"I can't believe you threw me under the bus like that!" Emmett groans.

I grin.

"A *hickey*?" Cassie tries out the word. "What's a *hickey*?"

"I'm *not* explaining that to her." His eyes are locked on the street ahead.

"What's a hickey, AJ?"

How *do* you explain these things to a girl who is almost sixteen but is still so innocent? I guess the same way you'd explain it to a ten- or eleven-year-old—with gentle honesty. "It means Holly kissed your brother's neck too hard."

"What?" Cassie's face scrunches up as she processes this. "So Holly's like a vampire?"

I burst out laughing and even Emmett can't help but smile. "Kind of, except she didn't bite him." At least, I don't think she did.

And I don't want to think about that.

"It's not something you talk about with people, okay,

Cassie? So don't tell your teachers or the kids in your class." Under his breath, but loud enough for me to hear, he adds, "Or *everyone* you know."

"Yeah. I know. Okay." I watch Cassie's face from my side view mirror as she considers this concept of kissing necks too hard. It's a good ten seconds before she frowns, gives her head a shake, and mutters, "Ewww."

CASSIE and I walk home that afternoon to find a tiny, white-haired lady and a giant car in Uncle Merv's driveway.

"Hello, Iris!" Cassie waves dramatically.

Iris. Aunt Connie's friend, a.k.a. the tuna casserole lady.

The lady shuffles her entire body around to regard us, and her wrinkled face splits into a grandmotherly smile. "Well, hello there, Cassie, how are you?"

"I'm good." Cassie jabs my shoulder with her finger. "This is Aria, but we call her AJ. That's her nickname."

Iris sets her purse in the driver's seat and then walks down the driveway to meet us, moving more easily than I'd expect of a woman in her seventies. Soft eyes land on me. "It's nice to finally meet you, Aria. I just finished having tea with your mother! Came by to see how Merv was faring and to drop off another tuna casserole."

Another tuna casserole. I force a polite smile. "*Yum.*"

"Well, I know it's Merv's favorite." The lenses in her glasses must be twice the thickness as the black frames, and they make her eyes look unnaturally large as she studies me. "How are you enjoying living here?"

"It's great, so far." That, I can answer honestly.

"Well, good. I'm glad to hear that. Your uncle was so

excited that you were coming. Listen, I'm going to let you two go now. I'll bet you have a lot of homework to do. And Cassie ... there *might* be something special waiting for you at home."

Cassie's grin falls off, her face turning serious. "Molasses cookies?"

"Better get them now before that brother of yours eats them all."

Cassie takes off, yelling "Bye!" as she gallops across the front lawn.

Iris laughs and shakes her head. "Oh, that girl and her sweet tooth. Well, you take care of that old grouch in there for me, Aria. Or AJ."

"Will do." I say goodbye and head inside, dropping my backpack on the floor by the stairs. Uncle Merv is in his chair, watching another black-and-white war documentary. "Hey, Uncle Merv," I call out on my way past, but I don't get a response. Sometimes he gets so into those movies that you have to stand right beside him to grab his attention.

My mom is at the kitchen sink, washing dishes. "Hey, hon. How was school?"

"Fine." A stack of Ontario law textbooks sits on the kitchen table. Next to them are a plate of crumbly brown cookies and a tall glass of milk.

"Iris made those," she confirms.

I slide into my seat and break a piece off. "I just met her outside."

"She's a sweet lady. We spent the past hour reminiscing about Aunt Connie. It felt good." Mom dries her hands with a tea towel and then, wandering over to peer around the corner at Uncle Merv first, she lowers her voice. "I think she's trying to woo your uncle."

"What?" I cringe. "But, she was Aunt Connie's friend. And they're *old*."

Mom's laughter fills the small, cramped kitchen. "That doesn't mean they don't want companionship. It happens all the time."

I match her low voice, though I doubt he can hear anything over the bomb blasts and plane engines. "You think Uncle Merv wants companionship?"

"I think your uncle wants someone to cook his meals and wash his clothes." She smirks, taking the chair across from me. "Okay, let's hear it."

I stifle my groan. Some days this is a real struggle, but Mom doesn't seem to care what I tell her, as long as I'm telling her *something*. "Number one: I told Ms. Moretti I'd join the cross-country team." I ran into her in the hall before third period.

Mom's eyes light up. "Oh, fantastic!"

"The first practice is tomorrow morning before school."

"Do you need a ride?"

"No. I'm going in with Emmett."

"Oh, well ..." She frowns. "How is Cassie going to get in?"

I shrug. "I don't know?"

She waves it off. "Heather will figure that out. What else?"

"Um, number two: I might go and see Emmett's hockey game on Thursday night. Cassie asked me to go with her."

"That's a great idea. Heather was telling me they try to go to all his local games. Maybe I should come, too. Get out of the house and meet some people," she muses, collecting her tea cup. "Oh! Before I forget, we're having the house repiped. I figure if we're living here for however long, we should be sure there's no lead in our water. Mick is coming next week. He said he could do it all in one day. I'm hoping that's true, because Uncle Merv won't like being without water for longer than that." She sighs, as if even the thought of dealing with Uncle Merv in that situation is exhausting. "Okay, one more," she asks and takes a sip.

"Cassie learned what a hickey was today."

Mom begins choking.

"Sorry." I wait patiently, picking at Iris's cookies, as Mom coughs up the tea she accidentally inhaled.

She clears her throat. "And how exactly did she learn that?"

I explain the morning car ride, giggling at the memory of watching Emmett fuss with his collar for most of first period.

The kitchen chair creaks as Mom leans back in it. "I guess I shouldn't be surprised that he'd be ... you know ..." She waves a casual hand.

"Having sex?" I say boldly. Maybe if I make this uncomfortable for her, she'll stop pushing for these daily chats.

She presses her lips together but then nods. "He's a good-looking kid and seventeen years old. Almost eighteen, I think Heather said the other day." She hesitates. "So, have you met any boys that you like yet?"

Yes, the one from next door with the hickey. The one with the girlfriend. The one I have to stop thinking about.

I pick at the last of the cookie crumbs and shake my head. "I'm going to start my homework now."

CHAPTER
EIGHT

Ten students linger by the front doors of school when Emmett and I pull into the parking lot at seven the next morning. My stomach flutters with nerves at the thought of walking up to a group of people who all know each other. Though, having Emmett by my side helps.

"Who is *that*?" I nod toward the stocky guy off to the side. A thick yellow headband—the kind a tennis player would wear—stretches over his curly brown hair and his socks are pulled up to just below his knees.

Emmett grins. "*That* is Richard. He's in my calculus class. Super smart."

"Is he for real?"

"Yeah." He chuckles. "I think he's channeling Jack Black, circa ... I don't even know, but he's intense."

"Uh ... *yeah*." Everyone else is chatting and laughing. Meanwhile, this Richard guy is rushing three steps one way, then spinning to rush three steps back, only to repeat.

"He comes out every year. Slow as hell, but he always finishes." Emmett half frowns, half smiles at the boy, now jumping up and down in place, shaking out his wrists and cocking his head from side to side. "He's a strange dude, but he's nice. Cassie loves him. Thinks he's the funniest guy in the world."

And with Cassie, I'm sure she's laughing *with* him, not at him.

By the time Emmett and I join the group, Ms. Moretti has emerged from the school. She's traded in her usual dress and heels for jogging pants and running shoes, and when she stands next to Emmett, who is at least a foot taller, I have to stifle my laugh. "Welcome, everyone! I'm excited to see so many of you back this year." She gives a gapped-tooth grin at the faces circling her. "And good news! We have an import from out west. *This* is Aria Jones." She gestures at me. "She's an old pro. She's placed in a provincial race before."

"She's gonna kick butt," Emmett pipes up.

"No, I won't," I mumble, feeling my cheeks flush as I cast an awkward wave.

Emmett leans in close, his chest bumping my shoulder as he mock-whispers, "We need to work on your trash-talking skills."

And my ability to breathe in your proximity.

I struggle to concentrate as Moretti spends a few minutes reviewing the rules—no missing more than two practices, must compete at three of the four mini-meets—before she claps her hands. "Okay, we're going to spend a few minutes warming up and then we'll do laps around the school property. Just for today. We'll venture off to our usual course around Miller's Park on Thursday—"

"Hey, Ms. M!" a female voice calls out. I turn to see Holly jogging toward us, her long blonde hair pulled into a ponytail, her Eagles T-shirt hugging her ample chest, her shorts showing off toned legs. "I'm sorry I'm late. My car wouldn't start."

Holly is in cross-country, too?

Emmett didn't mention that, did he?

"No problem. We're warming up."

"Hey, Aria!" she says, giving my forearm a gentle squeeze as she passes by me to fit in next to Emmett. "I'm so glad you've joined our team! Em said you're *really* good. You won provincials?"

"I came in second," I say.

"The second-fastest llama Alberta's ever seen," Emmett teases, grinning at me.

"Hey, you." She lifts to press a kiss against his lips.

I struggle to stifle my groan.

THE SMELL of stale sweat and popcorn permeates the air of Eastmonte's arena, an old brown brick building on the other side of town.

"Just a hot chocolate." Heather hands Cassie a five-dollar bill with an encouraging nod, but also a clear warning. "I'll see you two in there?" Pulling up the zipper on Cassie's hot-pink vest, Heather then heads for the rink on the right, pausing to greet a small cluster of mothers.

We head for the concession stand and the stern-looking older man running it.

The moment he sees Cassie step up, his hard mask cracks. "Finally! It's been a long summer of not seeing that smile. How are you, Cassie?"

"Good." She grins. "How's Coco?"

"Coco's good. Coco likes to chase cats."

Cassie laughs. "Yeah. That's because she's a dog." To me, she says, "I named her. She was a shelter dog and Frank adopted her."

"That's right. Cassie kept telling me about this small black poodle that came in. She was convinced that *I* needed a dog. Turns out she was right." Frank chuckles, reaching for a paper cup. "The usual?"

"One small hot chocolate, please." Cassie carefully places the five-dollar bill on the counter, leaving her hand on it as if it might fly away in a breeze.

"You want one, too?" His bushy eyebrows raise as he regards me and then, when he sees me waffling, adds, "It gets cold in there."

"Sure, okay. Thanks." I pluck a box of Junior Mints from the display and set it on the counter, then dig my money out of my pocket.

Cassie's eyes light up. "Do you like mint?"

"I do. I *love* mint."

"Me too." She pauses, smiling at them. I see the internal battle in her eyes before she finally blurts out, "I wish I could have some."

I can't help but laugh. That's the thing with Cassie—her intentions are obvious, but so innocent and simple. "Do you want to share the box with me?"

She nods in emphasis and her grin widens. "But don't tell my mom."

We gather our purchases, say goodbye to Frank, and make our way into the rink. The two teams are already warming up on their respective sides of the ice to the blaring music, skating in circles, firing shots on the goalie. I try to pick out Emmett but they all look the same.

A shiver runs through me from the sudden drop in temperature, and I'm thankful for the sweater Heather warned me to bring as well as the piping-hot beverage in my grasp. "Where should we sit?" I spot Heather's blonde head halfway down the blue bleacher-style seats, surrounded by a group of other moms, laughing and talking. Mark is standing at the top, talking to a man who fiddles with a video camera.

"We can sit with Holly."

"She's here?" *Of course she's here. To cheer on her boyfriend.*

Cassie's blue eyes search the heads in the stands before she announces with dismay, "I don't see her."

"Do you know if she's coming?"

"She's always here. Like me." Cassie shrugs it off. "That's okay. Sometimes she comes late. Can you help me with this?" She doesn't wait for my answer, thrusting her hot chocolate toward me so she can grip the rail with both hands and ease down the steep set of concrete stairs with great care.

"This is good," she declares, settling into a chair halfway down and over a section from the cluster of parents. She then takes her drink back and peels the lid open. "Mom! We're going to sit over here!" she hollers, earning several waves and smiles from surrounding parents. "This is AJ! She's our new neighbor!" She points at me, spilling her hot chocolate on her pants in the process. "Oops." She laughs and haphazardly wipes it away with a hand before dismissing it completely.

I'm fastening my sweater when a buzzer sounds and the teams race to kneel in front of a man who must be their coach.

"That's Emmett." She points at the gaggle of guys in helmets at the Home bench. "Number forty-four. He plays left wing?" she says as if she's not sure, her face scrunching up. "Emmett!" She waves at their backs.

"I think he's listening to his coach."

"Oh, yeah, he's not watching." When they finally break, five guys, including Emmett, skate into position. Cassie waves furiously again, calling his name.

He throws a hand in the air and Cassie points at me. "Look! It's AJ!" Another splash of hot chocolate hits her clothes, this time her pink vest. "Oops." She wipes once at it before ignoring it to take a sip through her straw. I've never met anyone who drinks hot chocolate through a straw.

But I've also never met anyone like Cassie before.

A whistle blows and the puck starts flying. "Do you understand the rules?" I ask.

"Yeah." Cassie nods vigorously, then laughs. "Actually, no. Kind of. Where is Holly?" She looks over her shoulder at the door.

Spilling hot chocolate on herself ... again.

"I don't see her," I confirm, silently admitting that I'm okay with that. I turn my attention to the game, to watch Emmett get the puck and race for his opponent's end, weaving deftly around the player trying to block him, and firing off a shot. It sails in, earning a round of cheers and claps from the stands.

"He's good," Cassie says, her head bobbing up and down as if to emphasize it.

"He is." I feel an odd and unexpected stir of pride in my stomach. I can see why a college team would want him.

"Yeah." Cassie grins. "Emmett's the best."

"Holly!" Cassie pauses in her careful climb up the stairs to wave. "We were looking for you. Where were you?"

Holly smiles from the top of the stairs. She's wearing a stylish quilted black vest and cute boots that I instantly want. "Hey, Cassie! I didn't think you were here! Where were you sitting?"

"Over there. With AJ." She points to our row.

"Oh, *nuts*. You're usually with your mom. I was sitting way over *there*." She points with a fuchsia-painted nail toward the opposite side.

Cassie shakes her head and laughs. "Okay."

"Next time, we'll sit together. *Promise*." Holly's blue eyes widen with that word and then she winks at me. "That was a good game but I've gotta say hi and bye to Emmett and then race home to do a bunch of homework. See you both tomorrow at school?"

"Okay. Oh!" Cassie's eyes light up. "Did you get that picture of Roger Dodger?"

Holly's head cocks to the side. "I *did*. He's *so* cute." Holly flashes one last brilliant, white-toothed smile and then rushes past us toward the exit doors.

"I sent her a picture of Roger Dodger, from the shelter, being *really* silly. He's my favorite."

"I thought they were all your favorite," I say absently, looking back to where we were sitting.

Wondering how Holly could possibly have missed Cassie's bright pink vest.

Dear Julia,

I think I like Emmett. Like, REALLY like him. But

maybe you already guessed that. He's easily the hottest guy in school. Maybe on earth. The real kicker is that he doesn't act like he knows it. And that smile ... Ugh. And then there's the whole hockey thing. I don't even like hockey! But seeing him out there tonight, as good as he is ... I don't know. It did things to me. I need to learn about hockey.

This whole crushing-hard-on-your-neighbor-when-he's-in-love-with-his-beautiful-girlfriend thing sucks, big time. But, at least I get to see him every day. Friendship is better than strangers, right?

I'm such a loser.

Hopelessly pining,

~AJ

CHAPTER
NINE

"I'll grab us seats," Jen offers.

"Thanks." I frown at the tiny ice cream cones on her shirt as she lumbers down the hall, her lunch bag dangling from her fingertips. Why does she wear clothes like that, anyway? Every day it's something unusual. Yesterday she came to school in a shirt with a giant smiley face across the chest. People stared. They frowned. They whispered. I haven't seen anyone be outright mean to her yet, but it's only a matter of time. She's a prime target for bullies.

What I haven't been able to figure out yet is whether she cares. She must not. But I also haven't seen her hanging out with anyone besides me and Josie, the quiet Asian girl who has said maybe five words to me total, though she sits with us at lunch every day.

Am I alienating myself in my new school and my new life, the more I hang out with her?

The girls' bathroom is empty when I enter. I head for the farthest stall, hanging my things on the hook and fishing out my phone to send a quick text my mother.

The outer door creaks open. "... trying to get him Leafs

tickets. My dad's company has box seats so if I could get two golds for the home opener ..." Holly's honeyed voice reverberates over the tile walls. "Oh my God, Emmett will *lose* his *mind!*"

Envy pulls at my insides. She's so lucky to have him. Does she realize how lucky she is?

"What do you think he'll get you?" another voice asks. I recognize it from the party as Mandy's.

This *has* to be about Holly and Emmett's upcoming anniversary.

I was midway through a text to my mother, but I quickly cancel out of that and open up the camera. Emmett did say that he'd owe me big time if I could find out exactly what day their anniversary was. How much would he owe me if I could tell him exactly what Holly wanted?

I switch to video and hit the red record button.

And then roll my eyes at myself as I silently acknowledge that I'm eagerly helping Emmett impress another girl.

"Knowing him? Something to do with hockey. Like a necklace with a hockey stick dangling from it, or something like that." She laughs. "I swear, I love the guy to pieces, but he can be so clueless."

I cringe.

"And that's if he even remembers our one-year anniversary. A hundred bucks says he misses it completely."

"Mention it to his sister," Mandy murmurs in a way that makes me picture her smearing lipstick over her puckered mouth. "*You know* she'll remind him."

"Oh, *I know. Every* day, until the thirtieth."

September 30. I smile. *Oh man, Emmett. I am saving your butt here.*

My thumb moves for the red button to shut off the recording.

"I feel like I've already gotten my anniversary gift with that new neighbor of his. That *AJ*."

My thumb freezes. The way my name sounds on her tongue makes my skin prickle. It's not her usual sweet tone.

"She came to Emmett's game last night. It was great. I hid up top on the Away side and got to watch the game in peace." Holly's musical laughter echoes through the bathroom, only it doesn't sound nearly as charming. "Cassie's finally got someone new to leech on to, so she'll leave me alone."

My heart is pounding in my chest as I sit on the toilet and witness Holly shed her angelic skin, unaware that someone aside from her trusted friend could be listening. "Yeah. Now if I can figure out a way to get her to stop texting me."

"Oh my God, she *still* texts you?"

"Like, *every* day. She texts me and tags me on stupid pictures of mangy dogs on Instagram, too. I *hate* dogs! And if I don't respond, she keeps texting! It's *so* annoying. I don't know why Emmett's parents let her have a phone in the first place. Someone's always with her and it's not like she has friends."

"What are you talking about? *You're* her best friend."

Holly scoffs and Mandy cackles viciously.

"I swear, if I'd known that I wouldn't be able to shake Cassie off, I would never have gone through her to get to Em. I could've met him some other way. Hey, no one's in here, right?" Holly suddenly asks, quieting.

Panic flares inside me. I hold my breath and pull my legs up, thankful that I chose the corner stall.

A moment later, "Nope."

"Cool."

I let out the slowest sigh of relief.

"So, what's the story with that Aria girl, anyway?" Mandy asks.

"I don't know, but she's weird."

My stomach clenches.

"Right? And she joined cross-country because of him?"

"And made up some story about winning provincials or something. I'm telling you, I've seen her run at our practices and there is *no* way. She's so *slow*."

My teeth grit together.

"Why did Emmett bring her to Zach's?"

"He felt sorry for her. She has, like, *no* friends. She and her mom moved in with that old, grouchy man next door. Emmett said her parents divorced. They probably have no money."

We have loads of money! I want to yell, my eyes burning with the cutting words. My mom's been a lawyer for twenty years. All she ever did was work.

And did Emmett say that? That he felt sorry for me?

"Do you think she has a thing for him?"

"Oh my God, for *sure* she does. Who doesn't though, right? He's, like, the hottest guy here. And he's all *mine*." Holly cackles. "She can have his sister. They're perfect for each other. Both weirdos."

"And Jen Ricci."

"Ugh! Did you see what that loser is wearing today?" Their laughter is grating.

It's a moment before I realize the bathroom is empty once again.

My hands are shaking with anger as I shut off the recording and tuck my phone away. I knew Holly was too perfect to be real. I knew there had to be an ugly side. *Everyone* has an ugly side. It's only ever a matter of how well they keep it hidden, and what makes it appear.

Has Emmett seen this side of her? Does he know that she used his sister to get to him?

Does she know how she talks about Cassie?

I wait another five minutes to make sure there's no chance Holly and Mandy are in the halls before I collect my things and head to the cafeteria.

I find Jen and Josie in our usual area. "That took a while," Jen says, already working on the second half of her sandwich.

I slide into my seat. "Yeah. Sorry."

She pauses midbite and frowns. "You feeling okay? You look pale."

"I'm fine. It's just ... it's nothing." It's just that Emmett's girlfriend is a full-fledged Regina George posing as Miss Congeniality. And she's got *everyone* fooled.

"Hey, Aria!" That saccharine voice calls out from behind me.

Tension ripples through my body as I look up to find none other than Holly and Mandy standing over our table. I swallow against the lump in my throat. "Hey. What's up?" Did she somehow figure out that I was in the bathroom, recording her as she exposed her toxic underbelly?

She shrugs. "Just wanted to say hi. You looked *great* at practice today, by the way. We're *so* happy to have you on the team." The way her eyes crinkle, the way her smile takes up her whole face ... it's like she's practiced her deception in the mirror for months, she's that good at appearing genuine.

But I know better now.

I offer her a tight smile. "Thanks."

"See you later. Bye, Jenni*fer!*" They don't even acknowledge Josie before strolling away to the other side of the cafeteria, their heads dipped toward each other conspiratorially, laughing about something. I no longer have to guess at what.

"Why don't you tell her that you go by Jen? That you don't like being called Jenni*fer*," I mimic, unable to hold the accusation from my tone. Someone needs to confront Holly about something. *Anything*.

Jen chews slowly—much slower than usual—which tells me she's stalling to answer. "She knows," she finally says, gulping down her Pepsi. She hesitates, then glances over at their table. "I've known Holly since I was six. We both used to live in Klemptville." Those owlish, gray eyes regard me for moment before she shifts her attention to her sandwich in her hands. "Holly is *really good* at pretending to be nice. But she's not. She's mean and competitive, and jealous of anyone who does better in school or sports than her. She made kids cry. She made me cry, and I'm a year older than she is. Called me fat and ugly. She started rumors about me —that I still wet the bed, that I kissed my cousin, Rob." She shakes her head, her face twisted with dismay. "I was miserable. It got so bad, I didn't want to go to school." Jen's head dips lower as she admits softly, "Some days I wished I wouldn't wake up."

My stomach tightens.

Jen *has* been bullied before.

By Holly.

"We moved to Eastmonte when I was twelve and life got better. I mean, sure, there's still jerks around here, but nothing like her. No one *that* mean." Her lips twist. "And then last year, who comes strolling down the hall but Holly Webber. I nearly puked." Her eyes flitter to me. "But when she saw me in the hall, she came up and *hugged* me, and told me how happy she was to see me."

"Did she apologize?"

Jen shakes her head. "She never acknowledged the things she said to me. But she was acting different. Like, over-the-top *nice*. So, I figured either she grew out of her mean stage, or she's taking some serious anti-bitch pills."

I snort. Even Josie, who has said nothing until now, smiles.

Jen's gaze sits on Holly's table for a moment. "She got a lot of attention right away. I mean, *look at her*. Miss Popularity almost from day one. She's smart, too. So, I think she figured out that a guy like Emmett wouldn't look at her twice if he knew she was a bitch."

"Do you think Emmett would want to be with her if he knew what she used to be like?"

"You kidding? See that guy sitting on the table over there?" With a covert finger, she points to a boy with spiky blond hair and a black T-shirt, sitting three rows over. "That's Adam Levic. Last year he said something mean to Cassie—I can't remember what—and Emmett knocked him on his ass. He got suspended for fighting. There was a rumor of him losing his big hockey scholarship because of it. I don't know if that was ever true but it was serious."

"I can't picture Emmett fighting anyone." I can't see him ever getting that angry.

"He's not the type," she agrees. "Not like Adam."

I watch as the caf monitor comes by and ushers Adam off the dining table, pointing at the chair. Adam rolls his eyes but drags himself off. Now that he's standing, I see he's at least a few inches shorter than Emmett, but he's stocky, with broad shoulders and thick forearms.

"Emmett is super-protective of his sister, if you haven't noticed yet. And Cassie's the kind of kid that Holly would torment." Jen's thin lips purse. "If Holly acted half the way she did in Klemptville, I can't see how he'd give her a shot, no matter how perfect her boobs are. At least, I have to think so, or it crushes every fantasy *I've* ever had about him."

You and me both.

"Me too," Josie chirps in a whisper.

I study that perfect, blonde head attached to that perfect body and that perfect smile for the rest of our lunch period.

What would Emmett do if he knew it was all a façade?

"THE PLUMBER IS at Uncle Merv's," Cassie announces as we round the bend of our street, toward our cul-de-sac. Sure enough, the battered red pickup truck sits in the driveway. "I wonder what he's doing."

"Fixing something."

"Yeah ... he's fixing something," she echoes, and it sounds like she's trying to match my tone. "Maybe we could watch a movie tonight? Emmett has a hockey game. I'm not going."

Which probably means it's out of town.

She says this like it's a bonus that Emmett won't be around the house. Meanwhile, it would be motivation for me to go. Normally. But now I have this recording of his girlfriend burning a hole in my pocket and I don't know what to do with it.

"I have a lot of homework to do this weekend. But definitely next weekend," I promise.

Her head bobs furtively, and I know she's logging that into her mind. It's a commitment that she won't forget.

"See you later, Cassie."

"Bye, AJ." She trudges off toward her house and I take the walkway up to ours, noting the orange and yellow flowers in pots sitting on either side of the rickety stairs.

I step through the front door to the high-pitched whir of a drill coming from upstairs, Uncle Merv and my mother bickering in the kitchen, and the smell of chocolate and spice lingering through the air.

"What do I need with all this damn kitchen stuff, anyway?" Uncle Merv says, waving his hands at the piles of small kitchen appliances, containers, and mismatched dishware hiding the countertop. "Donate it or toss it. I'll never use it."

"We don't have to keep *all* of it! I just thought there might be something of sentimental value here and—"

"Unless I'm gonna be buried with it, I don't need to keep it! I don't need a broken blender or a chipped plate to remember Connie."

"Fair enough. You're right." Mom gives his shoulder an affectionate pat.

"What's going on?"

Mom turns to smile at me. "Hey, hon! I'm doing some cleaning. Figured it was a good time, with Mick repiping the house next week."

I frown. "What's he doing upstairs?"

"Making a whole damn lot of noise and eating your mother's zucchini bread," Uncle Merv complaints.

Mom rolls her eyes. "He's replacing the shower faucet and valves." She nods toward the kitchen table—a slice of said zucchini bread and a glass of milk await. Such a different world from the one in Calgary, where she didn't step through the door until well after seven, long after I'd found myself something from the store-bought, premade options to heat up for dinner.

"So? What happened at school today?" She looks at me expectantly.

I flop into the chair. "Number one: if you don't go back to work soon, I'm going to be a thousand pounds by Christmas."

"What's wrong with that? It's a nice, *round* number." Uncle Merv rubs a hand over his protruding belly and hobbles out of the kitchen toward the living room where the TV still blares.

"Three things from your day *at school*," Mom reminds me, settling into her seat with one of her high-end collectible china cup-and-saucer sets—that used to sit in the display case, untouched, even on special occasions.

"Your *fancy* china, Mom? Really?"

She lifts it as if in cheers. "No point saving it until I'm dead."

"You sound like Uncle Merv." *Who is this woman sitting in front of me?* "Nice flowers outside, by the way."

"Aren't they? I saw them outside the grocery store today and figured I'd dress this old house up a bit. I haven't bought chrysanthemums in *years*."

"Yeah. Not since I've been alive."

"Quit stalling." She flutters her fingers at me.

I sigh. "Number one: I matched my worst time from grade nine at cross-country practice today."

"See? Told you. Not bad for a kid who just started running again."

"I guess. Number two: I had another surprise math test today and the questions were *nothing* like from the textbook examples. I think I failed it."

Mom frowns with worry. "How much do these surprise tests account for?"

"Five percent of my total mark."

"Maybe there's a disconnect between the curriculum in Alberta and here. I could talk to this teacher—"

"*Mom.*"

"*Exactly!* I'm your mother. If you need help, we'll figure it out. I'm sure you're not the only one who's having a tough time." She breaks off a chunk of zucchini loaf from my plate for herself. "What else?"

Zucchini in cake doesn't sound all that appealing but neither does telling Mom that I recorded Holly in the bathroom today. I shove a piece into my mouth, savoring the warm chocolate chips while I stall on my next words. "I told Cassie I'd go to the animal shelter with her next Tuesday after school," I say instead. There are some things my mother is better off not knowing.

Mom stares at me as I drag my finger through the melted smears of chocolate on my plate, and I begin to worry that she can tell I'm hiding something. But when I dare look up again, it's into eyes that shine with pride. "That's a great idea, Aria."

I shrug. "I need volunteer hours anyway."

"I was going to mention that. I had lunch with Heather today and she told me that every student needs forty hours of volunteer hours to graduate high school."

"Yeah, it was in the paperwork that Ms. Moretti gave me."

"So, maybe you should see if you can collect your hours there, too. Cassie goes twice a week to spend time with the animals. Apparently, they all *love* her there. Not that that's a surprise. That girl just has a way about her. I can't put my finger on it."

I chew the inside of my mouth. *Not according to Holly.*

"Any big plans for this weekend?"

"Homework." I collect my backpack and the laptop.

Hiding in my room while I figure out what to do about this recording I have on my phone.

"Why don't you start it here while I keep sorting through these cupboards?"

I give her a flat look.

"What? I like your company," Mom says innocently, collecting the dirty dishes and carrying them to the sink.

"No, you want to monitor what I'm doing, and who I'm talking to, and what's being said. You don't need me to sit in the kitchen to do that." She has a desktop spyware program that'll give her everything she needs—my location, my texts, my websites visited. Everything. She has become Big Brother.

She twists her lips. "You're right. I'm sorry. But we've talked about this already, Aria. I just ... I worry, and for good reason."

I swallow. "Things are a lot better here, Mom. *I'm* better. But I can't become that weirdo at school who's not allowed to have an Instagram account."

"Don't be ridiculous," Mom scoffs. "That doesn't make you *weird*."

"Yeah, it does."

"*I* don't have an Instagram account. Does that make me weird?"

"You're not in high school. Even *Cassie* has an account."

"She does?" Mom frowns with amusement. "What does she post about?"

"Dogs."

"Of course." Mom laughs, then shakes her head. "Fine. If you want to start a new Instagram account—if it's important to you—then you can. I'm not trying to stifle you, Aria. I'm trying to protect you."

"I know. But you don't have to worry about me like *that* anymore."

"I'm your mother. I will always worry about you."

I push my open phone to her, wary that she'll change her mind if I give her too much time to dwell on the past.

With a heavy sigh, she wipes her hands on her jeans and then begins punching in keys. "Seeing as I can monitor what you're doing anyway, I'm going to disable the parental control. Just make sure your account is set to private and don't use your name on your profile. Or your face." A year ago, my mother had no idea how Instagram worked. Now she's well versed in all the ways someone can send hateful messages.

"I wasn't going to anyway."

She holds up her finger in warning. "And I want the account info. Password and everything."

"Of course." I snatch the last bite of zucchini bread—I hate to confess that it's good—and head to my room, feeling a small surge of victory.

Dogs, standing.

Dogs, sitting.

Dogs, running.

Dogs, jumping.

I shake my head as I scroll through Cassie's profile. There's even a close-up of a dog's eyeball with a caption that reads "Bert's eye," followed by several laughing emojis. She's a one-girl publicity department for the Eastmonte Animal Shelter. Of course, she's only advertising to her circle of thirty-six people. Thirty-seven, now that she accepted my friend request, after I texted to get her handle and to give her mine: therunningllama.

I spy Emmett's profile in Cassie's list of followers—my real motivation for searching out Cassie. His icon is a professional photographer's action shot of him on the ice. Of course. I click on the link and my stomach tightens with excitement, seeing that it's not set to private. He has over two thousand followers.

Curling up in the window seat, I begin to scroll. He doesn't post often, and when he does, it's usually something about hockey or his team. Where there *is* the odd picture of him without a helmet, I linger, my heart rate spiking.

It's at least twenty pictures before I come across a picture of him and Holly, taken last Christmas based on their matching Christmas sweaters. There's another one of them, lying side by side in the snow, laughing.

I can't help myself—I click on the tag that takes me to Holly's profile.

It's full of pictures of Holly and Emmett, of Holly alone, and beautiful candid shots of Emmett that make my heart ache, all of them with a slew of hashtags that stake her claim over him.

He's all mine.

That's what she said in the bathroom today.

My teeth grit at that wide, toothy smile.

What a phony.

A horn honks outside and I peer out the window to see a black SUV waiting in the Hartford driveway. Moments later, Emmett strolls out of the house in a dark-gray suit and silver tie, his stick in one hand, his enormous hockey bag in the other. He rounds the truck to toss his equipment in the back before climbing into the passenger seat.

They wear suits to games? Hockey is *weird*.

I grab a nearby book and pretend to read as the SUV backs out of the driveway. It's Friday night. Will Emmett feel sorry for me if he happens to look up here and see me alone?

Did he actually say that to Holly?

My chest burns with equal parts anger and embarrassment.

Once the SUV is out of sight, I slide my earbuds in and replay the audio recording for the sixth time tonight, in all its unmistakable glory.

Proving that the only pretty thing about Holly is her big, fake smile.

CHAPTER
TEN

DEAR JULIA,

WHAT SHOULD I DO?

I know what I WANT to do—send that video to Emmett. I have his number. I could do it. But what will he think? Is Jen right? Will he be pissed with Holly? Will he dump her for what she said? She'd deserve it.

But what if he doesn't, and he's pissed at me for recording her? Plus, my mom will KILL me if she finds out I was hiding in a bathroom stall, recording conversations, which means I can't send this video to Emmett; she'd see it in her spyware.

So maybe I should just play it for her, and see what she says. Holly's a horrible person. My mom would see that in a heartbeat.

Or she could demand that I delete it. Then I don't have proof. Then Holly gets to keep strutting around being the Queen of Fake while talking trash about Cassie and me, and Jen, and who knows who else, all while pretending she's this sweet angel and sucking on Emmett's neck like a damn vampire (I've definitely been around Uncle Merv too much).

See the dilemma I'm in, Julia?

I know what I want to do. The thing is, I also know why I want to do it, and my reasoning probably isn't all that noble.

~AJ

EASTMONTE CROSS-COUNTRY TEAM, *Practice tomorrow morning (Monday) is cancelled due to inclement weather. Thx, Ms. Moretti.*

I fall back into my bed, surrounded by textbooks, and let the relief swarm my body. *Thank you, lightning.* Without that forecast, we'd be running in rain tomorrow morning and that is a crappy way to start off a week.

My phone chirps with an incoming text and my heart skips a beat when Emmett's name shows up at the top.

You see Moretti's email?

Between hockey and Holly, Emmett was out most of the weekend, which is probably a good thing because I haven't figured out what to tell him yet, if anything. There's a good chance that if I show Emmett the video, he'll break up with Holly, and I'd be lying to myself if I said I didn't want that. But the thing is, she deserves it for the things she said—not about Jen and me but about Cassie. The more times I listen to it, the more I convince myself that that's reason enough to out her.

Sure, Cassie's one of the most awkward girls I've ever met, but, funnily enough, she's grown on me. I may never be able to have a deep conversation with her, but she'll always be genuinely happy to see me. And if she heard what Holly said about her? Just the thought makes me want to march across the lawn and play the recording for Emmett.

But, if this were any other guy, if I'd overheard this conversation in the bathroom, would I care as much? Probably not. I'd probably tell myself to keep moving. I'm not interested in becoming known like that at Eastmonte. I don't want to bring attention to myself. Attention breeds whispers and whispers breed rumors, and rumors somehow become facts. Usually ugly and untrue facts that people *want* to believe.

But Emmett should know who he's dating. He deserves to know the kinds of things Holly is saying about his sister behind his back. And if he wants to stay with her after that ...

Jen said it best—the fantasy will be crushed. And maybe that would be a good thing for me, because pining for a guy I can't be with is not how I saw myself starting over in this new life.

I respond with *"Yup. See You at 8,"* and then toss my phone and count my stars.

MORNING ANNOUNCEMENTS CRACKLE over the PA system and my stomach curls as I watch Holly skate her fingertip over Emmett's collar, pausing to tickle the spot where the hickey has finally faded.

"*Still* not funny," he warns.

As if sensing my scalding gaze, she peers over her shoulder at me. "Hey, Aria! Ready for the first meet next week?"

"Yup." I struggle to keep the sharpness from my tone.

Her blue eyes flicker to Jen, to her shirt—a peach-colored, long sleeve with a unicorn wearing a party hat on the front. It's equal parts hilarious and embarrassing. "I *love* your shirt, Jenni*fer*. It's so cute."

Jen offers a tight smile, as if she can sense the inauthenticity. "Thanks."

Holly catches her friend Lindsay's eye and they share a secretive smile. Obviously, the catty conversation I overheard in the bathroom isn't the first of its kind. And, as much as I agree that Jen's wardrobe choices are an abomination, that Holly is mocking her makes my anger flare.

"She goes by Jen," I blurt out. "She doesn't like being called Jenni*fer*."

Holly's mouth gapes open. "Oh my God! *Are you serious?*" She presses her hand against her chest, over her heart. "I had *no* idea! I'm so sorry. I feel horrible!"

"It's not a big deal," Jen murmurs, her cheeks turning red as she glances around us, at the people who can overhear the conversation.

"Okay, everyone!" Ms. McNair calls out, prompting the class to begin.

Holly's face is a perfect mask of guilt—eyes round, forehead pinched.

Emmett reaches over to smooth an affectionate hand over her back. "It's okay. It was an honest mistake."

As McNair begins talking about this past weekend's reading assignment, Emmett glances over his shoulder to frown at me, shake his head, and mouth, "What was that?" before turning to face front again.

My stomach drops. I've managed to make myself look like the jerk in Emmett's eyes.

That was definitely not my intention.

I TRAIL Emmett and Holly out of first period, my stomach in knots, wishing I'd never corrected her for something so dumb as a name, especially when Jen doesn't have the nerve to speak up about it.

"Catch you later?" Emmett leans down to kiss Holly, and I duck around them to get to my locker, wishing I could just go home and curl up in bed. It's going to be an agonizing day of regret and pondering if I—

"What was that about, AJ?" Emmett's voice behind me startles me so much, I drop my textbook on the floor.

I swallow against the ache in my throat as he reaches down to collect it and hand it to me. "You made Holly feel like crap. And you embarrassed Jen in front of everyone. Why would you do that? I didn't think you were like that."

"I'm not! I just ..." I peer up into those dark-brown eyes staring down at me, the mix of confusion and disappointment in them unmistakable. That look, I can't bear. "Holly's not who you think she is."

"What?" He frowns and a doubtful smirk curls his lips. "What are you talking about?"

I glance around the hallway. Students shuffle along, teachers linger. "I can't show you right *here*. It's on my phone."

"Send it to me—"

"No." I shake my head furtively. My mother would see it. Plus, what if it somehow gets shared? Things like that have a way of getting passed along, and then people will think I sit in bathroom stalls and record students. Tension tightens my shoulders with that thought.

He huffs. "Fine. Follow me."

My heart pounds as Emmett leads me down the hallway, checking each classroom that we pass. As soon as we come across one without lights on, he tests the door handle to find it unlocked and leads me in, closing the door behind us. "Show me." His jaw is hard.

My hands are shaking as I pull out my phone and find the video. We only have a few minutes before the second-period bell goes. Luckily, math class is only three doors down. I talk fast as I explain. "I was in the girls' washroom at lunch, texting my mom, and Holly came in with her friend and they started talking about anniversary gift ideas. So I figured I'd get you some clues. Please don't tell anyone how you heard this."

I focus on my shoes, my blood pounding in my ears as Holly's fake sweet voice and cackle fill the empty, dark classroom, as Emmett hears the words that I've all but memorized. Even the embarrassing ones about me. If I had known *this* was going to happen, I would have edited the video to cut that part out.

I don't dare look up again until it's over. Emmett is staring at the screen, his jaw clenched.

"I *swear*, the only reason I recorded that was to help you with gift ideas. I didn't know if I should tell you or not—"

"Bell's about to go." His thumb moves fast.

"What are you—"

"I texted it to myself." He thrusts my phone into my hand.

My stomach drops. *See how fast that can happen, Aria?* "Please don't send it anywhere—"

"I won't. I promise." And then he's gone, out the door and down the hall, ignoring the nods and greetings of passing friends.

And I'm running to second period, praying I didn't just make things worse.

Dreading what my mother is going to say when she sees that video and figures out what I've done.

"It's raining!" Cassie announces with a hint of panic as we push through the doors after school, squinting up at the overcast sky.

"It's only spitting. But we should hurry home before it gets worse."

"Wait." She reaches back to pull her hood up over her head and yank the strings tight, until her face is tightly framed by her jacket. "Okay, I'm ready."

Despite my dour mood, I smile at her.

"What?" she asks, her face splitting into a grin. "Do I look funny?"

"A little bit. But it's okay because you'll stay dry. Come on." We take the sidewalk that leads past the parking lot, toward home.

"There's Emmett!"

I follow her finger to where Emmett stands, next to his open trunk, facing Holly. His arms are folded across his chest, his face carved in stone. Holly keeps shaking her head and swiping her fingers across her cheek, as if to wipe away tears.

"Hi, Emmett!" Cassie calls, waving frantically, oblivious to their bodily cues that scream, "Do not disturb."

Holly reaches for his arm and he jerks his shoulder away.

"No. We're done," I think I see him mouth.

Holy shit.

This is because of me, because of the video I showed him.

"Emmett!" Cassie calls again. "Holly!"

"You know what? They look like they're having a serious conversation," I say slowly. "So we should keep going and you can talk to him later tonight."

"Yeah. Okay," she agrees, but she doesn't move, her eyes narrowing. "I think Holly's crying."

"Yeah, I think she might be."

"Oh no! What's wrong? Is she hurt?" Rare and genuine grief fills Cassie's voice.

"I don't know," I lie. Callous as Holly's words may have been, I don't doubt her feelings for Emmett are real. Which means we're standing here, watching her heart get ripped out of her chest. "But we should leave them alone, okay?"

Emmett slams his trunk and climbs into the driver's seat. In seconds, he's pulling out, leaving Holly there, hugging herself, her face a picture of devastation.

"Holly! Hi!" Cassie waves frantically, as if either she didn't hear me or she's choosing to ignore me. "Are you okay?"

Holly looks over at us and then spins on her heels and marches toward her Civic, digging her keys out of her pocket.

Cassie watches, an odd mixture of hurt, confusion, and curiosity filling her face. What's going on in that head of hers at this moment? How is she's interpreting this?

"Come on. Let's go home."

She squints up at the sky again and pauses a few beats. "Is it raining?" she asks, as fat drops splatter over her lenses.

I sigh. "Yeah. It's raining."

My pant legs are soaked and my stomach is in knots by the time I step through the front door.

Uncle Merv is sitting in his usual spot, but his eyes are closed and he's wearing big black headphones, plugged into the tablet my mother bought him last week. To bring him into this century, she claimed.

"Hey, hon! How was your day?" Mom calls out from the kitchen, her voice light and unsuspecting. Not the voice of an angry person.

I find her seated at the old kitchen table with her tea, smiling. "Look at this old wedding photo of Connie and Merv. I found it in a pile of paperwork and had it retouched and framed." She holds up the picture for me to see. "Look how young Uncle Merv was!"

She hasn't listened to the text Emmett forwarded from my phone. Not yet, anyway. I exhale with the bit of relief this brings me.

"Young and thin." Toothpick thin, with long, skinny legs.

She chuckles. "I'm going to hang it up in the living room for him, as soon as I can find a hammer."

An array of pamphlets is spread out on the table in front of her. "What's all this?"

"Oh, I've had it with these dinosaur appliances. They're at least a hundred years old. That oven is uneven and the dishwasher doesn't clean a thing. Mick said he'd install it if I have it delivered. And ...," she waves a hand at the exterior paint catalogue, "I was thinking about having the front of the house freshened up in the spring. It always used to look so nice, with the flowers and the clean, white porch. Aunt

Connie would sit out there every afternoon and crochet." She smiles, more to herself. "It's time to bring back some of that charm to this old place."

I was half kidding when I told Uncle Merv that his house would be unrecognizable by the time Mom went back to work, but I'm not so sure that will be wrong. She's spending *a lot* of money for a person who's currently unemployed. I know she made a lot off the sale of our house out west. I overheard her talking to the realtor about how it was the best investment she'd ever made—a case of buying at the right time, in the right place. Plus, between my dad and her both being lawyers, and only having one kid, I never wanted for much.

I notice the plate of fruit on the table between us. "Is that for me?"

She shrugs. "You complained about needing a break from all the baking, so *there* you go. Plus, the freezer is full of zucchini bread. Sit, and talk to me." She smiles warmly. "Tell me about your day."

My day was horrible, Mom. Like crawl-under-my-covers-and-never-come-out horrible. There was nothing good about today. And I'm torn between confessing this to her—because I'll have to give details—and lying, telling her that everything is fine. Except, she's probably going to watch that video. Tonight or tomorrow, or next week. And when she does, it's all going to come out. I'll have no choice but to explain, and my mother will start to worry that I'm hiding things from her again.

I swallow my anxiety and fear. "Number one ..."

Mom sets my phone down on the table, having listened to the recording twice. Her face is unreadable as she takes a sip of her tea. "Well, that girl's a piece of work."

"She's awful. I don't care what she said about me. But it's Cassie and Jen." Mom listens quietly as I fill her in on Jen and Holly's history, of how cruel Holly has been to Jen in the past. And each cringe from my mother, each frown, each headshake emboldens me, makes me think that I did the right thing.

"This is not okay, Aria." She taps my phone. "Recording other girls in your school like that is *not* okay—"

"Mom, *I know*!" Tears prick my eyes. Of *all* people, *I know*.

"Of course, you do," she says, squeezing the bridge of her nose. "What did Emmett say?"

"Nothing to me, but he was mad. And I'm pretty sure he dumped her after school. That's what it looked like it in the parking lot, anyway."

She nods through a quiet sip of tea. "At least he has his priorities straight."

"He's the one who forwarded the video to himself, right after he watched it, before I knew what he was doing. *I* didn't send that to him."

She waggles a finger at me. "See how fast something like that can happen—"

"*I know*, Mom." I feel like I've said that a hundred times since sitting down. "He promised he wouldn't send it anywhere else." I just don't know if I can believe him.

She purses her lips. "I saw that text come through earlier today, but I didn't open it. I don't *want* to be snooping and monitoring you. Especially when it comes to Emmett and Cassie." She drums her fingers over the table's surface. "That's why you're telling me now, isn't it? Because you figured I might see it."

I shrug and avert my eyes to the table. *Guilty as charged.*

"I'm glad you told me, Aria. I'm not happy about any of this but your heart was in the right place, which is the important part here. Hopefully, this Holly girl will learn a valuable lesson from this." She spins the appliance pamphlet around. "Do you think we should go with all black? Or stainless steel?"

I blink at her. *Is that it? Is that all she's going to say?*

"Or there's this model that's a mix of black and stainless steel. That could be good."

"Uh ... What would Uncle Merv like?"

She waves that thought away with a laugh. "Oh, he doesn't care. I set him up with an audiobook account and he's been in that chair all day, quiet. He's in heaven." She gives me a pointed look. "And, now, so am I."

Emmett pulls into his driveway at nine thirty that night, as I'm curled up on my window seat, my textbook in my lap, halfway through my functions and quadratic equations homework.

He climbs out, pops his trunk, and hauls his equipment out, only to toss the bag haphazardly on the grass beside his SUV.

He looks up at my window.

Do I pretend I'm not watching him? Do I wave hello? Do I keep staring out my window, debating what I should do, until this gets *super* awkward?

He slides his phone out of his back pocket.

A moment later, my phone chirps with an incoming text.

Can you come out to talk?

A mixture of excitement and dread erupts inside me. I have no idea how this conversation is going to go. Marking my textbook page, I head downstairs to the tune of Uncle Merv's deep snore carrying from his bedroom. Mom glances up from the living room couch, an Ontario law textbook in her lap, her reading glasses perched on her nose. "Where are you going?"

"Outside, to talk to Emmett." I slip on my shoes. "Be back in a bit."

"Okay. I hope he's doing okay."

Oddly enough, I feel relieved that this isn't a burning secret between us. I hesitate. "I'm glad I told you."

She slides her glasses off to regard me. "I'm glad you told me too, hon."

With each step I take across our lawn and toward the Hartford driveway, where Emmett half leans, half sits against his trunk, his head bowed, my nervousness grows.

"Hey." I hug my body against the evening chill, wishing I'd grabbed a sweater. "How was practice?"

"Shit." He chuckles darkly. "Coach yelled at me to get my head into it. Actually, I had skating sessions with a bunch of seven- and eight-year-olds first and *then* a late practice. It's been a long night."

Uncomfortable silence lingers.

"So, about that video ..." He shifts to the far side of his trunk, making room for me.

I move in to settle next to him, inhaling his familiar, intoxicating scent. "Like I said before, I only did it because she was talking about your anniversary. I thought she might list a few things and I didn't want to forget. I wasn't sure I should even play it for you."

He sighs heavily. "I know Cassie can be a lot to handle. I lose my patience with her sometimes. A lot, actually. She's got all these weird little quirks and things about her and sometimes she seems more like a five-year-old than a fifteen-year-old. There are days that I wish she could be like everyone else." His throat bobs with a hard swallow. "But then she'd be a different person. She wouldn't be who she is, and I wouldn't want that either. And she's my sister. I just ..." He bows his head.

"You don't have to explain. I didn't like the way Holly talked about her either, and she's *not* my sister. Cassie doesn't deserve that." And I mean it, crush on Emmett or not. Cassie spent the entire walk home worrying about whether Holly was okay.

He kicks a loose stone with his shoe, sending it flying. "I broke up with Holly after school."

I temper my voice to sound sympathetic—the bubble of happiness I'm feeling is wrong, I remind myself. "Yeah, we saw you guys in the parking lot. It didn't look great."

"She didn't take it well. Drained my phone battery with all her texts tonight, apologizing over and over again. I haven't responded yet."

A dark, unwanted thought stirs in me. "Do you think you can forgive her?" What if he takes her back?

"She says she didn't mean it, but that's bullshit. And even if she's sorry about it, she still said it. And now I know the kinds of things she's thinking while she's smiling and pretending to be sweet. I can't trust her." He shakes his head. "You should have seen the look on her face when I played that recording."

My stomach clenches. "You didn't tell her where you got it, did you?"

"No, don't worry. She asked, but she doesn't need to know."

I sigh with relief. "Good. I don't need a rumor floating around that I hide in bathroom stalls and record people's conversations."

"When did it happen anyway?"

"Last Friday. I didn't know what to do. But then I figured you'd want to know."

He chews his bottom lip. "So that's why you were acting so weird." And then he cringes. "Not weird. Tense. You're not weird. Ignore what she said. And I didn't invite you out to Zach's because I felt sorry for you."

I shrug, even as my cheeks heat. Thank God for the dark of night.

Do you think she has a thing for him?

Oh, for sure she does.

What does he think about that part? Does the idea that it could be true bother him?

"I guess it's a good thing I didn't get that necklace with the hockey stick charm."

"I guess not." I'd wear it with pride.

He laughs, but it's not his usual laugh; it's a hollow sound. "I should get inside. I have a ton of homework to do and right now I just want to sleep." The car lifts as he stands. "By the way, I'm going to drop out of cross-country."

"Really?" My disappointment swells.

"I've got too much going on this year and I don't need to deal with seeing Holly any more than I have to. It's bad enough we have a class together. It's too late to switch out or I would."

Thank God for that.

119

He hoists the enormous hockey bag over his shoulder. "I'll still run with you on the mornings that you're not at practice, though. If you want. I need the exercise."

My eyes skim over his honed body and I struggle to not laugh. "Yeah, that'd be great. I hate running alone," I lie.

"'Kay. See you tomorrow?"

"Seven a.m." I feel my body lighten. Emmett isn't angry with me. All is right in the world.

"And Aria?" He's walking backward toward the house. He hasn't called me by my real name in forever. "Thanks. You could have deleted that and ignored it, instead of telling me."

I shrug. "Cassie deserves better than that." I hesitate. "And so do you."

I catch a hint of those dimples with his soft smile. "'Night."

CHAPTER
ELEVEN

I'm already halfway through my warm-up when Emmett emerges the next morning. I yank one earbud out so I can hear him.

He shudders, rubbing his hands together. "Damn, it's cold."

"This is my favorite weather to run in," I stretch my hamstrings. I was happy to trade in my shorts and T-shirt for my track pants and sweatshirt.

"What are you listening to?" He stops within my personal space, grabbing the dangling earbud and tucking it into his ear.

I shrug. "It's a mix."

"Nice." He drops the bud and moves away to begin his warm-up.

And I acknowledge with perverse pleasure that I can't wait to stick that back into my ear.

Maybe I *am* a weirdo.

"How are you doing?" I ask gently.

"Better, after sleeping." He lifts his arms over his head,

showing off a patch of taut skin above his shorts. My mouth instantly dries. "But Cassie's pissed at me."

I frown. "I didn't think she could be pissed at anyone."

He snorts. "Just me and my parents, I think. I was a bit of an asshole last night. I took her phone and deleted all of Holly's contact info, and told her she's not allowed to message Holly anymore. Of course, then she kept pushing to know why *exactly*, and it's not like I'm going to tell her. It would crush her if she found out that Holly was only ever friends with her to get to me." He frowns. "I don't even know if Cassie would understand. Sometimes I can't figure out what she *actually* understands."

I've thought those very same things. "That has to be tough." But I love that Emmett's opening up to me about it.

"Yeah. I'm dreading class this morning." He tucks his earbuds in and brings up his playlist on his phone. "Ready?"

I nod. "Let's do this."

THE FIRST BELL rings as Jen and I walk into social studies.

Despite my best intentions to avoid eye contact, I zero in on Holly right away. She's sitting at a desk near the back corner of the class, her puffy, tired eyes set on the door. Our gazes meet and hers quickly moves on, dismissing me entirely.

She's waiting for Emmett.

And when she suddenly sits up taller and bites her lip in hopeful pause, I know he has arrived. He was still at his locker a moment ago. He must have run to catch up.

"Hey, Jen?" He sidles up behind us. "Can I sit with AJ today?"

"Uh ..." Jen's eyebrows arch as they veer to Holly, her face a mixture of reluctance and confusion. I can't imagine her wanting to spend the next hour sitting beside her childhood bully.

I'm about to say as much when Emmett stops Holly's friend, Lindsay, who normally sits with a guy I've nicknamed Sleepy Steve, because he literally sleeps through first period. Even McNair has given up on trying to keep him awake. "Hey, you mind sitting with Holly today?"

Lindsay shrugs, though her eyes dart curiously to her friend. It seems that Holly hasn't shared the news of the breakup yet. Maybe she's still hoping to reverse it before anyone finds out. "Yeah, no problem." She heads to the back of the class.

Emmett gives Steve a look that might read as "You good with this, man?" Steve merely gives a lazy "I don't give a shit" shrug. His head will hit the desk soon enough.

Emmett slides into the seat next to me just as the second bell goes and morning announcements come on over the PA. "Thanks for doing this, Jen."

"No problem." Her eyes lock on mine, widening with question.

I hold my hands up in surrender, as if I'm an innocent bystander. But I *am*, I remind myself. I'm the conscientious messenger.

"You're good with this, right?" Emmett flips open his textbook. He peers at me with those gentle, dark-brown eyes. "If you want to switch back with Jen tomorrow—"

"No." I shake my head in emphasis. "This is fine." I smile.

And do my best to ignore the burn of scathing eyes boring into my skull for the next hour.

"SOMEONE RECORDED her saying crap about his little sister in the bathroom and then sent it to him."

I stare at Josie, momentarily dumbstruck. It's the most she's ever said in one sitting. And it's about me.

"I heard she accused Mandy Lovatt but they figured out that someone must have been *hiding* in the stall, listening to them," Jen adds.

Josie's delicate face scrunches up. "Creepy."

I lock my gaze on the homemade zucchini loaf Mom snuck into my lunch, picking it apart slowly as dread blossoms. What if people find out *I'm* the creepy one?

"I wonder what she said about Cassie." Jen takes a bite out of her ham sandwich, her curious eyes drifting across the cafeteria to where Holly and Mandy sit.

"Couldn't have been good because Emmett *dumped* her ass over it in the parking lot after school yesterday."

Wow. Josie's not only talking, she's swearing too.

I feel Jen's eyes shifting to me. Will either of them put two and two together and figure out why I was asking about Holly last Friday, after having gone to the bathroom? Will they remember that I was gone for a long time, that I came back pale-faced?

News of Emmett and Holly's breakup is spreading like flames through dry brush. I started hearing the whispers in math, when Beckett Smith leaned across the row to tell Morris Davenport that "Hartford's flying solo" again, followed by a fist bump.

By the time I went to swap my books for third period, a tall, raven-haired beauty was hovering at Emmett's locker, waiting for him to appear. And when he did, the flirtatious smile she was casting his way made me want to vomit.

Josie drags her french fry through her ketchup. "I always knew Holly had a mean streak in her."

Jen worries her bottom lip. "What's she going to be like now that she's done trying to impress Emmett?" Her thoughts are somewhere far off. Probably in her tortured past. It's a fair question, though. Was playing the part for Emmett the only thing that kept Holly's ugly side collared?

"We won't let her come after you like that again," I say with certainty.

She gives me a small nod and appreciative smile, though I get the impression she doesn't believe it.

I WRIGGLE my nose against the smell of bleach, wet dog fur, and cat urine as we step into the empty lobby of E.A.S—an old house that's serving as the Eastmonte Animal Shelter until they can rebuild the one that burnt down two years ago.

"*Hello,* boys and girls!" Cassie yells.

A wild chorus of howls and piercing barks from beyond a sky-blue door respond, making Cassie laugh.

A short, silver-haired lady emerges moments later. "You *love* to get them going, don't you?" Her eyes crinkle with her smile, not at all annoyed.

"Yeah. I can hear Bangles." Cassie laughs again. "Has Boots had her kittens yet?"

"Not yet. Any day now."

"Okay." Cassie nods. "This is my friend, AJ. She came to see the dogs and cats with me."

"Hi, AJ. I'm Pat." Pat pauses to straighten an array of pet insurance and adoption pamphlets in a rack on the desk. "You ready for this?"

"I'm not sure," I confess.

Pat leads us past the door and into a long, narrow room lined with portable metal cages of various sizes. The distinct smell of dog—sweat, fur, drool—is that much stronger back here, on account of the five dogs of varying sizes and color, already on their feet and panting as Cassie holds her hand out to their cages, greeting each one by name.

"Bangles already had his walk today, but Roger Dodger is ready for you."

"Hi, Roger Dodger!" Cassie exclaims in a high-pitched, excited voice, bending down to clap and greet a scruffy gray Lhasa Apso, who is attempting to cram his snout through the cage. She fumbles with the latch on the cage. "I can't do it."

I move in to help her, but Pat puts a hand up to stop me, winking at me. "Yes, you can, Cassie. Remember, pull up and then turn."

The dog is tearing around in circles by the time the gate pops open. He comes barreling out to jump on her legs.

"He's so excited!" Cassie laughs.

"He's always excited when you show up. You'll need to get him to calm down before you can get that leash on him. And ... AJ, right?" When I nod, Pat continues, leading me to a cage with a heavyset black Lab. "How about you take Murphy? He's much calmer. These two get along well enough. Come on, Murph."

The dog hobbles out, favoring his back leg.

"Is he hurt?"

"That's just hip dysplasia. His previous owners brought him in because he couldn't handle being in a house with little kids anymore. Too much noise and excitement. He got grumpy."

Sounds like Uncle Merv. "How old is he?" I scratch the gentle dog's graying chin. He peers up at me with sad, dark eyes. Wisps of silver fleck his face.

"Oh, he's an old guy. Over thirteen now. He just hangs out, looking for pats. Don't you, Murph?" She pets his head. "He's been here a while now. Will probably be here till the end."

I study the cage that is his home. "That's sad."

"Yeah, I know. But it's hard to get anyone to take a big old dog like this. 'Course Cassie would take the whole lot of them home with her, if her dad wasn't allergic. Right, Cassie?"

"Yeah. Whoa! Hold your horses, Roger Dodger." She laughs, letting him lead her toward the back on the leash she somehow managed to affix to his collar.

"Make sure you show AJ what needs to be done. I'll be with Boots if you need me."

"'Kay."

"And Cassie ..." Pat gives her a warning look.

"I know!" She grins and holds up a tiny roll of plastic poop bags, as if that's proof of her intention.

"I GO TUESDAYS AND SOMETIMES THURSDAYS," Cassie says, easing out of Heather's car. "You can come with me if you want."

"Two hours a week and you should have your community service hours by the middle of winter," Heather adds, grabbing her purse from the passenger seat floor. "Cassie, why don't you go in and wash your hands *really* well and change."

"I don't need to change," Cassie argues.

Heather makes a point of staring at Cassie's pants, drawing her daughter's eyes down to the muddy paw prints all over them.

"Oh. That's okay," Cassie says, bending down to wipe at them.

"No, it's not okay. Put them in your hamper, and put on clean pants from your drawer. Not from your floor."

"Mom! Shhh!" Cassie's eyes narrow with annoyance.

"I'll be there in a minute. I need to talk to Aria alone first."

Cassie lingers.

"I'm asking you politely to give us a moment."

Cassie doesn't move, her jaw setting with stubborn determination.

"Cassie!"

"Fine!" Spinning on her heels, she stomps up the path, pausing a few times as if reconsidering her compulsion to obey her mother, muttering something about not having to listen to her. Does she realize that she already is?

Heather sighs heavily, then turns her soft gray-blue eyes on me. "Do you know what happened between Emmett and Holly? All he told me is that they broke up."

"Uh ..." What do I say? *I know exactly why they broke up, and I can play the reason for you right here, on my phone?*

"I know. I'm sorry to corner you like this, but I'm not going to get more out of him, and he made Cassie *so* upset last night."

"Yeah, she seemed a bit annoyed with him." When Cassie and I passed the parking lot after school today,

Emmett was pulling out. He waved at us. Cassie lifted her hand partway to respond before abruptly dropping it, as if she had just remembered that she's still angry with him. And Cassie's facial expressions are priceless. Her smiles are wide but her frowns are equally deep, and as much as she sometimes has trouble showing the right emotions for the occasion, when she gets it right ... boy, does she get it right.

She outright glowered at her brother as he drove by.

"He's adamant that she stays away from Holly and, well, as you know, Cassie doesn't have a lot of friends to begin with. I wouldn't want her to lose a friendship, however shallow it may be, because of her brother's broken heart." There's a flash of raw vulnerability in her eyes. "If someone could help me understand—"

"You shouldn't. Let Holly near Cassie, I mean." I swallow. "Holly isn't as nice as she makes herself out to be. She's pretty horrible, actually. Some of the things she said recently about Cassie, and other people, were terrible. Or so I've heard," I add quickly, and hope she doesn't push for details. Though, there's a chance she and my mother will talk over lunch, and my mother will divulge the bathroom recording fiasco.

Heather sighs, her jaw tightening a touch. "I always did wonder about that girl. She seemed *too* perfect, but she was always outwardly nice to Cassie so what could I say?"

"She is nice. Outwardly."

"I've spent the last ten years, since Cassie started school, trying to shield her from the kids who might be cruel to her. I can usually see it in their eyes—the way they look at her. Or the way they brush her off. It's always so nice when she finds someone who's willing to give her a bit of time and respect. And patience." I can't help but notice the way her eyes gloss over and she blinks repeatedly.

"Mom! There's no clean pants!" Cassie calls from the front door of their house.

Heather seems to search her thoughts. "Oh, that's right. I haven't folded them yet."

"Mom!"

"I'll be there in a minute!" Heather smiles at me. "Thank you for being a friend to Cassie, and for looking out for her."

"Mom!"

"As much as she may test you sometimes." She takes the same path toward the house that her daughter so insolently stomped up not long ago.

"Bye, AJ! See you tomorrow!" Cassie waves wildly at me, the smile on her face infectious.

CHAPTER
TWELVE

Dear Julia,

I'm conflicted.

I HATE cross-country mornings, because I don't get to run with Emmett, or drive in to school with him. BUT on the mornings I don't have practice, I get Emmett all to myself in the morning for a half hour—no Cassie, no McNair—BECAUSE of cross-country.

Deep thoughts at 1:00 a.m. as sleep evades me, yet again.

Tomorrow's a cross-country morning, and I'm dreading it. Holly missed last Wednesday's and Friday's practices. I was hoping she'd dropped out, but I overheard Ms. Moretti telling someone she'd be back tomorrow. Even if she isn't, I can't see Moretti kicking her off. We're already down one runner, now that Emmett's gone, and Holly's a decent runner, as much as I hate to admit that.

So, I have to assume she'll be back tomorrow morning, which means either I run behind her or deal with burning-hot laser beams drilling into the back of my head, and let me tell you, I'm getting tired of feeling those all first period, for just sitting next to Emmett.

And if she's going to hate on every girl who goes near Emmett, she had better make a long list because, oh my God, Julia ... You would not believe how many girls are suddenly lurking around him, batting their eyes and bumping into him in the halls. And they're ALL pretty.

And every time I see him stop to talk to one of them, I convince myself that she's the one he's going to fall for next.

~AJ

I spot Holly warming up when I reach the school the next morning.

I intentionally head for the opposite side of the group to avoid her.

"Hey, AJ. How was your weekend?" Richard bounds back and forth from one leg to the next, lifting his knees with each step. He has swapped his usual yellow sweatband for an orange one.

I stretch out my hamstrings. "Quiet. What about yours?"

"Oh, it was just the best weekend of my entire existence. No big deal."

I can't help but chuckle. Richard's intensity goes beyond his efforts with cross-country. There's a lot of "extra" with *everything* he says and does. It's earned him some uncomplimentary looks along the hallways but, much like Jen with her odd clothing choices, either he doesn't notice or doesn't care.

I think I respect him for it.

"I'm almost afraid to ask."

"Me and the guys clocked in an epic twenty-two hours straight of *Dungeons and Dragons*. We were delirious."

I frown. "Dungeons and Dragons? What's that?"

He pauses, his mouth agape. "'What's that?' she asks. It's only the greatest role-playing game known to mankind."

"Hey, Aria, can I talk to you for a sec?" Holly's voice is especially sweet as she cuts into my conversation with Richard.

I stifle my groan. So much for avoiding her. As much as I want to call her out for the crap she said about me, it won't help matters. It sure as hell won't help team dynamics. Still, I struggle to keep my own voice light. "What's up?"

"Katie said your time is *really* improving."

Something tells me Holly doesn't care about my time. "I've been training hard."

"With Emmett?" she asks innocently.

Now I see where this conversation is headed. "Sometimes." *Always.* I reach toward the ground, mainly to avoid eye contact.

"How's he doing?"

She obviously thinks I don't know about the recording, about how she belittled me. It also means she doesn't suspect me as being the culprit in the bathroom stall.

I choose my words knowing they'll strike hard. "He seems fine. Happy."

Her face pinches, as if she was hoping for a different answer. The front doors slam and we turn to see Ms. Moretti marching toward us. "Hey, so for social studies today, swap seats with me, okay? I *really* need to talk to him."

"You want to talk to him during class about why you broke up?"

"Well, that way he can't walk away when I try to apologize. *Again*, for like the *thousandth* time." She rolls her eyes, as if annoyed. "Let him sit down first, and then, when morning announcements come on, you can get up and—"

"No. I don't think so."

Holly's eyes flash with anger.

"He'll talk to you when he's ready, which I'm guessing is going to be long time from now. You really hurt him. And his family," I throw in for good measure, Heather's watery eyes flashing through my mind.

Thankfully, I'm saved from whatever response she might have when a sharp blow of Ms. Moretti's whistle cuts through the air. "Okay, you've had time to warm up. Let's go, ladies and gentleman!" She claps her hands.

I take off down the path, trying to put as much distance as possible between myself and Holly.

My thighs are throbbing by the time I reach the end.

"Term project time!" Ms. McNair announces, brushing at a streak of white chalk dust on her navy suit jacket. "As discussed at the beginning of the year, a sizable chunk of your overall grade will be based on your class project. To make it easy, you'll be partnered with your tablemate."

I steal a glance Emmett's way and my stomach flutters with excitement.

"You'll be required to present on a social issue and how it affects teenagers in society today. Expectations for this assignment are posted on the class portal. I have the topics here." She holds up a stack of quote cards and then walks around, setting one on each table. "I like for my students to be passionate about what they're learning and presenting so, for today only, you can swap with another group."

A curly-haired guy named Sidney holds up his card with the word "abortion" displayed in bold black block letters. "Hot topic for anyone daring enough, right here! Anyone ... anyone ..."

"Many of these topics are big and contentious," McNair continues, ignoring him. "You are to approach this from an unbiased angle. Work on this project is to be done mainly outside of regular class time, with thirty minutes given each Friday for prep and discussion. Presentations will happen the week of November 18 to 24."

I catch a waft of her floral scent as she passes by our desk, setting down an index card with one word scrawled across it in bold, black ink:

BULLYING.

A sinking feeling hits the pit of my stomach.

McNair taps her fingertip over it. "Timely, for you two, given that happens to be Bullying Awareness and Prevention Week." Louder, she continues. "Please fill out your names on the bottom of the card and drop it off on my desk on your way out."

Emmett slides the card between us and reaches for a pen.

"Did you want to try to swap that?" I ask.

"No, this is a good one." He pauses. "Unless you don't want it?"

I force a smile. "I'm fine with it." Can he tell I'm lying?

"Great." He grins, and my attention is pulled to those adorable dimples. "How easy is this going to be to work on, living next door to each other?"

"So easy." I watch him scrawl "Emmett Hartford and Aria Jones" across the bottom and my mind instantly drifts away, into a direction where those two names belong together.

The bell rings, ending class.

Emmett drops the card on McNair's desk as we pass, and then trails me out to my locker. "What'd you and Steve get?" he asks Jen.

"Racism."

Emmett whistles. "That's a big one."

"Yeah, especially when I'll probably be doing all the work."

I can't disagree with her. I don't think I've seen Steve take notes once in class yet.

"Hey, AJ, I should be home from practice by five. Do you want me to come over after so we can talk through this?"

My heart flutters. "Sure." Where, though? In the cramped kitchen that Mom is overhauling? On the hideous living room couch next to Uncle Merv while he listens to his audiobooks or watches war documentaries, trying to drown out the sound of Mick drilling and sawing? And then I remember. "Oh, wait—they're redoing the plumbing at the house today." Mick showed up this morning with another guy as I was leaving for cross-country. "So it depends—"

"Let's make it easy. Come over to my house. I'll just ask my mom to keep Cassie busy, so she's not distracting us."

"Sure." I grab my math textbook.

Emmett's eyes flicker to the next bank of lockers over. "Walk me to my next class, 'kay?" He drops his voice and leans in. "Patricia Morgan's on the prowl again."

With a covert two-step glance, I look first to Jen, and then behind her, confirming that the tall, beautiful, raven-haired girl lingers at her nearby locker, no doubt watching Emmett from the corner of her eye. It sounds like he's not as eager to spend time with her as I expected. My heart soars with relief. "Sure. I guess."

"What? You too cool to be seen with me all of a sudden?"

I slam my locker shut. "Let's get something clear: I've *always* been too cool."

He bumps my shoulder playfully as we stroll down the hall.

Curious eyes are on us the entire way.

"DON'T FORGET. Dinner's at six *sharp*!" Mom calls out as I step out the front door, leaving the mouthwatering aroma of her homemade spaghetti sauce behind. Mick and his guy weren't able to finish everything today, but they did enough to turn the water back on at around four, in time for Iris to drop off Uncle Merv. Mom figured it best to send him to a quiet house with working toilets. Not sure what she's going to do with him tomorrow.

"Going next door?" Uncle Merv frowns at that same bush I've seen him tending to a few times now, a spray bottle in his grasp.

"Yeah. I have an assignment with Emmett. What are you doing?"

"Trying to save this rosebush from certain death." It sounds all the more ominous in his dry, gruff voice. "It was Connie's favorite. It gives off these big fuchsia-colored blooms, the size of your hand." He holds his hand out in front of him to emphasize. "We've had it for years. Connie knew how to take care of it and then she passed and ... well,

I started seeing these black fungus spots on the leaves in spring. Not sure I'll be able to save it."

Sometimes I forget that Uncle Merv had a whole other life before we showed up. That he wasn't always alone. "You must miss her a lot."

It's a moment before he responds. "We were married for sixty-one years. And all we ever had was each other. Weren't blessed with kids." He spritzes the mottled leaves. "It's funny, we spent our lives hoping we'd live long enough to grow old, and now here I am—my body aching and my eyesight going, wondering what fresh hell tomorrow's got in store for me, and which day is the one I'm not going to wake up to. At least when Connie was around, we were wondering together."

Sixty-one *years* with someone, only to lose them in an instant. What must that feel like? Is that why Uncle Merv is so grumpy?

An idea strikes me. "You need a dog," I blurt out.

His unkempt eyebrows arch as he peers at me. "You think I should replace my dead wife with a *dog*?"

"No! There's this dog at the shelter. Murphy. He's old and alone and, I don't know, maybe you could both use the company."

"Hmm ... We had a dog once. I remember it being a lot of work," he mumbles, aiming the spray nozzle. "You're beginning to sound like Cassie."

"It was just a thought." I sling my backpack over my shoulder and I cross our front lawn and then the Hartfords'.

"AJ!" Cassie's face stretches with a wide smile as she greets me at their front door, crumbs from whatever she was snacking on coating the corners of her mouth. "This is a surprise! I didn't know you were coming." She backs up to let me in, then points to the two cans of paint sitting on the floor. "My dad is going to paint my bedroom just like yours."

"That's cool. When's he doing that?" I ask, sliding off my running shoes.

"This weekend! And I'm getting stars, too!" Excitement radiates off her.

"AJ!" Emmett pokes his head out from his bedroom. "Come up."

"Okay?" We're doing this in his bedroom? Is Heather okay with this? My mother wouldn't be. My heart pounds as I climb the stairs, Cassie in close pursuit.

Heather rounds the corner, a tea towel in her hands. "Hi, Aria. Cassie, I need you to come down here and help me peel the carrots."

"Not now, Mom. I'm going to hang out with Aria and Emmett." I guess she has gotten over her anger with her brother.

"No. They're doing *homework*. It's not chitchat time. We already talked about this." Heather is still calm, but there is an edge to her tone that says this isn't negotiable.

It appears Cassie catches it too, because she turns and eases down the stairs, making a point of stomping her socked heels against the hardwood floor as she passes by her mother.

Heather rolls her eyes, then heads back to the kitchen.

And I head for Emmett's room.

It's across the hall from Cassie's and slightly bigger, with slanted ceilings like mine and a window that overlooks the street. There's no built-in bookshelves or reading nook, though. As bubblegum pink and girly as Cassie's room is currently, Emmett's room is shades of navy blue and burgundy, and hockey *everything*.

"Wow." My eyes roll over the hockey sticks mounted to

the wall with brackets, countless medals dangling from the ends.

And in the center of it all is Emmett, his long body looking especially good in jeans and a faded T-shirt, sprawled out on the navy-blue patterned rug, his back propped against his bed frame, his laptop open on his legs.

His feet bare.

"Hey, have you looked over McNair's expectations yet?" He's frowning at his computer.

"I scanned it." I set my backpack on the floor and kneel beside him. Sitting next to him for an hour each day has helped me learn to control my breathing, but where there was once mind-blanking nervousness, now there is wild excitement. Equally distracting.

He runs his index finger across his screen, open to the Social Studies 12 portal page. "It says here minimum seven minutes, maximum twelve minutes, and we'll be penalized for going outside of that."

"I guess that means we have to rehearse the slides."

"Yeah. And they have to be in PowerPoint, with a maximum of twenty-five words per slide, and a maximum of ten slides in total. So, basically, she doesn't want us reading off slides to the class."

"Those are always the worst presentations to sit through, anyway."

He snorts. "Right? Still, this is going to take planning."

"But we're allowed to have talk sheets to guide us."

"Thank God." He frowns as he continues reading.

Meanwhile, my eyes involuntarily veer to his feet, to his toes that are long and touched with dark wisps of hair at the knuckles. His nails are neatly trimmed. All in all, they're not awful.

"Why are you glaring at my feet like that?" Emmett asks suddenly.

"What? I'm not," I deny, feeling my cheeks flush.

"Liar." He laughs. "You were looking at them like you want to cut them off at the ankle and throw them in a Dumpster."

I cringe at the visual.

"They're clean. I *did* shower after practice." He's staring at me, waiting for an explanation, amusement dancing in his eyes.

"I *hate* feet," I finally confess.

"What?" His thick, dark-brown eyebrows pop. "You *hate* feet. How can you *hate* feet? They're feet! They help you run those cross-country races!"

"I'm not arguing that they're useful. But they're ugly."

"You're saying that my feet are ugly."

"No, *yours* are ... not bad." *Because I doubt there's an ugly inch on your entire body.*

He pauses. "What about *your* feet? Are they ugly?"

I shrug.

His full lips twist in thought. "Only one way to find out." Setting his laptop aside, he leans over to seize one of my legs, his firm grip wrapping around my ankle.

I shriek as he effortlessly drags me closer to him, using his free hand to slip off my ankle sock.

"*Wow.* Look at this hideous thing! I can't believe you leave the house with these!" he teases, inspecting my toes, painted with a sparkly blue nail polish.

"Shut up!" I laugh, tugging on my leg, trying to free myself. It's in vain; he's too strong.

"Seriously though, they're *freakishly* small. How do you run so fast with these tiny things?" He drags his finger over my insole, making me jolt. "Freakishly small, *ticklish* feet, huh?"

Oh God. "No!" I cackle as his fingertips dance over the bottom of my foot, torn between mortification and exhilaration, knowing that within moments my face will turn an unsightly mottled pink as it did when my dad would pin me down and tickle me, years ago.

"Hey! What are you guys doing?" Cassie steps in, her eyes flashing back and forth, grinning at us.

Emmett releases his grip of my leg. "Nothing. Aria was showing me her ugly feet and she's right. They're horrible."

Cassie pauses, as if weighing that. "You're joking."

Emmett sighs. "Yes, I'm joking. Aria has cute feet. Mine are ugly. What's up, Cassie? We're working on a project."

"About ugly feet?"

"No. Aren't you supposed to be helping Mom?" I hear the forced patience in his tone.

Cassie holds up an orange flyer. "It's the Fall Fair this weekend."

"Right." Emmett's smile wavers. Is he thinking about Holly right now?

"Can we go?"

"Oh, so now you're talking to me again?" He gives Cassie a knowing look.

"Can we go?" she repeats, and I can't tell if she's ignoring him or if she's missed his point altogether.

"I don't know. I'll have to see my hockey game schedule."

"You don't have a hockey game on Friday. Mom said. So we can go on Friday night. AJ can come. And Zach, too."

"We'll see. I have to talk to him."

"Okay." She pauses, stares at him. "Can you call him now?"

"No, Cassie! Right now, AJ and I are working on a project for school. I'll call him tonight. But I need you to let us work on our project for now. Go and help Mom set the table or something. Come on, Cass ..."

She finally relents, slowly easing her way down the stairs, one cautious step at a time.

Emmett groans, his head falling back to show off the jagged point of his throat. "And now I feel guilty."

"Why?"

"Because she just wants to be included, and now she thinks we're excluding her from something fun. She doesn't have any real concept of this." He casts a hand at the laptop. "Most of her work is in class."

"We can call her back and let her listen to how boring this is," I offer.

He rubs his hands over his face and then grabs his phone. "Lemme text Zach. See if he's around for Friday."

"She likes him, huh?"

"Yeah. Pretty sure she has a crush on him."

"*Really?*" I'm struggling to picture Cassie fawning over a boy—like I am over her brother at this very moment. "She can't even handle watching people kiss in movies."

"You should see the way she blushes sometimes when he teases her." A small smirk touches his lips as his fingers fly over his keypad. He sends the text. "Zach's great with her. His mom works with special needs kids and he has a cousin with autism so he gets it." His phone chirps with a response. "Cool. He's in."

"That'll make her really happy."

"Yeah ... it's kind of lame but we go every year. They have the usual carnival rides." He chuckles. "And they have this haunted house that Cass was begging to go in for years so I finally took her last year and she lost her mind. They had to turn the lights on and guide us out through the emergency exit. I thought my mom was going to kill me."

"Is it scary?"

"Not for me or you." He shrugs. "She mostly goes to play the games. Every year she spots one stuffed animal that she has to win and then spends all her money trying."

"You don't win it for her?" I can't help the accusation in my tone. I'm surprised.

"I used to, but we're trying to help her boost her confidence, which means not doing everything for her. Plus, she's not five anymore. She has to learn that things won't always get handed to her." He shakes his head. "Of course, she comes home from the fair in tears without a toy, and I feel like a jerk." He pauses. "You're gonna come, right? Friday night?"

"Yeah, sure. After the mini-meet." I keep my voice nonchalant.

Meanwhile, my heart is racing.

CHAPTER
THIRTEEN

Dear Julia,

I think my mother is having a midlife crisis. That, or she has lost her identity without her job and has decided to assume Martha Stewart's.

No sooner had Mick finished putting the last pipe in place than she was asking how long it would take to renovate the bathroom upstairs. When I came home from school today, I found them sitting on the porch with tea and a plate of cookies, planning how to replace the steps and what front door would look best. And now that the old appliances have been swapped out for shiny new ones, she's talking about installing new cupboards. Or at least painting them. She can't chill.

Plus, she bakes every day. EVERY DAY, Julia. I know ... first-world problems.

I can't help but wonder how Uncle Merv really is with all this. He grumbles about the noise but then tells her to do whatever she wants because he can't take the damn house to his grave. He loves talking about his grave. It's morbid. Is that what happens when people get old? Is that all they do?

Talk about dying? He doesn't go anywhere. Mom finally got it out of him that they suspended his license because he ran down five pylons in a construction zone. He's lucky that's all he ran down. Iris is the only one who visits every so often. If she was trying to woo him, I think she has given up.

I came home from school today to find him sitting in his chair with his headphones on, listening to an audiobook, and staring up at that wedding picture Mom had framed (she found a hammer: Mick's).

I think he really misses Aunt Connie.

~AJ

THE WIND IS brisk as we lead Murphy and Roger Dodger in through the back door of the animal shelter, their tongues lolling and their tails wagging. Despite his hip impediment, Murphy managed to keep up with the little Lhasa Apso during our trek across the farm field behind the shelter property.

"Did you remember to pick up after him, Cassie?" Pat calls out from the front desk.

"Yes!"

I give her a flat look.

She grins. "AJ did it for both of us."

And I think I've been manipulated. Last week, she struggled with holding the bouncy dog still while she bent down to collect, so I did it for her. This week, she didn't even bother trying. She simply smiled, handed me a bag, and asked, "Oh, could you help me again? I'm having trouble."

"Teach a girl to fish, Cassie ..." Pat scolds softly.

"Yeah, I know." She laughs, bending down to pat Roger's head. "But I don't like dog poop."

"Neither do I." I lead Murphy to his kennel. But when I open the door, he backs away, lifting his nose to graze my hand, leaving a wet trail across my palm. "I'm sorry, Murph."

Gloomy brown eyes peer up at me.

"I know. It's not fair. But you've gotta go. Come on."

He bows his head and ambles in, easing himself down to settle his chin on the piece of ragged remnant carpet that lines the bottom.

And my heart aches, looking down at him. He's going to lie there until he's taken for his next walk, whenever that is. Sit here, in this drab room. His home, until he dies.

Is he counting down his days like Uncle Merv?

"Aww. He looks so sad." Cassie's brow furrows deeply as she studies him. As much as she misses human emotional cues, she seems acutely in tune when it comes to animals.

"He does, doesn't he?" An idea strikes me. "Hey, Pat?"

Pat pokes her head around the corner.

"Are dogs allowed out of the shelter for the night?"

"I WISH I could bring Roger Dodger home," Cassie pouts as Heather pulls into their driveway. Emmett's SUV is gone. So is my mom's, I note. She must still be out grocery shopping.

"Well, we *can*, but we'd have to get rid of your father." Heather smiles at her daughter. "Should we do that?"

"Yeah." Cassie grins. "Let's get rid of him and bring Roger Dodger home."

Heather chuckles. "You know, I'm not sure you're joking." Her wary blue-gray eyes peer through the rearview mirror at the big old Labrador in her back seat. It took both Cassie and I to help him in. "Are you sure Merv and your mom are going to be okay with this?"

I shrug. "You know Merv."

Those eyes in the mirror shift to me. "*Exactly*. I know Merv."

"I already suggested it to him, and he didn't say no." Both are true facts. "And it's only for the night." For now. I'm crossing my fingers that Uncle Merv will like having Murphy around. I can't believe Pat went along with the idea in the first place, but I think she feels as sorry for the poor old dog as I do. I guess it's not the worst thing if I have to take him back tomorrow.

"I'm pleading ignorance." Heather sighs. "It is a nice thing you're doing for him, though."

"Maybe you can remind my mother of that in case she brings this up."

Cassie giggles as she climbs out and opens the back door. "Come on, Murph!"

"We might have to help—oh, maybe not." I watch as he carefully picks his way down, first to the floor of the back seat, before hopping out of the car. His nose lifts in the air to inhale the crisp scent.

I collect his leash, though I don't bother to put it on. He's not going to run.

"Can I come with you?" Cassie asks.

"That's a good idea. You can be a witness if Uncle Merv kills me."

She bursts out laughing. "You're joking. Mom! I'm going next door!"

Heather smiles after her. "For a minute. You're helping me with dinner tonight. Send her home in five, Aria."

Murphy hobbles along beside me as we cross the front lawns, his nose to the grass, his tail wagging. He slows by Uncle Merv's prized rose bush, sniffing around its base.

And then he lifts his leg.

"No!" I whisper-cry, checking the bay window off the living room to make sure Uncle Merv's not watching, wishing now that I had put on his leash. Not that I'd be able to drag the seventy-pound dog away without hurting him.

Meanwhile, Cassie laughs hysterically.

"Whatever you do, *don't* tell Uncle Merv," I warn her with wide eyes. "He'll get mad."

Her face goes slack, the humor gone in an instant. "At me?"

"No! At Murphy."

"Oh. Okay." She nods solemnly.

"Not a smart move if you want to stay, Murph." I climb the porch steps. He limps up behind me.

Cassie opens the front door as if she lives there, gesturing for Murphy to follow her. "Hello, Uncle Merv!" she bellows. "Guess who came to visit you?"

"Eh? What's that?" comes the gruff response from the living room.

I hold my breath.

"What the hell is that?"

Cassie laughs. "This is Murphy. Say hi, Murphy."

I dare poke my head around the corner to see Uncle Merv frowning at Murphy as he ambles around, sniffing everything. "So, remember that dog I was telling you about?"

"I remember you telling me about him," he grumbles. "I don't remember telling you to bring him *home* with you."

"It's just for the night. Murphy's been in that shelter for over six months, and he looked so sad going into that *tiny* little cage in the *horrible* dark, lonely room." I lay it on thick as I reach down to scratch the dog's graying head. "I thought he'd like a change of scenery and you might like the company. He's easy and quiet, and don't worry, I'll walk him later tonight, and tomorrow morning."

Uncle Merv grunts. "Does Debra know about this?"

"I thought it would be a nice surprise?"

I get a bark of laughter in return. "It'll be a surprise all right," he mutters, watching Murphy mosey up to his armchair and sniff his pant legs.

"So ... I'll be upstairs doing my homework if you need me. Cassie, you need to go home."

"Bye, Murphy!" Cassie waves to the dog, waits a few beats as if expecting him to respond, and then trudges off across the front lawns.

I take my time climbing the steps, bending to steal a glance between the railings. Murphy has settled onto his haunches beside the chair.

"You're an old guy, aren't ya?" Uncle Merv finally reaches over and scratches Murphy's head. "Old like me ..."

I smile to myself as I dive onto my bed and pull out my phone. I have hours of math and biology homework to do tonight. But for now, I need a few moments to stare longingly at the screenshots of Emmett's face that I stole from Holly's Instagram.

Only to see that Emmett has sent me a follow request.

Butterflies stir in my stomach as I approve it, bumping my total follower count to two—the Hartford children.

He hasn't added any new pictures, but I spend a few minutes scrolling through his feed anyway. On impulse, I switch to Holly's, curious to see if she's posted anything post-breakup. If she has finally acknowledged it.

All the pictures of Emmett are gone.

Every last one of them. She has combed through her collection and removed all traces of her ex-boyfriend.

Maybe that means she's finally moving on.

Maybe she'll stop trying to murder me with her eye-daggers.

I smile at the tacky stars above my head. Tomorrow is my first cross-country mini-meet, against Baylor Oaks Secondary School. And tomorrow night I'm going to the Fall Fair with Emmett.

And Cassie and Zach.

But ... Emmett.

I'm still smiling up at my ceiling twenty minutes later when the front door creaks open. My mother's home.

I brace myself.

"*Aria!*"

SWIRLS AND FLASHES OF BLUE, green, and red neon carnival lights compete with the steady stream of brake and headlights, as cars slowly snake in and out of the Fall Fair parking lot—nothing more than a grassy field in the middle of nowhere, along dark, quiet roads. Traffic controllers in fluorescent orange vests wave batons, directing us down the long, bumpy makeshift laneway to the available spots.

I find myself smiling at the chaotic scene as I climb out of the back seat of Zach's car, fragments of a distant memory resurfacing—of me, dangling from my father's hand, my other hand gripping a bag of cotton candy, of our laughter.

Long before he decided he wanted a new life, a new family. Does he take his stepdaughter, Charlotte, to the fair?

I'm sure he'll take my half-brother, Teddy, when he's old enough.

I push those dark thoughts aside because I have a new life, too, and so far it's shaping up to be everything that I could ever want.

"So, what's your favorite ride, AJ?" Zach tugs on his black toque and zips his jacket. A bitter cold front blew in last night, bringing with it a forecast of single-digit temperatures and the threat of frost, according to Uncle Merv, who is fretting over his pumpkins and squash, and whatever is left in the garden that my mother hasn't managed to bake into a loaf.

"I don't think I have one?" I huddle in my quilted vest, wishing I'd worn a hat, and peer up at the Ferris wheel. "Not *that*."

Emmett grins down at me. "Why? You afraid of heights?"

"No," I deny, too quickly to hide my lie.

In the next moment, he's stooping to wrap an arm around my thighs, and then I'm off the ground and falling over his shoulder. I squeal with a mixture of surprise and delight, all while demanding that he put me down. Cassie's howls of childish laughter carry through the parking lot.

He sets me back down again with deft hands, so fast that it takes me a moment to regain my balance. I stumble a touch, and he grabs onto my shoulders.

"Sorry. I forgot you had the meet today. Are your legs sore?"

"No. They're fine." They're tired. Tomorrow they'll be sore. But if Emmett wants to throw me over his shoulders, I'll gladly let him.

I placed third, which isn't first but it also isn't fifth, which is where Holly landed, and I'd be lying if I said I didn't enjoy beating her, even if she's on my team. So much for me being "so slow."

"Good." He grins and I lock my legs before my knees buckle.

"Hey, guys, I am *not* going in the haunted house," Cassie declares, fussing to adjust her scarf and mitts. It's the fifth time she's said it since Zach pulled into our driveway tonight.

Emmett hooks an arm around her shoulders, pulling her against him. "We know, Cassie. We know."

Her joyful giggles blend into the carnival sounds.

"Can I try again? *Please?*" Cassie's eyes are on the bug-eyed, pink-and-white stuffed animal dangling from the hook as she pleads with Emmett, the strip of game tickets gripped tightly within her fingers, as if afraid she'll lose them to the breeze.

"Yeah, but this is the last shot, Cass. We're out of money for games." He adds with a grumble, "We could have *bought* three of them for what we spent on trying tonight."

With a determined nod, she hands the skinny middle-aged guy behind the counter five tickets—for the fourth time—grinning at him as he sets three softballs in front of her.

"You know the drill," he mumbles, his hands tucked into the front pocket of his hooded sweatshirt, his bored gaze rolling over the crowd. He doesn't look particularly happy about being here, though I'm guessing the life of a traveling carnival operator isn't a particularly easy or glamorous one.

"I have to get two balls in," she confirms as she lifts the first one.

It lands in the woven basket, earning her squeal of glee.

"Okay! See? You can do this! Just one more." I watch the man's attention flitter to Cassie, studying her. He can tell she's different. But can he tell what a big deal it'd be for her to win? Does he care?

The next two balls do a lap inside the basket before spiraling out.

Cassie's shoulders slump with disappointment. And so do mine, I realize. Unlike this guy, I *did* really want to see her win.

I catch the guy's cold, gray eyes and ask, "Hey, what's that thing about fourth time's the charm?"

He looks at Cassie and then out to the crowd, and I'm ready to lead her away so she doesn't have to hear him tell us to beat it, that she lost fair and square.

But then he reaches below the counter to grab one more ball, and he sets it in front of Cassie. "Make it count, kid," he warns, offering nothing more than the smallest of nods my way.

"Oh. Okay." Cassie picks up the ball. I'm not sure she comprehends what just happened—that she's getting a free shot.

She tosses it at the woven basket.

It does a lap before settling inside.

"Hey! You did it, Cassie!" Emmett cheers from behind.

"I did?" Her face is serious as she looks from him to me, to the ball, to the guy. "Did I win?"

"Which one do you want?" The game operator asks by way of answer, throwing a thumb at the stuffed animals.

She doesn't miss a beat, thrusting her hand forward to point out the cat-fox *thing*, her gray-blue eyes bright, the smile on her face contagious.

Even the man's stony face cracks for a second as he tosses it to her waiting grasp, just before he slaps an "on break" sign on the counter and ducks away.

"I can't believe it! I won!" Cassie holds the stuffed toy up to examine it closely before hugging it close to her chest.

I meet Emmett's coffee-brown eyes then, and my heart stutters at the soft look in them as he regards me. "Thank you," he mouths.

I shrug, as if it's no big deal. Meanwhile, blood is racing through my veins.

Zach wanders up, shoving a fluffy wad of blue cotton candy into his mouth. "You win that, Cass? Seriously?"

"Yeah." Her grin somehow grows wider.

"Way to go. High five!" He holds up a hand and she meets it with a resounding slap of hers. "So, where to next? Haunted house?"

The smile falls off abruptly. "I'm not going in there." She punctuates the refusal with a vigorous shake of her head.

Zach laughs. "I know. I was only kidding. You don't have to." He holds his bag of cotton candy out for her to take some. "AJ and Emmett will go. You and I can hang out here."

"Is AJ scared?" she asks Zach. She does that sometimes, I've noticed—ask questions about people as if they're not there. It's usually when she's too excited to focus.

"I don't know," Zach says patiently. "But she's standing right beside you, so you should ask her."

She turns to me, her eyes bright with amusement. "Are you scared, AJ?"

"No."

"Oh. Good." Her attention veers back to her prize, wrapped tightly within her arms. She's smiling at it as she warns, "Watch out for that man."

I frown. "Which man?"

"The one who ..." She sticks her tongue out and makes a licking motion in the air.

"Excuse me?" I feel my eyebrows climb my forehead. "A man is going to *lick* me?"

Emmett laughs and seizes my biceps from behind. "No one's going to lick you. It's a wet sponge," he promises, leading us to the two-story, rickety wooden façade. A roped path leads up to the fake porch where the entrance is curtained off. He hands the operator our tickets. "You ready?"

"I'm not sure anymore," I say warily.

With a grin and a nod toward the attraction, he lingers long enough for me to pass him, his hand skating across the small of my back for the briefest moment. Just long enough for my heart to skip a few beats, just quick enough for me to question if he meant to do it. "Don't worry, the whole thing's pretty lame. That part freaked her out because it's pitch-black and, well, she's *Cassie*."

"Wet things touching me in the dark would probably freak me out, too." I push past the heavy black drape, only to find myself caught in another one.

Emmett snorts. "No comment."

I playfully elbow him as my cheeks heat. "God, how many curtains do they need?" I fumble through layer after layer until I finally break free.

A skeleton with glowing red eyes pops out from the wall to the left, the accompanying recorded cackle startling me enough to make me yelp and lurch backward, into Emmett's hard body.

He laughs as he grips my waist. "I knew that'd get you." His hands linger a few beats longer than necessary before he releases me. My heart is pounding, and it has nothing to do with the collection of plastic bones and electrical wire dangling from the wall.

We follow the narrow corridor, painted black and pitch-dark save for the red rope lights that mark either side of the floor. I hold my breath and brace myself as I sweep through the next heavy curtain, expecting another Halloween prop to jump out at me. Nothing jumps out this time, though, as we step into a small room that glows neon purple from black light. Creepy dolls line shelves on either side of us, trailing us with radiant eyes and maniacal laughter carrying over a crackling speaker.

"Where is this licking man, exactly?"

Emmett laughs. "It's not for a while but after last year with Cassie, I'll bet they got rid of him. By the way, I hear you guys have a dog now?"

"Yeah, as long as I feed and walk him twice a day." That was the deal my mom and I struck this afternoon, after Uncle Merv spent the day rambling to Murphy about Aunt Connie and his forty years working in agriculture and the folly of youth today. When Mom made a comment about taking the dog back, Uncle Merv insisted that, if he's just going to sleep in a cage until he dies, he might as well sleep in our living room until he dies.

So now we have a dog.

"Cassie told me all about it. That was a pretty cool thing you did."

I smile to myself as we move past the doll room and into the next blackened corridor. We round a corner, and a guy with a Michael Myers mask steps out to loom over us, forcing me back to bump into Emmett again. I giggle as we edge around him and move on, past another heavy curtain and into a room of mirrors. "This is neat." I wander deeper in, slowly spinning to take in all the tall panels, the countless reflections of Emmett and me, standing side by side.

Could we ever pass for a couple?

He's the most beautiful guy I've ever laid eyes on, even more so now because I know he has a heart. He's not a hot jerk; he's not full of himself. He's ... Emmett.

And he's watching me as I stare at his reflection.

"You figure it out yet?" he asks softly, smiling like he can read my mind.

"Uh ..." *That we should be together? Yes, I've known that from the start.*

"The way out."

"Oh." My face flushes. "Yeah, it's easy. This way." I reach out, only to have my knuckles smack the glass.

Emmett's reflection grins at me.

Determined to find the path, I search around us. "*This* way. No ..." I note fingerprint smudges ahead. Another fooled occupant. So I turn the other way and pass through. We continue like this, me fumbling for direction, until another draped threshold appears before us.

I'm more curious than nervous as I push through the curtain this time.

That is until we step into utter darkness. I can't see my hand in front of me. "Is this the room?" I whisper, my body shrinking into itself.

"Why are you whispering?" Emmett whispers back, his voice filled with amusement.

"Because—"

The space ignites with a flash of light, just long enough

to show us a square room of maybe fifteen-by-fifteen feet and someone dressed as Pennywise standing in the far corner before falling into complete darkness again.

"Well, he's new," Emmett murmurs as eeriness settles over me.

"What do you mean?"

"I mean they didn't have him last—"

Another flash and Pennywise is there again, only this time he's standing a few feet closer.

"Oh man, thank God Cassie didn't want to come in here." Emmett chuckles. "She would've lost her mind."

My heart races with anticipation. That light is going to flash again soon and Pennywise will be that much closer. "Where are we supposed to—"

My words cut off with the flash. He's only maybe four feet away now.

"I don't like clowns." I back up and into Emmett before sidestepping to edge behind him and use his body as a shield, my hands shamelessly gripping his vest. He laughs.

One ... two ... three ... I count in my head, pressing my forehead against him, inhaling the faint smell of his body wash and cologne as I wait, the muffled screams and carnival rides from outside so far away.

The light should have flashed by now.

Where is Pennywise?

Why hasn't the light flashed?

Finally, I lift my head. "Okay, is this going to be over soon—"

Something wet slips across my cheek.

I shriek and dart around the other way, to press myself into Emmett's chest.

His arms are around me in a flash, pulling me in close. "Did he get you?"

"Are you sure that was a sponge?" I grimace, wiping furiously at my cheek with my hand.

His chest shakes with laughter. "They're not allowed to lick people's faces. Trust me, it's a sponge. That's what they use at these things. Someone hides in the corner. I looked it up after last year's disaster."

Oh God, they did that to Cassie? "It felt like a tongue."

"I'll take your word for it."

"Is this over? I'm ready for it to be over."

"Yeah. They'll turn on the lights in a sec."

I haven't pulled away and Emmett hasn't released me yet, and now that I'm over the shock of the face-licking, I'm acutely aware of how close we are.

I peer into the darkness, imagining where his mouth might be. A good six inches away, at least. Still ... so close. Would he hold a female friend so protectively? "How did they know where I was anyway?" I ask softly.

"There's a second person hiding in the corner behind us, wearing night vision goggles." Emmett's voice has dropped to a low, gravelly timbre, and I can feel his breath skating against my skin.

As if he's peering down into the darkness at me.

He still hasn't let go.

"That's so creepy."

"Right? Imagine having that on your résumé?"

"Carnival face-licker, 2002 to present."

Our laughter mingles, the sound a sudden blend of nervousness.

"Are you sure they're going to turn the light on?"

"Yeah." His hard swallow fills the eerie quiet.

And I feel his heart hammering in his chest, pressed against mine. I sense his body leaning toward me, his head tipping forward.

His lips brushing ever so faintly past mine, almost as if by accident ...

The strobe light flashes nonstop then, filling the room with—

I shriek as I look into Pennywise's face directly over Emmett's shoulder.

"Shit!" Emmett senses him and jumps a touch. Laughing, he grabs my hand and we both run for the black curtain now visible. In seconds, we're outside and rounding the far end of the haunted house, laughing in between our ragged breaths.

"You *knew* he was going to be there, didn't you!" I jab at Emmett's chest.

"I didn't. I swear." Emmett holds both hands up in the air, but then he doubles over with laughter.

"I *hate* you right now."

With a devastating grin, he seizes my hand and pulls me into him. "No, you don't."

It takes me a moment to gather my courage and tip my head up to meet his eyes. "I do, though. A little bit."

His gaze flitters to my mouth, making my heart race all over again for him. He shakes his head. "Not even a little bit."

"No," I finally whisper, swallowing against my rash of nerves, aching for him to kiss me. To *really* kiss me.

"Did he lick you?" Cassie yells from behind me, loud enough for plenty of nearby carnivalgoers to hear, misinterpret, and laugh.

Emmett chuckles as his eyes shift to his sister. But then his smile drops off and his hands release mine.

When I turn around, I see why.

Holly is standing a few feet away from Cassie and Zach, a candy apple in her grip.

A mixture of pain and fury in her blue eyes as she regards us.

And a wave of guilt overwhelms me, though I remind myself that they're no longer together, that *she* caused their breakup. And nothing has happened between Emmett and me.

Not *really*.

Not yet.

Still, it would be a kick to the stomach to come to the Fall Fair and see your ex standing so close to another girl.

As if remembering herself, Holly lifts her chin and strolls forward. "Hey."

Emmett's attention wanders around the crowd before finally settling on her with a reluctant sigh. "Hey."

"Can we talk? Please?" She's practically mewling, she's made herself sound so docile.

He shakes his head but then mutters, "I guess. They're shutting down now, though."

"I drove."

Of course you did.

He chews the inside of his mouth, seemingly in thought, before nodding at Zach, who nods back—an unspoken understanding passing between them.

He turns to me. "Cassie should probably get home, anyway. You mind going with her and Zach?"

"Of course not." I force a smile as my gut clenches. "Thanks for letting me tag along. It was fun." I hesitate. "Except for the clown and the face-licking thing. That was not cool. I will get you back for that."

A devilish spark flashes in his brown eyes. "Can't wait to see you try."

"Okay." I take a deep breath and stroll past Holly,

unable to avoid meeting her eyes. Her contrite act disappears just long enough to offer me a scathing look.

Yeah, I don't feel so guilty about that near-kiss anymore.

I want to scream at Emmett, to beg him not to fall for whatever lies and tricks Satan has planned to win him back.

But instead, I follow Cassie and Zach out of the fairgrounds.

Mourning the loss of an otherwise perfect night.

CHAPTER
FOURTEEN

Dear Julia,

I think Emmett was going to kiss me tonight. Scratch that, I KNOW Emmett was going to kiss me tonight. Damn that Pennywise. Couldn't he have waited another five seconds?

And now Emmett is somewhere with HER. Sitting in her car, listening to her convince him that they need to get back together. She's persistent, I'll give her that.

Oh, God.

What if Emmett forgives her? Do I have the right to be upset?

I toss my journal to the floor, not bothering to sign off, my stomach in knots. It's after eleven and I have yet to see Holly's car roll into the Hartford driveway. They've been "talking" for an hour.

What does that mean?

My chest tightens with dread as I pick up a novel from

my pile of library books and curl up in my window seat with a blanket.

Knowing I'll only stare at the pages.

MY MOM HAS BEEN USING a distinctive knock lately—one firm rap, followed by two shorter, softer sounds in quick succession.

When I hear it against my bedroom door on Saturday morning, I pull my covers over my head and groan.

The door creaks open. "Nice try. It's almost nine."

"It's the weekend!"

"Murphy doesn't care."

"Can't you take him? Please?"

"Two walks a day. That was the deal for keeping him and you happily committed." The curtain rings slide over the metal rod. "Come on, up you go. Unless you want to take him back to the shelter."

"I'll be down in five minutes," I say from beneath my dark duvet, sensing the kink I earned in my neck after drifting off in the window cubby last night, my forehead pressed against the cold windowpane. I woke up at three to a quiet street and no evidence that Emmett had returned. Not that there'd be a flag mounted or anything, but I was hoping for a text, at least. After dragging myself to bed, I tossed and turned for hours, and now I just want to sleep all day.

"I'm glad to see that you're taking Dr. Covey's advice."

My diary.

I bolt upright so fast, my head spins. My mom is holding the teal-blue book, the one where I've divulged all my inner thoughts, including exactly how hard I'm crushing on our neighbor. "Mom!"

"*What!*" She jumps, startled.

I reach for it, waggling my fingers with impatience.

She sighs with exasperation as she tosses it onto my bed. "If I were going to read your diary, do you think I'd do it in front of you?"

My mouth drops open. Has she found my hiding spot?

"Relax. You haven't given me any reason to invade your privacy. Besides, I haven't learned how to pick a lock." Her eyes rove over my sweatshirt. "I'd say get dressed but I see you're still wearing yesterday's clothes. Good! You can take Murphy out now, before Uncle Merv feels compelled to."

"He could use the exercise," I say under my breath, digging out my discarded socks from the tangle of sheets.

"... WORKS WITH TEENAGERS." Uncle Merv's gruff voice carries up the stairwell, along with the delicious waft of something.

"You told Iris!" my mother hisses.

I freeze, my ears perking to listen, knowing instantly that this has to do with me.

"No! Of course not. She was prattling on about her granddaughter and mentioned that she had some *emotional* issues—"

"Aria worked with a therapist at home. I don't want to keep pushing her to talk about it when she clearly wants to move on. And now that we're far away from those people and all the reminders, and I'm here and present in her life, I really believe she's going to be fine."

"That wasn't your fault, Debra. If anything, I blame that lousy father of hers."

"Oh, come on, Merv. Of course it was my fault." The kitchen chair legs drag along the linoleum floor. "I'm to blame for at least part of it. Between the divorce and my career, I was *never* around. I assumed too much; I didn't know what was *really* going on with her until it was too late. That wasn't *my* Aria. But she's back, and trust me, she never wants to go through something like that again."

"All I'm saying is these teenagers get good at hiding things. I know Connie and I didn't have any of our own, but I've seen and heard a lot in my years."

"I know, believe me. But I'm watching her carefully and we're talking now and—"

The floorboard creaks under my foot, cutting off whatever my mother was going to say. Not that it's a mystery to me.

Murphy is waiting for me at the bottom of the stairs, his tail wagging off-tempo, as if he's hoping for a walk but isn't sure he's going to get one. When I grab the leash off the hook, he heads for the door. I could probably get away with not leashing him, if he'd stop going straight for Merv's struggling rosebush.

"No, Murphy!" I hiss, steering him toward the line of hedges so he can relieve himself. He has a slight spring in his hobbled step that wasn't there on Thursday, I note. A more confident tail wag to replace the tentative one, multiple swipes of his wet nose against my hand that feel like signs of affection.

I smile despite my bad mood, knowing I did the right thing for Murphy, even if meant risking the wrath of Uncle Merv.

We're halfway to the main street when Murphy lifts his

nose to sniff the air. He stops to peer over his shoulder and a stripe of hair rises along his back.

"What's up, buddy?" I follow his line of sight to see the tall form jogging toward us in a long-sleeved shirt and track pants.

My stomach flutters the way it always does in that first moment of spotting Emmett.

I scratch behind Murphy's ear in a soothing way. "It's okay, he's our friend."

Emmett comes to a stop five feet away. "Hey," he offers, a touch breathless. His hair is untamed, as if he just rolled out of bed. "Your mom said you were out walking him." He leans down to let Murphy sniff his hand before giving the top of his head a pat.

Emmett went to my house looking for me. Why?

"So, *obviously*, Zach got you and Cassie home all right?"

It takes me another beat to push aside my question. "After he stopped to buy a bag of weed from his dealer, yeah."

Emmett's eyes widen.

"I'm kidding."

His shoulders sink with his chuckle. "I was gonna say ..."

"Thanks again, for taking me to the fair. It was fun. Hey! Murph!"

The dog has found a scent trail and is tugging me down the sidewalk with surprising strength.

Emmett falls into step beside me. "I'm sorry about how the night ended."

I take a deep breath, stuck halfway between wanting to ask what happened and never wanting to hear his answer. But I need to know. "How'd it go?"

He pushes a hand through his wild hair, sending it into further disarray. "Exactly the way I expected it to go."

Which means ... We turn right at the end of the street. And I wait for him to elaborate, holding my breath.

"It was a *long* night." He shakes his head, his eyes wandering over the quiet houses. "Three hours of sitting in Holly's car in the Tim Hortons parking lot while she cried and said sorry *over* and *over* again and tried to—" He presses his lips together to cut his words off, and dips his head, a sheepish look filling his face.

I can only imagine how that sentence might end, and it likely involved roving hands and eager lips.

A flash of memory—of being pressed against that broad chest, our hearts pounding against each other, his mint-laced breath skating across my mouth—hits me then and my cheeks burn, even as my stomach roils.

I give Murphy's leash a light tug and he continues on, moseying along the sidewalk at a leisurely pace, only to pause another five feet away to sniff at a shrub.

"She gave me some lame excuse about being caught up in the moment and having a crappy day." He chuckles but the ring of humor is absent. "She actually tried to give me the Leafs tickets for our anniversary. She thinks there's still a chance we'd get back together. But how can I ever trust what's going on inside her head? I mean, *you* heard her. You heard what she said about Cassie and Jen ... and you. That didn't sound like being caught up in the moment."

More importantly, it doesn't sound like they reconciled last night, a realization that leaves me struggling to keep the smile of relief from showing.

It's a few seconds before I realize he's waiting for me to say something.

"Maybe she feels she needs to act a certain way with her

friends?" I offer halfheartedly, because agreeing too quickly with him would be self-serving.

"And what does that say about her choice in friends? No. I'm done with Holly. I think she finally figured that out by the time she dropped me off."

"What time was that?"

"Late. After one." He pauses. "You were sitting in the window."

"I fell asleep there." I reach up with my free hand to rub the back of my sore neck.

"Figured. You know, with all the drool."

My mouth drops open. "I was not drooling!"

"Oh, yeah. There was this big gob, dripping down here." He reaches out to drag his finger playfully down my chin, earning a swat and my laugh.

"Like you'd be able to see drool from down there anyway." My mind searches my vague, sleepy memory of coming to, curled in a ball, my face cold from the glass. There could have been drool.

"You like that spot, don't you?"

Yes, because I can watch you. "It's comfortable. And it's kind of neat that Uncle Merv built it for my mom, and she used to read there too. My room back home was boring. A rectangle with two plain windows, and stucco on the ceiling. Painted lavender. But this one has personality. I like it."

"Do you miss it? Calgary, I mean."

"No," I say without missing a beat.

"Really?" He hesitates. "Your dad still lives out there, doesn't he?" He's fishing for information.

"Yeah, but he has a new family and he has no interest in being a part of my life anymore, beyond the required monthly child support payment." I feel Emmett's gaze on my profile but I keep my eyes on Murphy as he sniffs around a bramble of bushes.

"He sounds like a loser."

I swallow the rising lump and give the leash another light tug. "He wasn't always that way. But things happen, people change."

"Not parents. They're not supposed to change like that."

I shrug. "Maybe." That whole concept of unconditional love seems to have evaded him.

"What about your friends?"

"They're still there." I shrug. "My mom and I needed a change. This was a good one."

Emmett nods slowly. "I can't imagine leaving Zach and Mower, and all those other guys. I guess I'll know what that feels like next year, though."

Eastmonte without Emmett. Just the thought brings an ache to my chest.

"I'm sure you'll have *no problem* making new friends." *Plenty of Hollys and Patricias to chase after you.* A sour taste fills my mouth.

He pulls his bottom lip between his teeth, and I feel an overwhelming urge to know what Emmett's bottom lip between my teeth would be like. "I keep telling myself that it worked out, having things end with Holly now, before I'm gone. Long-distance relationships never work."

His words are a sharp needle to this intoxicating bubble I imagined growing around us last night. The last thing he wants is to get into another relationship.

He dips his head. "So, about last night, in the House of Horrors—"

"That was scary, right? I don't know what the hell happened. And honestly? I don't think wiping wet sponges on people's faces is sanitary." *Topic change now, please.* So I don't have to stand here and listen to Emmett tell me that I'm a great person and he likes me as a friend but it was a mistake *almost* kissing me and *blah, blah, blah.*

He sighs. And then smiles. "No, it probably isn't."

Murphy whines and burrows his nose deeper into a bush then, his tail wagging. A deep growl responds and a second later, a gray-and-black-striped cat springs out and tears off across the street. Murphy goes after it, wrenching my arm and jerking me forward with his burst of strength.

Emmett's reflexes are as swift as the cat's. He dives in, seizing the leash to keep Murphy from running in front of a small red hatchback as the driver slams on the brakes and the car comes to a jarring halt.

Adrenaline races through me as the car rolls by, the lady giving me a dirty look on her way past. "Oh my God, that was close."

"Yeah." Emmett is well within my personal space, much like he was at the carnival. It hurts, knowing last night was a freak occurrence, never to happen again.

I take a calming breath. "Did the cat make it?"

We both peer to the opposite side of the street just as the striped furball bounds over someone's front lawn.

"Little asshole is fine." He peers down at me with those warm, deep-brown eyes. "You good?"

"Yeah. Thanks. He's stronger than I thought. He never pulled that hard when we were at the shelter." I take a step back into safer, more platonic territory. Where Emmett wants to stay. "I should get him home. Pat said to keep the walks short because of his hip."

"Oh, yeah. Of course." Emmett's lips press tight. If I were a fool, I'd mistake that look for disappointment.

We head back, the leash wrapped twice around my fist in case of more kamikaze cats.

"What do you have planned for the rest of the weekend?"

"Not much. Homework, probably." I frown at the red pickup truck that turns onto our street. "What does she have him doing now?"

"Is that the handyman?"

"Yeah. My mom is, like, renovating Uncle Merv's entire house. I don't know if it's because she's bored, or because she feels guilty for not visiting all those years and this is how she thinks she can make it up to Uncle Merv. But it's Saturday."

By the time we round the bend in our street five minutes later, Mick is parked and standing casually on the porch with my mother, cradling a mug in her hands. She's wearing her favorite mustard-yellow cable-knit sweater and, even from this distance, I can see the way her hair spills over her shoulders in fat waves.

"Hot rollers." Things begin to click like puzzle pieces. The soft laugh to cap off the "please call me Debra," the Mick-this and Mick-that, all the projects ... "Oh my God. My mom has a crush on the *handy*man!" I don't *mean* to sound appalled by the idea.

Emmett and I linger on the sidewalk, watching the exchange—the way Mick shifts his body, his crinkle-eyed smiles at the porch floorboards, the way my mom giggles and fusses with her sweater collar, her gaze holding his intently, her smile effervescent. She has a thing for him and I think it's reciprocated.

"Now we know what Mick's working on today." *My mom.*

Emmett chuckles. "And you're not okay with that?"

"No, I am. At least I *think* I am?" I pause to consider it for a moment. "It's just *weird*. I've gotten used to the idea of my dad being with someone else. But my *mom*?"

"I can't picture my parents apart, let alone dating other people." Emmett peers over at his house, as if trying to imagine it at that moment. "It'd be weird," he finally agrees. "Is this guy nice, at least?"

I shrug. "Seems like it, but I haven't talked to him. I don't know anything about him. Like, has he ever been married? Does he have kids?" Is he a closet drinker? A serial cheater?

One thing's for sure—my mom is going A-to-Z opposite from my partner-at-a-busy-law-firm dad if she's chasing after Mick. But wouldn't that fit with this new life she's taken on? It's like she's making a concerted effort to become the exact opposite of who she was in our old life.

Mom bursts out in a strange, youthful laugh and then, spotting us standing on the sidewalk, casts a casual wave.

"How long before they do it, do you think?" Emmett asks suddenly.

My jaw drops and then my hand flies out to swat against his hard chest. "Ew!"

He winces, rubbing the spot where my hand made contact.

"Oh, *please*." I roll my eyes. "I watched a guy ram his entire body into you on the ice."

"I wear padding!"

"All that muscle is basically padding." *And now he knows that I've spent a lot of time ogling his body.*

By the time we reach my driveway, the awkwardness from earlier has made its way between us again. "So, I guess I'll see you around?" Where do we go from an almost-kiss?

Back to being just neighbors and running buddies and social studies partners, I guess.

Just friends.

He hesitates. "Hey, I've got a game tonight in town, if you're not doing anything. I'm sure Cassie would love for you to come." His eyes are steady on me.

Is he really asking me for Cassie's sake? Not that it matters. I'd accept either way.

Still, I try not to sound too eager. "Only if you score ... three times." I pull the number out of the air.

His lip curls with amusement. "You expect a hat trick for gracing us with your presence?"

"Sure?"

Emmett's head falls back with his laughter. "You *really* don't know a thing about the game, do you?"

"You put the puck in the net." I shrug. "I've never lived next to a hockey family before. You people are *weird*."

He smirks. "I'll see what I can do." Bending down to give Murphy a scratch, he takes steps backward toward his house. "But *only* if you come."

He just wants to be friends so why does it feel like he's flirting with me?

With reluctance—because I could spend the whole day standing here, talking to Emmett—I turn and lead Murphy toward the house.

"Hey, Aria! Mick and I were talking about your closet," my mom says through a sip of coffee.

"I don't have a closet."

"*Exactly.* He thinks he can frame out the left corner by the door and build you something nice, with shelves and cubbies. Custom. Wouldn't that be great?"

"That'd be awesome. Hey, Mick." I offer politely.

"Hi, Aria. How's the water pressure holding up for ya?"

"It doesn't take me ten years to rinse the shampoo out anymore, so ... good?"

By his nod of satisfaction, I guess that's the right answer.

Mom's eyes flicker to Emmett's retreating back. "He found you, did he?" A secretive smile touches her lips.

Oh, she *so* knows about my crush on Emmett.

My cheeks burn. Has she been reading my diary after all? A flash of panic tightens my stomach.

No. There's *no* way she found it.

"Murphy likes to chase cats," I blurt, wanting a change of topic, especially in front of our handyman. "And he's a lot stronger than you'd think, so be careful, if you're ever walking him."

"Noted."

Mick reaches down to scratch beneath Murphy's chin, earning himself a lick. "Hey there, old man. How you doin' today?"

Mom studies Mick's face. Now that I'm closer, I see that she not only did her hair in the time between waking me up and now, but her cheeks are rosy with blush and her lashes are coated in mascara.

She suddenly looks up and catches me watching her gawk at Mick. She gives her head the slightest shake. "Before I forget, Heather and Mark invited us for Thanksgiving dinner next Sunday. I know it's your birthday but I thought a family dinner would be *nice*." Her forehead furrows. "I can't remember the last time we had a turkey."

Because turkeys have always been too much work and so messy and "God, what do you do with all the leftovers?" complicated.

And none of that matters because it means I get to spend at least part of my sixteenth birthday with Emmett. "That's fine."

"Good, because I've already said yes." Mom's lips quirk. "I figured you'd be more than agreeable."

Now she's teasing me.

I plaster on a wide smile. "You look *really* nice this morning, Mom. You did your hair and makeup and everything. Were you expecting someone?"

Mom's eyes flash first to Mick and then to her coffee mug, her cheeks glowing. "I thought we'd go out shopping when you got back from your walk. For a new couch and wine and stuff."

"You want your fifteen-year-old daughter to help you shop for *wine*?"

"What? No! And *cheese* and groceries and ..." She's flustered. My mother is never flustered. She laughs and shakes her head, flashing me a warning glare. "Go on inside, Aria. There's a plate of pumpkin bread on the table."

"Pumpkin bread today. *Great.*" I drag my feet up the stairs.

"Your mom is quite the baker," Mick offers.

"Yes. All of a sudden, it would seem. It's like she's trying to impress someone."

"Okay. Off you go!" Mom shoos me inside with a wave of her hand.

CHAPTER
FIFTEEN

I SHOULD HAVE DRESSED WARMER.

Heather warned me that the rink would be much colder tonight than last time, back when summer still lingered in the air. I misjudged and now I'm left shivering in my fleece sweater and my fall vest, my only source of warmth the watered-down hot chocolate I grabbed from the snack bar.

I'll gladly freeze if it means watching Emmett play, though.

He flies down the ice with the puck, passing it to one of his teammates. Cassie and I were late arriving. He hasn't looked up here yet, he's so focused on the game. I doubt he knows I've come. We're sitting apart from Heather and the group of moms again, at Cassie's request. She says it's because they yell and swear too much, but I think it's because Cassie doesn't get a lot of time away from Heather's watchful eye, and she relishes every opportunity.

I can't blame her.

Suddenly there's a chorus of loud shouts and a whistle blows and the ref points at one of the players on the other team, then makes a hand-chopping gesture. "Hey, Cassie.

Do you know what that means?" My words drift as I take in her face. I can't help but laugh.

She giggles and licks her lips. "I have a chocolate mustache, don't I?"

"Yup. An *extra* big one."

"This is why I need a straw!"

"You should bring one from home next time." I reach for the box of Junior Mints between us.

And scowl as the last one tumbles into my palm.

"Oh. Yeah." Cassie pauses to peer down at my hand. "I ate them all." She's grinning broadly, her front teeth coated in the chocolate evidence.

I crumple the box as I watch Emmett race for the puck, deftly maneuvering his stick to swipe it from the opposing player.

"Are you mad?" There's a hint of panic in her voice, as if the idea of me being angry with her is sinking in and causing her anxiety.

"No, I'm not mad. I'm *annoyed*. Do you know what that means?"

She searches her thoughts. "When someone does something that bothers you?"

"Exactly. It *bothers* me that you ate all the Junior Mints." *In five minutes.* "They're my favorite."

She swallows. And then her face breaks into a sheepish smile. "I'm sorry."

A round of cheers explodes and I glance back in time to see Emmett clapping gloves with another player. "Did Emmett score?" Dammit, I missed it!

He turns toward the stands and points in our direction.

I freeze for a moment. "Me?" I mouth, covertly gesturing at myself, my cheeks heating.

He's pulled his glove off and holds up one finger.

I feel the big, dumb grin stretch my lips. *One goal down. Two to go.* I did demand that earlier.

"What is Emmett saying?" Cassie frowns. "Why did he do that?"

"Nothing. It's a joke between us."

One of his teammates follows his gaze up to the stands and then gives him a playful shove against his shoulder.

He knows I'm here, all right.

"I was there on Saturday! *The creepy Pennywise clown?*" Jen's blue eyes widen as she squeezes my biceps. "I hate normal clowns. But *that* clown? I almost cried!"

I laugh, spinning my combination lock. "Same here." Had I not had Emmett's strong chest to bury my face in, I might have.

Then again, if not for carnival Pennywise and the face-licker, I wouldn't have found myself in Emmett's arms that night. They deserve giant raises.

"Ready for the chem test, Jen?" Emmett sounds breathless as he sidles up beside me to lean against the lockers, his textbook casually tucked under his arm. He smells of soap and the perfect amount of cologne, like he *just* stepped out of the shower, even though his hair is barely damp anymore.

"Probably not. You?" She slams her locker shut and adjusts her shirt collar. She's wearing a turkey print today and, as hideous as it is, I've found myself looking forward to discovering what Jen is wearing on any given day. I've noticed that not *all* the looks from students are negative. A girl walked by us minutes ago, her eyes narrowing on Jen's back just long enough to decipher the tiny birds, before a genuine smile touched her lips.

Emmett smirks. "Probably not." Those intoxicating brown eyes shift to me. "How was practice this morning?"

I catch myself practically fawning as my head falls back. Emmett truly towers over me. I've never had a thing for tall guys, but now that I think about it, none of the fourteen- and fifteen-year-old boys I hung around with reached six feet. I was taller than half of them. "Fine. I ran with Richard."

"Why? You're way faster than him."

Everyone on the team is faster than Richard, including the ninth-grade girls. Short of every other racer injuring themselves midway through, he'll never place.

I shrug. "My calf felt tight. Didn't want to overdo it." In truth, running alongside Richard guaranteed that I wouldn't have to deal with Holly's scathing glare. She was leering at me when I arrived at school this morning, in a way that set me on edge.

"Fair enough." He seems to buy it.

The first bell goes.

"Crap. I'm going to be late." I rush to dig my books out of my backpack.

"Here." Emmett reaches for the bag, his fingers grazing mine as he holds it open for me.

My heart stutters. "Thanks."

"No problem." He peers at me from behind a fringe of long, dark lashes, the look unreadable. "So, I heard it's your birthday this Sunday."

"Yeah." I feel my face reddening. *Why am I embarrassed?* "Whatever. It's no big deal."

"What are you gonna do?"

"Eat turkey at your house?"

He rolls his eyes. "A food coma for your sixteenth birthday, with your neighbors. That's awesome." The sarcasm in his voice tells me it's not.

"Well, I don't know." I hesitate. "Do *you* have something in mind?" I reach for my backpack to chuck it into my locker. But he doesn't let go immediately, and my fingers linger against his, amping up my adrenaline.

"Maybe. Do you trust me?"

"Yes," I quickly add, "as long as there aren't clowns or face-lickers involved."

He smirks. "I'll promise no clowns."

Oh my God. What is that supposed to mean?

A streak of blonde catches the corner of my eye and I glance toward it.

To meet Holly's blue eyes, flaring with rage and accusation as she sizes us up.

I know what this must look like.

I *wish* it was what it looked like.

"*Wow.* Didn't waste time, did you?"

Is she talking to me or Emmett?

She sneers at me, at my jeans and faux baseball shirt. "And with a major downgrade, too."

Definitely Emmett.

"This isn't what it—" Emmett begins to say, but Holly spins on her heels and marches into class, past McNair, who mutters something about teenage hormones under her breath and then taps her watch in silent warning.

He shakes his head. "Just ignore her."

I'd love to. I really would.

I trail him into class and settle at our usual desk just as the second bell goes. It's ironic that given the freedom to sit anywhere, everyone subconsciously falls into a routine.

"Good morning! I hope you all had a wonderful weekend and are ready to learn," Mr. Keen says over the PA system, his voice crackling with static.

I *did* have a wonderful weekend. Now, though, Holly's harsh slight is going to hang over my head. Maybe I should start making more effort with what I wear to school. I've always liked this shirt, though.

I feel Emmett's eyes fixed on my profile and I turn to offer him a reassuring smile—to pretend that I don't care what Holly thinks—before returning my attention to the front of the classroom where McNair is jotting down notes on the blackboard.

"At last Friday's cross-country mini-meet at Baylor Oaks, three of our team members placed ..."

Mr. Keen's voice disappears as Emmett leans over to whisper in my ear, so close that his bottom lip grazes my earlobe. "By the way, you are definitely *not* a downgrade, in *any* meaning of the word."

My heart pounds in my chest.

I walk out of class an hour later, having missed every word that McNair said.

I didn't even take notes.

DEAR JULIA,

Things between Emmett and me have been weird since last Friday. Tense. Even though he basically told me he wants to be just friends, I'm starting to wonder if that's really the case? Or is that my delusional, wishful thinking? Am I setting myself up for crushing heartbreak?

McNair used the old "elephant in the room" saying

during class today, and now that's all I can think about. There's this giant elephant standing between Emmett and me. It's looking at us with its hooded eyes and it's waving its long trunk. Emmett sees the elephant. I see the elephant. We're both pretending that we don't see the elephant.

The elephant wants peanuts.

Sooner or later, someone's going to have to feed it. Should I be the one to take that risk? I'm not brave like that, Julia. I wish I was that girl.

If I were, maybe I wouldn't be sitting here, writing to you.

~AJ

I LIFT my hand to knock when the door suddenly flies open.

"Aria!" Heather exclaims, startled. She's wearing a navy wool jacket. "I didn't know you were coming over tonight. Not that it isn't great." She steps back to allow me entry.

"Yeah, Emmett texted to see if I had time to work on our project. I figured I'd better take it." As usual, the Hartford house smells mouthwatering. This time it's the lingering scent of roast beef and rosemary.

She shakes her head in a knowing way as she grabs her purse and keys from the hook. "His schedule is impossible to plan around, isn't it? Cassie, come on! Let's go!"

A moment later, Cassie rounds the corner, her jacket dangling from her fingers. "Oh, *hi*, AJ!" She grins. "Are you coming with us?"

"No. She and Emmett are studying. Get your coat *on* and let's go. We're already late for swimming!"

"Okay, *okay!*" Cassie shoves her arms into her sleeves, scowling with annoyance at her mother, who merely sighs. "Emmett, Aria's here! We'll be back in an hour. Dad's in his office on a call with the Vancouver office."

"'Kay!" comes the deep voice, stirring my nerves.

Heather smiles warmly at me. "See you in a bit."

I kick off my shoes and climb the stairs, acutely aware that Mark's office is in the basement—two floors below us. For the next hour, Emmett and I are basically alone.

I'm going to be in his bedroom.

And Heather doesn't seem at all fazed by that.

Of course she's not. It's me, Aria from next door. The fact that I'm majorly crushing on her gorgeous, popular, athletic son isn't a concern for her, because she figures he'd never go for me.

Would he?

"By the way, you are definitely not *a downgrade, in any meaning of the word."*

I've been replaying his words from social studies for days in my head, searching for meaning between the words. Was he just being nice? That would be like Emmett, to be aware of how cutting Holly's words were, to try to placate my ego.

Taking a deep breath, I bang my knuckle on the ajar door once before pushing it open. "Hey—" The simple greeting comes out as a croak, caught in my throat as I watch Emmett slide his T-shirt over his head, giving me a glimpse of the web of muscle in his back. His bedroom smells of his potent, masculine body wash.

"Hey. Sorry. Had to shower after practice." He reaches for a pair of socks on the bed. "The arena showers aren't the same."

"That's fine." I exhale slowly, trying to refocus on the

task at hand. I hold up a notepad covered in my scribbles. "So, I pulled a bunch of data from the province's website that I think we can use?"

"Cool." He nods toward the small pile of books and his laptop, haphazardly set up on the floor. A few feet over is a pile of pamphlets from University of Minnesota. How excited is he to be going away to college next year? To be on his own, living in a dorm or wherever hockey-scholarship guys live, no one to worry about but himself.

Emmett groans and stretches his arms high over his head, the move lifting his shirt to hint at the V-cut of his pelvis.

I can't help but stare.

He catches me—his return smile is playful. "Let's get to it. We have an hour of peace before Cassie gets home."

"DIRECT AND INDIRECT BULLYING. That's important." Emmett types those two words into the squares of the flow-chart. "We should list them, too, with stats."

"I couldn't find any for Canada. Only the US."

"Yeah. Me neither. But we can keep those in our back pocket, for impact. Like this one." He taps the screen with his pen's end. "An estimated 160,000 students miss school every day in the US. So, if we assume ten percent of that for the Canadian population, that'd be 16,000 students. That's like, what, ten times our entire school population, staying home *every* day."

I punch numbers into my phone's calculator. "Nine point six zero four times, to be precise."

Emmett's eyebrow rises in question.

"Apparently, I'm student number 1666, according to Keen."

He chuckles softly, jotting down notes in blue pen. "I think we should focus on cyberbullying. It's changed the whole dynamic. Made it that much easier for people to hide behind screens and be assholes to each other."

My stomach turns. "Sounds good."

"And we should do a couple slides about suicide, seeing as that's the most drastic outcome of bullying."

The room sways, even though I'm sitting. "We only have seven to twelve minutes, remember?" *Can we please move on from this topic?*

"Yeah, you're right. That's not a lot of time. Okay, so let's dedicate one slide to suicide. The basics. The increasing rates, the top three methods, which are"—he glances at his notes— "hanging, gunshot, and poisoning." He frowns. "What does that mean, exactly? Poisoning?"

My throat feels thick. "Pills."

He shakes his head. "Man, I can't imagine how bad it has to get for someone to do that to themselves."

My heart hammers in my chest as a swirl of emotion—pain, mortification, and *so much* regret—swells. "They're usually already depressed. And then being attacked and ridiculed ..." A lump forms in my throat. "It's the perfect storm."

"Yeah, for sure." Emmett's fingers fly over the keyboard as he types bullet points for that slide. "Hey, you don't have any pictures on Instagram."

"Uh ... what?"

"Your Instagram. You have no pictures on it."

"*Oh*. Yeah." My relief for the sudden change in topic threatens to bowl me over. "I just started the account."

"Yeah, figured as much. I was just surprised, is all. Even

Cassie has had an account since she was in, like, grade eight."

"Yeah, well ..." I pick at a loose thread on my shirt sleeve. "You know how my mom is."

"Fair enough. There are a lot of crazies out there. We have to keep an eye on Cassie's account to make sure she's not talking to anyone she's not supposed to."

"Do you really think she would?"

He snorts. "We've had the stranger-danger talk with her a million times, enough that she gets pissed off when we bring it up—she *hates* being lectured, if you haven't noticed."

"Don't blame her. So do I."

"Yeah, I guess. But with Cassie, we *think* she gets it, but then she goes and does something that makes us think she doesn't. Like, a few months ago, my mom was scrolling through her contact list on Instagram and there was some dude in there. Cassie accepted him because his profile picture was of a little girl hugging a dog." Emmett gives me a knowing look. "The guy's entire feed is of him posing shirtless in front of mirrors in public bathrooms."

I cringe.

"Yeah. So that's what she was looking at every time she scrolled through her feed. She agreed that it wasn't right, but she couldn't figure out to take the next logical step and block him. So now she has to come to me or my parents every time she gets a follow request. We walk her through deciding whether she should accept it. We're trying to teach her how to think critically, but that's one of her challenges. Everything is black or white, absolute yes or absolute no for her. Anything outside of that, she has a hard time grasping."

"Does she get a lot of requests from creepers?"

"No, thank God. She'll get invites from kids she's chatted up at school every once in a while. I make sure they're not the kind who would drop mean comments on there, or be coming around to find things to mock her for behind her back." He snorts. "Didn't do the greatest job there, did I?"

He's referring to Holly.

Does he know that she deleted him from her feed?

Does he care?

"So, how come *your* profile's not protected?"

"I'm not worried about attracting predators." He scrolls through the bullying website, searching for more nuggets of information.

"No. Just adoring female fans," I mutter under my breath.

"What was that?"

"Nothing."

His dimples divot his cheeks with his grin. He heard me, all right. "So, tell me something about Aria Jones from Calgary, since you're basically a ghost online."

I study my socks. "Am I?" I know as much, but is he confessing to sitting here in his room, perhaps lying in his bed, looking me up?

Out of mere curiosity?

Or interest? The more-than-friend kind?

My thrilled heart is at odds with the wariness creeping into my spine, of what he could probably find out about me if he knew where to dig.

I take a calming breath. "There's not much to tell. I like running, and reading. And apparently, zucchini bread."

He laughs and I laugh along with him, my chest warming. "What else do you want to know?"

"Have you ever had a boyfriend?" He asks it so casually. "Are you allowed?"

"Of course I'm allowed!" I sound indignant. Truthfully, my mom never knew about my two short-lived relationships. She was never present enough to notice the days where I was floating on a cloud, or the nights where I drowned my sorrows in tubs of mint chocolate ice cream.

Emmett sets his laptop aside and settles back against the rail of his bed. He swallows hard, the sound carrying through his bedroom. "Can we talk about it then?"

The elephant.

The air in his bedroom has turned thick with anticipation. "About what?" I hesitate, gathering my courage before I turn to meet his beautiful brown eyes, so open and earnest as they skate over my features, stilling on my mouth.

"About *this*." He leans in, until the tips of our noses touch, his lips an inch away. He holds there a moment.

Long enough to give me the chance to stop this from happening, I'm guessing.

Long enough to make my blood rush to my head and my heart thump wildly and my breathing just ... stop.

And then he presses his lips against mine.

Kissing Emmett is an out-of-body experience; it doesn't feel real. His lips are somehow both warm and cool, both soft and firm. When the tip of his tongue touches mine for the first time, I realize I'm still holding my breath. I exhale and with it escapes the softest sigh.

Emmett leans further in, pushing me back to rest against the frame of his bed, the slight stubble on his face scratching deliciously across my chin and my cheeks as he kisses me deeply, with an expertise I can't possibly match.

I'm dizzy when he finally pulls away.

"Is that going to be okay, with your mom? You know, because you're fifteen."

"*Almost* sixteen," I manage in a harsh whisper. And Emmett will be turning eighteen in less than three months. We're not even two years apart. "That was unexpected."

He grins, still leaning into me, his fingertips grazing my cheek. "*Really?* I thought you had figured it out."

"What? No!" I giggle with disbelief, my head swimming in shock. "You said you wanted to stay single. You know, because you're leaving next year?"

"Yeah. Next *year*. Plus, you never let me finish what I was going to say."

I pull my bottom lip into my teeth to hide the stupid grin that threatens to surface. "What were you going to say?"

His brown eyes settle on mine. "Just that the first night I came to your room with the boxes, I thought you were adorable."

"Yeah. *Right.*" I roll my eyes. "Aria with a green face."

He laughs. "You were. And I liked running with you, and hanging out with you. And I didn't expect to be breaking up with Holly, so I couldn't see myself with anyone else at first. But, I don't know ... Zach kept asking me if I'd mentioned him to you at all, and then he said he wanted to ask you out to a movie. I got jealous."

"*Really?*" I thought I was the only one.

"I told him to stay the hell away from you. That's when I realized that it was because *I* wanted to be with you."

"Really?" I sound like a doe-eyed dimwit.

He weaves his fingers through my hand, stroking my palm with the tip of his thumb, and I can't describe the way my heart surges with happiness. I don't think I've ever been this excited about anything in my life. "Yeah. I mean, you're funny and sweet and cute—"

I groan.

"In a *hot* way, trust me." His mouth is on mine again, this time more urgently, the palm that was cupping my face earlier now settled gently against my neck. It'd be an easy slide down. What it would feel like to have Emmett's hands on me like that?

The very thought sends heat through my core.

Gingerly at first, I let my fingers wander as our mouths and tongues tangle, smoothing over his strong arms, marveling at his hard muscle. Not long ago I was fantasizing about touching this body and here I am, free to do so. The question now becomes, how fast is too fast?

I'm not sure which order it happens in—if his mouth shifts to my neck first or his hand slides up my shirt, but soon my body is being inundated by Emmett, who may be a decent guy but is *not* a shy one. I let my head fall back against his bed, close my eyes, and sigh my pleasure as his tongue leaves a trail across my throat and his palm smooths over my abdomen, slowly moving upward, until cool air skates across my skin. His palm settles over one of my bra cups, and I silently thank my choice of pink lace today.

I vaguely hear a door creaking open somewhere in the house, but I'm too far gone, my hand now having found its way through Emmett's thick mane of chestnut-brown hair, my body a live wire.

"*Hello*, Emmett and AJ! We're *home*!" Cassie's voice carries from the bottom of the stairs.

Emmett pulls away with a heavy exhale, his hair tousled, his eyes wild, his breath ragged. A soft curse slips from his lips as he settles back into his prior position—hauling the laptop back to rest on his lap.

The stairs creak with Cassie's slow and steady approach. She appears in the doorway a few moments later, her hair damp from the pool. The subtle smell of chlorine drifts in along with her. "What are you guys doing?"

"Homework," Emmett says in a croaky voice. He clears his throat. "How was swimming?"

"Good. No one pushed me into the pool today."

My eyes widen in surprise. "Someone pushed you into the pool at swimming lessons?"

"Yeah." She nods. "Ranjeet. He thought he was helping."

"That happened four *years* ago," Emmett reminds her.

She shrugs.

"Cassie, start the bath!" Heather calls from downstairs, earning her daughter's huff of irritation. Still, Cassie listens, disappearing into the bathroom.

My phone chirps with a text from my mom.

How's the project going? Murphy needs his walk soon.

"Man, she's holding me to this dog-walking thing." I gather my books. "I should probably get going." I don't see us getting any more work done on our presentation tonight.

"Yeah, I've got a calculus test to study for." Emmett laughs at my cringe and walks me to the door, pushing it almost shut to block my way. "Talk to you later?" His voice is low, each word somehow touching my body in an intimate way.

"Yeah." I clear the shakiness from my voice under the weight of his gaze. "Just so you know, my mom monitors my phone. Like messages and all that."

"Wow. *Really?*" The expression that takes over his face makes me want to shrivel from embarrassment. What if he second-guesses this thing between us? What if he decides he needs someone older, less supervised?

I don't have much choice; I have to explain. "There was this *thing* back home." I hesitate, dread swelling in my chest as I try to temper my voice, "I was getting these messages from people for a bit."

"What do you mean? What kind of messages? From who?" he asks warily.

"Just kids from school sending me things." *Prayers for death, wishes for broken limbs, dreams of tragic afflictions, general hatred. Those sorts of things.* I clear the thickness from my throat. "My mom's paranoid, but as soon as she realizes that none of that is going to repeat itself here, she'll ease up. So, just for now, know that she'll probably be reading whatever text you send me."

Emmett's face fills with pity that I don't want. "Seriously, it's fine. It's over. I'm here now." My eyes skate to his full lips. "Things couldn't be better."

"I can make them better." He leans down to press a long, leisurely kiss against my lips. "Run, tomorrow morning?"

"I can't," I pout. "I have practice. With regionals coming up soon, Moretti's on a mission."

"Okay. I'll see you in class, then." He kisses me one last time and I force myself out of his room, half-expecting to float down the stairs.

The tub water is running in the bathroom but the door is open and Cassie isn't in there. She's still downstairs and, when I start my descent, she darts down the hall to the kitchen, the distinctive rattle of candy in a box trailing her. "Mom! You have to hide it from AJ!" she says in a harsh whisper that may as well be a yell.

She's up to something and, if I had to guess, it has to do with my birthday.

She reappears as I'm sliding my shoes on, her grin suspect.

"We're going to the shelter tomorrow, right?" I ask, feigning oblivion.

"Yup." She presses her lips together, looking ready to burst from excitement.

"Get lots done?" Heather calls out, strolling toward us.

"Uh ... yeah?" I bend down to collect my things from the bench, and to hide my pink cheeks.

"This weekend is kind of big. Your sixteenth birthday, eh?"

"Shhh!" Cassie presses her index finger against her mouth as she follows me to the door, suddenly urgent to get me out. "See you tomorrow, AJ." The door practically closes on me, and I hear Cassie lamenting, "Mom! You almost ruined the surprise!"

"I did not, but *you* are going to." Heather's laughter fades as I move farther way from the Hartford house, picking a path through the front lawns to home, glancing up at Emmett's bedroom once. I would do anything for my window to meet his.

Then again, that would spell doom. As it is now, it'll be *hours* before I'm able to drift off.

Too busy staring up at my glow-in-the-dark stars and pinching myself over and over again.

Wondering if this is what I deserve.

DEAR JULIA,

I told Emmett. Not EVERYTHING. There's no way I'll ever tell him—or anyone here—the whole story. God knows he'd never look at me the same way again. But he knows enough.

I wish I had a time machine, Julia. I'd do anything to go back in time.

To erase it all.

~AJ

CHAPTER
SIXTEEN

Jen's round face pinches. "You are, like, *super* happy this morning. What gives?"

I struggle to shrink my grin as I pull my social studies textbook from my backpack and chuck everything else into my locker. "Nothing. I had a good run today." Even Holly's scowls and huddled whispers and suspicious laughter with her friend couldn't dampen my spirits. I blew past her to lead the pack, beating my best time. *Ever.* I couldn't wait to finish, couldn't wait for first period to start, so I could see Emmett again.

A hand grazes my back a split second before I catch the scent of his body wash.

I spin around just as Emmett leans in, pressing his lips against mine. "Hey," he whispers, his brown eyes twinkling with a secretive smile.

"Hey." And my wide grin is back as I peer up at that stunning face I could stare at all day, a face that is no less striking today than it was the first day he walked through my door.

I still can't believe this is happening.

The first bell rings.

"Be back in a sec." He gives my side an affectionate squeeze before peeling away to speed to his locker.

It leaves me reeling.

"A good *run*, huh?"

I turn back to meet Jen's gaping mouth. I shrug, not trusting my own voice.

"When did *that* happen?"

"Last night." I watch Emmett as he sheds layers and tosses in textbooks, sharing a laugh with a guy standing next to his locker.

Is *he* really mine now?

Are those broad shoulders mine to wrap my arms around?

Are those strong arms mine to graze?

He hip-checks his locker shut and, with a grin at his friend, heads back my way, holding that devastating smile.

Is that beautiful face mine to touch, to kiss, whenever I want?

Adrenaline rushes through my veins at the thought of the next time we're alone together. When exactly will that be? How long do I have to wait?

Holly strolls past Emmett, cutting in front of him and forcing him to halt.

He gives the back of her head a mildly amused look, but she doesn't acknowledge him, let alone apologize. Her head is held high as she strolls into our classroom, as if she doesn't have a care in the world.

Maybe an act of indifference? There's no way she's over him so quickly, purged social media or not.

"Does *she* know yet?" Jen asks.

"I don't see how. You're the first person I've told." And Emmett's a guy. I can't see him texting all his friends to share the "big news" the second I left last night. And Holly wasn't at her locker when Emmett kissed me. My chest tightens with anxiety. "What do you think she's going to do when she finds out?"

Jen slams her locker shut. "For your sake, hopefully nothing." There's no mistaking the worry in her voice.

"Hopefully nothing what?" Emmett is next to me again, leaning in for another kiss.

"See you later," Jen says somewhere in the distance. Far, *far* away from this euphoric cloud I find myself floating away on.

"Okay, you two. Second bell's about to go," McNair warns sharply, yanking me back down to earth, her tone likely less to do with punctuality than with the school's policy on PDA.

Emmett pulls away with a groan. "So, when are we getting together to work on our project again?" he asks softly.

"I was just wondering the same. Are you free—"

"*Mr.* Hartford. *Ms.* Jones."

Emmett's jaw clenches with annoyance but he takes a step back, eyes rolling.

I stifle my laugh as we move toward class, sucking in a breath as his fingers graze the small of my back.

We step in to plenty of curious eyes settling on us.

And one set that glares suspiciously.

Whatever. If she has a problem with this ... it's her problem.

The second bell rings and announcements blast over the intercom as we take our seats.

The next sixty-five minutes are a blur.

A blissfully happy blur.

Mick is taking me to see some tile options for the kitchen this afternoon. That orange linoleum has to go! I'll be back around five.

A date?

I watch the three dots dance on my screen as my mom types her answer.

No, of course not. What kind of date would that be?

But what if Mick thinks this is a date? Would you be okay with that?

More dancing dots.

Would YOU be okay with that?

Will YOU stop making zucchini bread if I say yes?

I get a flat-mouthed emoji in response and then,

I'm asking seriously, Aria. You've been through a lot.

It always comes back to me.

Mom ... Dad had a baby with another woman. You should date if you want to.

I hesitate before sending the next text.

And Mick seems like a nice guy.

Not that I know him at all.

Doesn't he? I don't think he charged me for replacing the broken lock on the back door.

That's because he cut himself a key so he can sneak in at night.

Aria!

Gotta go. Jen will think I fell into the toilet.

I smile and tuck my phone away before finishing up in the bathroom stall. I step out and round the corner.

And find Holly standing in front of the tiny mirror, dabbing at the tears that run down her cheeks. I hadn't heard the door creak open, hadn't heard her make a sound. At least she's alone.

And I can guess what those tears are about.

I quickly wash my hands, intent on getting the hell out of there. She deserves it, I remind myself. She brought this on herself.

I'm two seconds from the door, thinking I'm going to avoid an awkward confrontation.

"It was you, wasn't it?" Her silky-smooth voice rings with a sudden realization.

"I don't know what you're talking about." Guilty. I sound guilty. Can she hear it, too?

"That's why you were *staring* at me in the caf that day, at lunch." Each word comes with more conviction. "That's why you called me out in class over Jen's name. You were in here, hiding in the bathroom stall, *recording* my *private* conversation."

"Your *private* conversation in the girls' *bathroom*?" I scoff, trying to shrug it off, daring to face her now.

Disgust twists her beautiful face. "And then you sent it to Emmett so you could break us up. So *you* could have him."

"That's ridiculous, Holly." A tiny twinge deep inside me flares at her accusation, as if she hit somewhere too close to the truth. "I heard what you said." I add quickly, "Emmett played the recording for me," though I don't know if I'm fooling her anymore. "He deserved to know who he was dating. That's why *whoever* sent it to him did it. So he'd know the truth about the kind of person you are."

She takes two steps forward, moving into my personal space, her eyes filled with rage. "You're going to regret it."

"I haven't done anything wrong." I hold my stance, setting my jaw, meeting her glare, hoping she can't see the dread in mine.

The door swings open and two girls stroll in, stopping short at what must look like a fist fight that's about to break out. I use the interruption as my excuse to hightail it out of there.

What will Holly's next move be? She has no proof that it was me.

I remind myself of this, even as the weight of her promise settles in my gut.

This is not supposed to be happening again.

It's five thirty when Heather pulls into the driveway after picking Cassie and me up from the animal shelter. My mom and Mick are leaning against the posts on opposite sides of the porch steps, my mom's stance casual as she laughs at something Mick said. She's swapped her usual yoga pants and T-shirt for dark-wash jeans and a soft-pink long-sleeved knit top. Her hair and makeup are done.

She looks ... different.

Happy.

Murphy moseys around the front lawn, his nose to the grass, his leash dangling from his collar as if my mother thought to take him for a walk but gave up.

"What is Mick doing now?" Heather asks, parking next to Emmett's SUV.

Her.

Emmett's lewd comment from the other day rings in my ear and I stifle my cringe. How long before she's staying over at his house? "The kitchen floor, I think. Mom wants tile."

"That'll freshen it up." She eyes them shrewdly. Does she suspect that there's more going on than rendered handyman services?

Cassie pushes the door open. "Murphy!"

The old black dog's tail wags as he hobbles toward us, giving Cassie's hand a quick lick before coming to me, his tail's wag quickening.

I scratch the top of his head. "How was your day with Uncle Merv? As exciting as usual?"

"Aria! I need you to peel the potatoes," my mom calls out, throwing a casual wave toward Heather, who's heading up the porch steps with two bags of groceries.

"You, too, Cassie. Carrots," Heather calls—earning

Cassie's exaggerated groan—as Emmett steps out the front door.

"Hey, you." Heather angles her cheek up, prompting a kiss from her son.

He appeases her with a quick peck. "Is there more in the car?"

"Three more bags. What time are you leaving tonight?"

"Practice is at eight." Our eyes meet and his face splits into a smile as he saunters down the stairs, heading toward me.

My stomach flips with anticipation. Is he going to kiss me again, like he did this morning? In front of our mothers and Cassie? Oh God, I hope not. I don't want to deal with those questions yet. It's bad enough everyone in school knows already. As quickly as news of Emmett and Holly's breakup spread, by fourth period I felt eyes from every angle, and whispers of "That's her" trailing me. People asking who the new girl is and what Emmett sees in her, likely.

But seriously, doesn't anyone have anything else going on in their lives? The only person who seems to have no clue yet is Cassie.

I scoop up Murphy's leash and take steps backward, toward the sidewalk. "Hey, Mom, I'm gonna walk Murphy around the block and then I'll be in to help. Five minutes."

"Yeah. I'll bring the rest of the groceries in as soon as I'm back," Emmett echoes, for Heather's sake. "We need to go over a few things. About our project."

"I'm coming, too!" Cassie declares, tossing the bag of groceries to the grass, and marching toward me.

I school my expression to hide my frustration. If she knew her brother and I were together, would she still insist? Definitely.

"*Mom.*" Emmett gives Heather a pleading look.

Heather presses her fingertips against her forehead, as if the task of mediating between her kids causes her pain. "Cassie, you've been with Aria for the past hour. Let's give them five minutes to talk about their project."

Cassie scowls and keeps walking toward me, ignoring her mother's request.

"*Cassandra Jayne Hartford*, get in this house *now*," Heather demands, her typically serene tone sharp and leaving no room for argument.

Cassie's face hardens as she whips around and stomps her feet.

"On your way by, please pick up that bag you threw," Heather calls out, tempering her tone again. I can hear the weariness in it. How exhausting must it be dealing with Cassie's childish outbursts?

Cassie bends down to grab the bag's handle and then runs in her off-balanced way up the path, letting the contents of the bag bear the brunt of her anger, smashing against the stair rails as she clomps up the steps, mumbling something at her mother that I can't decipher but that can't be good.

Emmett sighs deeply, as if to shake off his frustration with his sister, and then throws a hand in the air. "Hey, Ms. J."

"Hello, Emmett." She watches him curiously as he closes the distance toward me.

"Be back in fifteen." I walk ahead but slow enough for him to catch up.

My mom folds her arms over her chest. "Fifteen now ..." But the small, knowing smirk touching her lips tells me she's not bothered.

"Hey." He nudges my arm with his.

My heart skitters. I've been waiting for this moment all day. "Hey."

"They still watching?"

Ever so casually, I glance over my shoulder to see Mom's gaze following us. "*Still* watching."

"Have you told her yet?"

"About what? *Oh.*" That Emmett and I are now a thing. *Are we officially a thing?* "No." I'm not sure if *I* believe it yet. "Does your mom know?"

He shrugs. "She'll figure it out soon enough. She'll be happy. She loves you."

I feel the conflicting swell and tightness in my chest. Would she want her son with me, if she knew *everything* there was to know? Would she want Cassie as my friend?

"What's wrong?" Emmett asks.

I swallow my anxiety. I haven't had a chance to talk to Emmett for more than five seconds since first period. A few passing words in the hall before fifth period. Now's as good a time as any to fill him in. "I ran into Holly in the bathroom today. She figured out that *I'm* the one who recorded her conversation. I denied it but I don't think she believed me."

He waves a hand dismissively. "Whatever. Ignore her. It's not like she's gonna do anything."

"Are you sure about that?" Because girls like the one Jen described don't just roll over and move on. "She thinks I *stole* you from her."

He snorts. "We broke up because I found out she's a bitch."

"And she told me I'm going to regret it." I kick at a loose stone on the sidewalk. "I'm kind of hoping to avoid being a target here. Been there, done that. It's not fun."

I feel Emmett's steady gaze on my profile as we round

the bend in the street, but I keep my eyes on Murphy, his nose prodding the bushes that line the sidewalk.

"Maybe we should cool it for a bit, until she's moved on."

"No! I mean ..." I temper my panic at that terrible suggestion. "I don't want to do that."

His lips twist in thought. "Is your mom still out there?"

"Uh ... I can't see the house from—"

Emmett's mouth captures mine in a searing kiss that pulls me right back into the headiness of last night in his bedroom. His one hand slips beneath my hair to cradle the back of my neck while the other snakes around my waist, easing me into his body. I forget all my worries—my past life, the C+ on my math quiz, the kamikaze cat waiting in the bushes, the potential wrath of Holly—as I sink into his warm body, tasting mint on his breath as his tongue slips over mine in a seductive dance.

A car gives a light honk on the way past, reminding me that we're standing on the street.

"Did you actually want to talk about our project?" I ask in a shaky voice.

"No." He laughs, releasing me from his hold, glancing around. "Mower's having people over Saturday night. You think your mom will let you go?"

"Maybe?" I'll beg and plead if I have to.

He shrugs. "I figured it'd be a good way to ring in your sixteenth birthday."

"Sixteen minus an hour. My curfew's eleven," I admit with bitterness.

His face pinches. "Even on your birthday?"

"We'll see." Maybe I'll ask when I get home, while she's still buzzing from her tile-shopping non-date with the handyman.

"Try. His parents are going away for the weekend so it'll be a good time."

"I'll probably leave that detail out."

Emmett chuckles. "Good idea. And he lives over there." He points to a side street up ahead, lined with grand oaks and sizable houses. "So we can walk. No worries about driving."

Which, I'm guessing, means Emmett's planning on drinking. "You don't have hockey?"

"Not on Thanksgiving weekend. It's one of the only weekends I can let loose."

What does that mean? Is he planning on getting drunk? What is Emmett like when he's drunk?

Jen's words hit me then, about how he and Holly were known to "go at it" at parties. I witnessed it firsthand. Well, I witnessed the prelude and then the hickey aftermath.

What's going to happen at Mower's house this weekend? What is Emmett going to expect from me, still very much a virgin?

When do we have *that* conversation?

Murphy squats.

"Oh, shit," I mutter.

"Yeah. *Literally.*"

"No ... I mean, I didn't bring a bag!" I check my jacket pockets in case there's an extra one from the shelter visit.

There isn't.

As discreetly as possible, I glance around at the houses, to make sure no one's watching.

The moment Murphy has finished, Emmett declares, "Run!" and we take off at a slow jog toward our houses, allowing Murphy to keep up.

We laugh the entire way.

CHAPTER
SEVENTEEN

DEAR JULIA,

I'm petrified of this Saturday night.

Is that stupid? Because it feels stupid to be so nervous. It's Emmett, after all. But ... IT'S EMMETT. I don't want to screw this up by saying or doing the wrong thing, or doing something the wrong way. Do all teenaged girls worry about this kind of stuff or am I strange? This is when I wish Denise and I were still friends. Maybe I should ask Jen. I'm guessing she's still a virgin, but she's also smart and level-headed. She'd probably give good advice. I don't know if Mom will let me go anyway. Mick ended up staying for dinner tonight, so it didn't feel like the right time to ask. Or maybe it would've been the perfect time, with Mick there and her in a bubbly, non-Mom mood. But I was getting creeped out with all the secret looks they kept giving each other, so I ate and then hid up in my room.

Mick's okay, by the way. A bit of a dork—he tried to strike up a conversation with me about Star Wars—but he seems nice enough. He doesn't have any kids. That's a bonus.

I don't need any more stepbrothers or -sisters. The ones in Calgary are more than enough.

So ... I guess I'll ask her about Mower's house tomorrow, after the cross-country meet.

~AJ

"Did you double-check your laces?" Richard points a stubby finger at my running shoes and I look on instinct. "Yeah. Twice."

"All right! Go whoop some Xavier ass for us." The second cross-country mini-meet is at a conservation area near Xavier Secondary in Klemptville. They're a big rival high school for Eastmonte and also where Jen and Holly both came from before moving.

I size up the runners readying on the start line. Most of them are tall—one looks like she's teetering on six feet. "I don't know. I'm guessing some of those girls can go the distance."

"So can you. *And* you're fast. That's a *deadly* combination in this sport. Stay with the pack." He pats my shoulder. "You're Aria Jones and you can do this."

I laugh, though I don't think Richard was trying to be funny. "Thanks for the pep talk. See you in a bit." I take my place in our team's box at the starting line—a white streak of chalk marking the trail—ever aware of Holly settling in directly beside me. Almost as if she was waiting for me to find my spot before taking hers. *Now I'm being paranoid,* I tell myself.

I edge a step to the left, to put some distance between

us, but it's futile as the rest of our teammates move in, eating up the space.

"Runners, ready!"

We take our starting positions. Adrenaline courses through me.

"Good luck, SWF," Holly murmurs in that faux sweet voice a second before the official fires the starting pistol.

I launch myself forward to fall into place with the herd, careful to avoid getting tangled in the encroaching knees and legs. The start of these races has always been the most stressful and my least favorite, ever since I watched three girls trip over each other in seventh grade. One ended up with a broken ankle.

SWF?

What the hell does that mean?

I roll the initials in my head, coming up with random words.

Stupid? Whore? Fake?

The only thing I can be sure of is that it wasn't intended to be kind, and Holly intentionally threw it at me right before the gun went off to rattle me.

Screw her.

I set my jaw with determination and push Holly's jab out of my mind as we pass the official at the fifty-meter mark. A few girls are outpacing the group ahead. As much as I want to put distance between myself and Holly, I avoid the urge to run faster just yet. Moretti warned us that this trail would be challenging, the hills steeper, the terrain rough.

Slut? Is that what the "S" stands for?

Wouldn't that be a little ironic, given—unlike her—I'm still a virgin.

I sense someone closing in on my right, getting too close for my liking.

And then the next few seconds happen in a blur. There's a swish of a blonde ponytail as my foot catches a heel. I stumble, fighting to regain my balance.

But I fail and tumble to the ground, my knee landing on the sharp gravel.

The runners behind me maneuver last minute and continue past as I struggle to get to my feet. Ahead, Holly glances over her shoulder once before continuing.

As if to make sure I'm down.

There's no way that was an accident. How the hell she managed to trip me like that, and to stay on her feet, though …

Frustration and anger—at her, but mostly at me—flares, my eyes prickling with tears. My focus was broken, that's how.

And we've passed the hundred-meter mark. They won't restart the race, but maybe I can still catch up. I take a step forward, and pain lances through my knee.

"Aria!" Moretti's standing at the sideline, her raven bob swishing with her head shake. She waves me over.

I hobble off the course much like my old dog would.

"It's a mini-meet—not worth it. Not with regionals coming up." Her face twists with sympathy. "That looked like it hurt. Are you okay?"

"I think so."

Richard has procured a folding chair from somewhere. I offer him my thanks as I settle into it, peeling my pant leg up.

Moretti winces at the quarter-sized patch of missing skin and the blood. At least it's not *dripping* with blood. "Can you try to bend it for me?"

I hiss from the sting as I do as asked.

"Okay. Clean that well and ice it for tonight. Fifteen minutes on, fifteen off." She frowns, her gaze on the runners in the distance. They're climbing a slight hill, spread out now, the leaders of the pack making their move. "It looked like you and Holly got tangled but I couldn't see clearly. What happened?"

She ambushed me.

It's on the tip of my tongue.

"I tripped," I say instead.

"You sure?" Her eyes narrow in a way that makes me think she saw more than she's letting on, that she suspects more than she's saying.

But I'm not stupid. I already know how this is going to play out—Holly will return after the race, all doe-eyed and full of worry, apologizing profusely for "accidentally" crossing paths with me. She'll swear she didn't know what to do—hang back or keep going. She'll be so thankful that I'm okay. Maybe shed a few tears to cement her innocence.

And, in the end, suspicions or not, Moretti will believe her, because Moretti *wants* to believe her. She doesn't want to think that one of her runners could harm another like that, and all over a boy.

I'll end up looking like the problem.

And if I bring up the SWF reference?

Holly will deny it. Her face will become a portrait of innocent confusion. *I have no idea what she's talking about, Ms. Moretti, I swear! I just wished her good luck!*

Or she'll have an innocuous answer for what that might stand for. Something kind and flattering.

This is what girls like Holly do. This is how they get away with their cruelty—they hide their toxic underbelly with a honeyed veneer for adults, and adults buy it because they want to.

Or they shrug it off as typical teenage behavior.

The Hollys get away with it.

And then they do something else. Something worse.

And the cycle continues.

I study the grass at my feet. "Yeah, I'm sure. We got tangled."

Dear Julia,

Single white female. That's what SWF stands for. I Googled it. As in, I'm some sort of stalker.

Holly basically called me a stalker. And then she tripped me!

Of course, like I expected, she pretended to be "oh so sorry!" (insert apologetic, concerned treacherous doe eyes here).

Maybe I can use this as my excuse to quit cross-country. Though, I think I'll get so much more satisfaction from beating her at regionals. Is that too catty a thought? I can't tell anymore.

All I know is that I hate Holly Webber and I don't feel an ounce of guilt over showing Emmett that video anymore. In fact, I'll be sure to stick my tongue in his mouth the next time she's—

Mom's signature knock sounds on my bedroom door and then she pokes her head into my room. "How you doing?" Her concerned eyes shift first to my knee—cleaned, bandaged, and propped atop the desk chair I dragged over to my window seat, bag of frozen peas chilling the ache—and then to the diary on my lap.

I shut the book. "I'm fine. It's already feeling better." Because it's numb.

"Good. I'm glad to hear it. Listen ... so ..." She edges in, folding her arms over her chest. "Mick asked me out to dinner tonight. To that cute little Italian place we drove past the other day. You remember—Nonna's? The one with the red-and-white-checkered awnings."

"Okay?"

"But I don't have to go," she rushes to say. "I can stay home with you. If you need me to."

"Why would I need you to?" I pause. "Unless you're looking for an excuse to turn him down, in which case I am dying and they may need to amputate, so you should stay with me. I'm on board with whatever. Just let me know what to say."

She chuckles. "No, it's not that I don't *want* to." Her gaze searches the cluster of yellow stars stuck to the ceiling above my bed. "I spent twenty years married to the wrong man. A complete schmuck. *Twenty years*. And here I am, going on a first date again. I don't know if I'm ready. Plus, Mick is a *good* man but he's never been married and, at his age, that raises alarm bells."

"It's *just* pasta."

Her lips twist in thought. "It's just pasta. You're right." Shaking her head at herself, she stands taller. "So, you'll be fine at home alone tonight, then? Well, Uncle Merv is here, but he'll be in bed soon."

"Yeah, of course."

"Oh!" Her eyes flash. "And I was thinking, if your knee is good enough, we could get mani-pedis tomorrow morning and then, I don't know, maybe head into the city to go shopping? You know, make a day of it, for your birthday."

"Umm ... Yeah, that sounds great." *It's now or never.* "And there's this guy at school who's having a few people over to his house tomorrow night. It's around the corner. Like, a five-minute walk. So, I was thinking of going." I figure the key to this is telling her, not asking her.

"Will this boy's parents be there?"

I bend my knee intentionally, so I'm forced to wince and have an excuse for shifting my eyes when I lie. "As far as I know."

She shrugs. "Okay. Sounds good."

My phone chirps with an incoming text.

How was the meet?

I can't keep the wide grin from showing when Emmett's name appears, despite his question.

"Let me guess ... a certain boy from next door?" Mom smiles knowingly. "So, what's going on between you two?"

I shrug, trying to act nonchalant. "We're hanging out."

"Right. 'Hanging out.' That's what the kids call it." She bites her bottom lip. "Maybe we should have a conversation soon, about what it means to have a boyfriend—"

"I've already had a boyfriend, Mom. Two, actually."

"Oh?" Surprise fills her face before she smooths it over. "Anyone I know?"

"No. They were from my old school. But ... no."

"I see." She hesitates, then asks, "And have you ever ...?" Her eyes widen.

"*Mom.*" My face flares with heat. "Let's stick to the daily three for now." As much as she's pushing for this whole open-and-honest communication, we're not at the chatting-about-our-sex-lives stage. I kind of hope we never get there.

She purses her lips. "Fine. Just know that you can come and talk to me about that kind of stuff."

"Uh-huh." *No, thank you.*

"And remember, Emmett is older than you and probably—well, *hopefully*—more experienced."

I groan and close my eyes. I *so* regret ever telling her about the hickey.

"I want to make sure you're being careful and—"

"This *just* started." And I want this conversation over with.

"Yes, well, these things have a way of moving fast when you really like the boy. And I can tell that you really like this boy." She smiles. "And for the record, so do I."

My phone chirps with another text.

So, what's the plan for tonight?

My heart flutters. He assumes we're doing something tonight.

"Actually, I'm probably going to hang out with Emmett tonight."

"You need to be off that." She points at my leg.

"I know. I'll see if he wants to watch a movie or something."

"At their house. Where there's an adult present who doesn't go to bed at eight and sleep like the dead," she warns, heading for her bedroom, her hum carrying through my open door.

I read the texts again, and decide how I should answer. There's no way I'm telling him that Holly did this. He might do something crazy again like suggest we take a break from us. *No way.* "In case you were wondering how psychotic your ex is ..." I say to myself, aiming my phone at my leg. I snap the picture and hit **Send**.

A FORM HOVERS inside the Hartford front door as I approach, Murphy toddling beside me, his leash dragging on the ground. I was surprised Emmett told me to bring him for Cassie, given his dad's allergies, but I guess they can't be *that* severe.

"They're here!" Cassie's voice carries and then the door flies open and she steps out, her focus going straight for the dog. "Hi, Murph! You're going to watch a movie with us!" she exclaims, dismissing me entirely.

His tail wags.

"Oh, you're hurt." Cassie's eyes dart from the grocery bag in my hand to my leg as I ease up the porch steps, wincing. "Mom! Emmett! AJ's *hurt!*" To me, she demands, "What happened?" Her expression waffles between concern and curiosity, as if unsure which to land on.

"I fell at cross-country. It's no big deal. I'll be fine."

"Oh. Okay." She nods, reassured, her attention shifting to Murphy again to scratch behind his ear. "Does it hurt?"

"Yes." I point to my tightened face. "That's why I'm wincing."

"Yeah. Okay." Another nod. A smile. "Was there blood?"

"A bit." I step into the warmth. The delicious scent of apple pie tantalizes my nose. A candle, I note, with disappointment.

"Can I see?"

"See what?"

"The blood." She's already bending over, her hand tugging on my pant leg, intent on pulling it up.

"Cassie ..." Emmett stands at the top of the stairs, looking as gorgeous as ever in a fitted black long-sleeved shirt and dark-wash jeans. "Sorry, she has a weird obsession with blood and injuries." He descends with casual effort, and the candle's aroma vanishes as the scent of his body wash envelops me. If there is a benefit to all the hockey—besides his honed body—it's the multiple showers he takes after practices and games.

"AJ hurt her leg," Cassie announces.

"I know. Hey." He stops just within my personal space, tilting his head at the plastic bag dangling from my fingers. "We have frozen peas here, you know."

I shrug casually, hyperaware of his proximity. "My mom bought extra so I could swap them in the freezer."

"AJ has to put her peas in the freezer!" Cassie's attention is momentarily on the back of the house, long enough for Emmett to steal a quick kiss.

My cheeks flush, the ache in my knee vanishing with his parting smile.

"Why don't you guys go downstairs? I'll be there in a sec."

"Come on, Murph! Let's show you the basement. You're going to like it." Cassie takes his leash and leads him toward the stairs. "Here, let me turn the lights on for you. Oh, okay, Murph." Her giggles carry.

"You're okay with her hanging out with us, right?" Emmett asks softly.

"Yeah. Of course. I figured as much." Truthfully, it was *because* I knew Cassie would be with us that I'm relaxed right now. She's a buffer, until I get used to this thing with Emmett being a reality.

"Cool." His eyes drift to my mouth a second before he leans down to kiss me again, this time lingering a bit, the tip of his tongue teasing the seam of my lips.

He's *such* a good kisser; I could do this all night. But is he thinking the same about me? My heart pounds inside my chest, a potent mixture of intoxication and panic, of lust and self-doubt.

This is exactly why I need Cassie there.

"Emmett told me that you—tripped," Heather stutters as she rounds the corner, catching the tail end of our kiss as Emmett pulls away. A tiny smile flickers across her lips. "Will you be okay for regionals?"

My face flames. "I think so. It's already better. I have to keep icing it."

"I'll put one of these in the freezer for you." Emmett leans down to collect my bag, his fingers grazing mine, seemingly unbothered about getting caught by his mother.

Heather's steady gaze is on her son as he passes her, and I hobble down the stairs.

"Please don't forget that she's *our neighbor* and Merv's *family*." My ear catches Heather's whisper.

"I know."

"And Cassie's *friend*."

"Yup."

There's a pause. "And she's *only* turning sixteen. I don't know if Debra is going to be okay with ..."

Heather's voice has faded by the time I've reached the landing, unable to linger without the risk of getting caught eavesdropping. But I can guess how that sentence ended. The Hartfords are a tight-knit family. Heather and Mark know their kids. There's no way Heather didn't figure out that Emmett and Holly were doing it "like rabbits." *Thanks, Zack, for that mental image.*

The basement is finished and warm—two things that the dungeon in Uncle Merv's house is not. On the right is a closed door leading to Mark's office. Around the corner on the left is a family room with an impressive flat-screen TV mounted on the wall and a lumpy chocolate-brown sectional that has probably catered to a lot of lazing kids over the years. The kind of couch that, once you sink into it, you have a hard time pulling yourself out.

Deep, gray walls, a soft beige Berber carpet, and mismatched tables fill the rest of the space. Furniture that has seen better days—pieces that Heather and Mark won't fuss over spills and scratches. All in all, it's the perfect lounging area for teenagers.

"What movie do you want to watch?" Cassie has already burrowed into the corner of the sectional beneath a woven blanket, next to a bowl of Cheetos. Her arm dangles over the edge toward a resting Murphy, her fingers on his head. If ever there was a person who should own a dog, it's Cassie. I'm sure it'll be the first thing she gets when she moves out.

Will she ever move out, though?

What will Cassie be like at twenty-one, when she finally graduates high school?

"What movie do you want to watch?" she repeats.

"Oh, I don't care. You guys can pick." Because no doubt I won't be watching a moment of it with Emmett in the room.

"Okay. But *not It* because I do *not* like that clown." She shakes her head with conviction, her face a mask of grim resolve.

I sink into the cushions. "Good thing you didn't go into the haunted house, then."

EMMETT GENTLY POSITIONS the bag of frozen peas on my propped-up knee and settles in next to me. A thrill courses through my limbs, making me shudder.

"Here." Emmett retrieves a plush blanket from the basket beside the couch and spreads it over my body.

That's not why I shuddered, though it *is* chilly down here. "You want some?"

"Nah. I run hot." He pauses. "Well, maybe a bit." He edges in closer, until our sides are pressed against each other. "How's that for your leg?" He juts a chin toward where my ankle rests atop a pillow on the coffee table.

"It's perfect."

"Good." He lifts his arm up and over to stretch out on the back of the couch behind me. He aims the remote. "You seriously haven't seen *Alien* before?"

"Seriously." My body sinks into his, thanks to his weight and our proximity, until I'm leaning against his hard chest. He's right, he does run hot. And I love it. "Isn't this, like, *old*?"

"Still amazing, though."

"The alien's not real," Cassie declares. "Don't worry, AJ, it's fake. They're all actors."

"Well, that's a relief. I was worried." I doubt she catches the sarcasm in my tone.

"Okay, you guys are sitting close." She tacks on that odd little laugh at the end. But if she's aware there's something more than casual friendship growing between her brother and me, she isn't letting on.

"So are you and Murphy," I tease.

"Hi, Murphy!" Cassie exclaims, suitably distracted, her cheese powder–coated fingers reaching for Murphy's nose, earning a lick in return.

The opening credits roll and Emmett adjusts his body, as if to settle into the cushions for the long haul. His free hand slides under the blanket, his fingers curling through mine.

"Let's watch the second one!" Cassie exclaims as soon as the closing credits appear.

"I think I'm *Alien*'d out for tonight." Emmett slips his fingers from mine to stretch his arms over his head.

I miss his touch instantly. I've had it all to myself for the past two hours, through acid-spitting, human-eating, close-your-eyes scenes, save for the few times he was fussing with the bag of peas, or swapping it out for a fresh one from the freezer.

I had so many excuses to bury my face in Emmett's warm chest, and I greedily accepted every last one of them.

"I think Murphy needs to go out." Emmett eyes the near-comatose dog. He must have eaten half the bowl of Cheetos, one by one, as they tumbled from Cassie's grip onto the floor. Accidentally or otherwise, I can't be sure because she giggled every time she heard his crunch.

"I'll take him!" Cassie kicks off her blanket. "Come on, Murph! Let's go for a walk!"

The old dog lifts his head at that word, and then struggles to ease himself to a standing position, staggering a few steps before he gets his bearings.

"Just make sure you hold onto the leash tight and watch out for cats," I warn.

"Which cat? Tiger? Oscar?" Her brow furrows in thought as she rattles off names of the neighbors' pets. "Misty?"

"We don't know, Cass. Just watch out for all cats." Emmett watches her lead Murphy up the stairs and then his head flops back. "I knew that would work." He turns to me, his eyes skating over my features, an intense look in them.

"What?" My voice is shaky as my own eyes trail his hard jaw, the sharp jut of his Adam's apple, the cut of his collarbone peeking out from his shirt. Two hours of being pressed against him and holding his hand has made me desperate for more.

"Nothing. I'm waiting for you to kiss me."

My stomach flips.

He laughs—as if he can sense it—and shakes his head. "I can't remember the last time I *just* held hands through a movie. I think I was ...," his lips twist with thought, "*thirteen*, maybe?"

"Shut up. It was nice."

"It *was* nice," he admits, his voice earnest. "And I promised my mom I wouldn't piss off our neighbor by corrupting her sweet fifteen-year-old daughter."

"Sixteen, in two days."

"Sorry, *sixteen in two days*," he corrects with a smug grin.

Adrenaline courses through my lips as I study the lines of his face in the flickering light of the movie credits. "And I'm not *that* sweet."

"No?" His jaw tenses as his gaze flips to my mouth. "Well ... I'll follow your lead, then."

"Is that what you want?" There's sultriness in my voice that I didn't think myself capable of.

"Yeah, like, *really* want."

Steeling my nerve, I lean forward to press my chest against his. I can feel his heart hammering in his chest, can hear the shakiness of his breathing. It sends a thrill through my body, the knowledge that Emmett may not be so cool and confident and experienced, and that this overwhelming edginess isn't just mine to bear.

My first kiss against his lips is soft and unsure—teasing, really—as I feel him out, my fingers skating over his cheek, marveling at the light stubble. He shaves. I don't think any of my other boyfriends shaved.

Is that officially what Emmett is now? My boyfriend?

"Watch your knee." He shifts his muscular frame to loom over me, my back sinking into the plush couch cushions, his arm still stretched out along the back of the couch. I feel small and cocooned as his free hand wanders over my throat and along my collarbone, down to graze my side before settling on my hip.

Who knows how long we have before Cassie comes back but I'm desperate to venture beyond the feel of his arms, and so I waste no more time, my hands heading straight for his chest, smoothing over the planes of hard muscle and down over the ridges of his stomach. I curl my fingers beneath the hem of his shirt.

I press a palm against his hot skin over his belly button, holding it there.

He pulls away a touch to rest his forehead against mine, his ragged breathing skimming over my lips, his eyes steady on me. Waiting to see where I'll venture next.

"Murphy pooped!" Cassie announces from the top of the stairs, followed by her careful footfalls.

Emmett curses and pulls away with a groan to sink into the couch, pinching the bridge of his nose as if he's in pain. "I'll bet there's a mound of dog shit somewhere on one of our front lawns right now."

I laugh, though I probably shouldn't. I'm the one who has to walk home in the dark.

It's two minutes to eleven when Emmett and I reach my front porch, Murphy moseying beside us.

The Tiffany lamp in the living room glows through the front bay window and my mother's car sits in the driveway. A low hum carries from the television. The news. She likes having the TV on in the background.

"I wonder how her big first date went," I say, more to myself.

Will she be floating as high as I am right now? What if she and Mick kissed? My nose crinkles at the image that produces. *Not* what I want to be picturing.

"Have you asked her about tomorrow night yet?"

"Yeah. She's fine with it. I'm waiting to bring up the curfew."

A shadow passes in front of the front door and Emmett takes a step back, as if expecting my mom to pop out any second. She doesn't, though I sense her hovering.

"So ... I guess I'll talk to you tomorrow?"

Biting his bottom lip in thought—a simple move that makes my good knee threaten to buckle—he whispers, "I wish I could text you whenever I wanted."

"You can."

His eyes are dark and intense as he stares at me. "But I can't say the things I *really* want to."

Breathe, Aria. "Me neither."

His hard swallow carries through the still night. "What are you doing tomorrow, during the day?"

"My mom's taking me birthday shopping. You?"

He nods toward the street. "Annual Thanksgiving weekend road hockey game in the afternoon."

"Of course." I roll my eyes and he laughs.

"So, I'll talk to you tomorrow?"

I nod, watching his lips as they approach mine. He presses a chaste but sweet kiss against them.

The front door creaks open.

"Murph! There you are!" my mom exclaims, bending over to pat his head, a glass of white wine cradled in her other hand.

"I told you I was taking him with me."

"Hey, Ms. J.," Emmett offers cordially.

"Oh! Hi, Emmett. I didn't realize you two were out here."

I give my mom a flat look.

She ignores it. "How's the knee, Aria?"

"A lot better."

"She's been icing it on and off all night. Hopefully she can run in regionals." He says that part while looking down at me. "'Kay, well ... good night, AJ." With a small wave and smile, he takes the porch steps two at a time and heads for the sidewalk. Neither of us feels like stepping in a pile of Murphy's dog shit tonight.

Mom's eyes trail him. "He's a nice boy."

She's in an awfully good mood. "How was your date?"

"Good." She smiles secretively. "We're going out again

next week."

"Wow. A *second* date."

"I know. So ... we'll see." Her lips press together. "I'll put the peas in the freezer if you don't need them? You should go and get some rest. Tomorrow's going to be a long day."

Yeah. A long day followed by an exciting night. I find my own lips pressing together, the feel of Emmett's against them still alive.

"'Night."

I'm curled under my blanket, staring up at the glow-in-the-dark stars, unable to sleep, when I pick up my phone and text Emmett.

Thanks. Tonight was fun.

That seems safe enough for any parental filter.
He answers not ten seconds later.

Tomorrow night will be even better. Good night.

I grin, my fingers itching to type out so many other things. *You're an incredible kisser. I'm head-over-heels crazy about you. I wish we could have stayed on your couch all night.* Thoughts I wouldn't have the nerve to send, even without my mother's supervision.

But she *can* see these messages and, for the first time since we shut down my old social media accounts and disconnected my Calgary number—basically, since we deleted me from online existence—this bothers me.

I'm three thousand miles away from my old life. Things are good now.

I finally settle on a simple *Good night*.

CHAPTER
EIGHTEEN

THE DELICIOUS SCENT OF HOT COFFEE AND FRYING pancake batter meets me at the top of the stairs the next morning.

"I don't need a new bed! Stop wasting your damn money!" Uncle Merv's gruff voice booms, followed by Cassie's burst of laughter.

Murphy stands at the kitchen's threshold, brushing his wet nose against my fingers in greeting when I enter.

"Sleeping Beauty's awake *finally*," Uncle Merv grumbles, but then he follows it with a smile that lifts his loose jowls.

"Oh, *hello*, AJ." Cassie grins at me as my mom sets a plate of pancakes in front of her, the bottle of maple syrup gripped in her hands.

"Hey, Cass." I glance at the clock on the wall, though I know it's only a few minutes past the time I last checked—9:42 a.m. "Mom, why didn't you wake me up?"

"I figured I'd let you sleep in. Cassie took Murphy out." She pours pancake batter from the soup ladle onto the hot griddle. "How's your knee today?"

I lift and bend it. "A bit sore but it's okay. I should be good for regionals." My speed and endurance is another story. But, if there's anything I dwelled on last night besides thoughts of Emmett—of his smile, the taste of his mouth, the warmth of his body against mine—it was running in that race.

And beating the hell out of Holly's time.

"Here. Why don't you take this seat." Uncle Merv slowly eases out of his chair, collecting his plate and mug. He hobbles toward the sink. "That was good, Debra. Thank you."

"Just leave it there. I'll load the dishwasher after," Mom instructs. "I found that audiobook you wanted. The one about the Vietnam War? It's all set up and ready for you on your tablet." Another purchase my mother made that he insisted he didn't need, along with the Bose headphones that he uses daily.

"Well ... good."

"What's the Vietnam War?" Cassie asks, her eyes laser-focused on the steady stream of maple syrup she pour onto her pancakes.

"A big war in the 1960s." He shuffles toward the living room.

"Did people die?"

"It was a war. Of course people died."

"How many?"

"Lots."

"Did you know any of them?"

"Nope."

"Have you been in a war?"

"Nope. Murphy?" Merv snaps his fingers. The poor dog peers back and forth between him and Cassie, looking

230

reluctant to leave when staying will guarantee him at least one pancake from the floor, the way Cassie eats.

"I used too much maple syrup," Cassie announces, licking her finger and eying the pool of sticky liquid on her plate with delight.

Maybe it's the sickly sweet smell of it that finally drives Murphy away, toward the beckoning of the other old man in the house.

My mother lifts the edge of one pancake, tipping her head to the side to check its readiness. "So, Aria, I made an appointment for manis and pedis for eleven—"

"Can I come, too?" Cassie blurts out.

"Uh ..." My mom shrugs, exchanging glances with me, as if to ask, "Are you okay with that?"

I shrug, not sure how to answer. "Have you ever been, Cassie?"

Cassie's head bobs vigorously.

"That means they'll be touching your hands and feet," my mom adds warily.

Cassie grins, holding up her hands to show off her chewed-up fingernails, the cuticles torn and red. "I won't pick. I promise."

"Well ... if your mom says it's okay, then we'd love to have you come along. Right, Aria?"

"Yeah, that'd be great."

A rare, somber expression washes over Cassie's face, her gaze shifting between her plate and the back door off the kitchen, her thoughts unreadable. And then she's pushing away from the table in a panic and rushing for her shoes.

My mom laughs. "You can finish your breakfast *first*."

"I just have to ask my mom and then I'll be back. I just have to—don't leave without ..." Her words trail as she bolts out the door and races across the lawn, her elbows out and legs jutting.

My mom chuckles as she watches her go. "I don't think I've ever seen anyone so happy to get a manicure."

"I hope Heather lets her come." I pour myself some coffee and wipe down the table before sitting, hugging my body against a sudden chill.

"*So*, I gave it a lot of thought last night and ..." Mom pauses to flip the pancakes over, leaving me hanging.

And my stomach tightening.

If you're about to tell me that I can't date Emmett ...

"Now that we're here and things are going well, and *you're* doing well, you should have some of your privacy back. I know you and Emmett probably want to be able to text each other without your mother reading your messages."

"No more spyware?" I hold my breath.

She snorts. "No more spyware. I'm still going to keep a GPS tracker on your phone, though, and I want all your passwords. And if I ever ask to see your phone because I'm worried, you will give it to me immediately, no questions asked, or there will be serious consequences, understood?"

"Of course. So ... when will—"

"Already done. I disconnected it last night."

I sink into my chair, a grin stretching across my face. "Thanks, Mom."

Her phone rings as she's setting a plate of pancakes in front of me. "Hey, Heather," she answers. She looks out the window toward the Hartford house as she listens. "No! Of course. We'd love to have her come with us ... No, I promise, she *did not* invite herself." Mom's eyes flash to mine, amusement in them. "Yes, we're going to go after breakfast. Tell her to come back before her pancakes get cold ... Yes, she has a whole plate waiting for her, here ..."

I tune out their conversation, sliding my phone from my pocket to text Emmett.

Hey ... What are you doing?

Emmett answers almost immediately.

Still in bed. Being lazy. You?

My stomach flips. Emmett's lying in bed right now. What does he sleep in? What does his hair look like?

Eating pancakes.

Nice. Will I see you before tonight?

I smile.

Maybe. FYI, my mom isn't reading my texts anymore.

There's a long pause as the three dots bounce and stop, and bounce again.

So I can tell you how crazy you made me last night?

"Sounds good, Heather." My mom ends her call with a chuckle. "She says she hasn't seen Cassie this excited in a long time."

"Cool," I murmur absently, punching out a response.

Yes. You can tell me that a thousand times.

When we arrive home from shopping around five that afternoon, parked cars line the street and a cluster of guys in jerseys linger in the cul-du-sac, hockey sticks in their hands. Two nets are set on either end and Mark stands at the sidelines in a black-and-white-striped shirt.

"What's going on here?" Mom eases her CR-V past them and into our driveway.

"Annual Thanksgiving weekend road hockey game." I smile as I spot Emmett in the center, laughing over something with another guy.

As soon as Mom has thrown her car into park, a whistle sounds and the game is back on.

"Sounds like fun." She peers at four girls from school who linger at the sidelines, bundled in sweatshirts against the cold, their hands gripping various mugs and paper coffee cups. Lindsay is among them, in a cute pink sweater and UGG boots. Cassie is watching as well, sitting in the open trunk of Emmett's Santa Fe, holding a set of purple pompoms. When we dropped her off after the nail salon appointment, she bolted for her house to show off her painted fingernails.

"Kids from school?" Mom asks as Emmett smacks the ball into the net and his teammates cheer.

"I think so. A few, at least."

Mom checks the clock. "I better start dinner. You know how Uncle Merv is."

"I'll be there in a sec to take Murphy out."

Her eyes drift to the street hockey game in progress. "No, you should hang out here. With your friends." Relief radiates off her. That I have friends. That I have a boyfriend.

That I have a new life.

I smile. "Thanks for today. I had a great time."

She takes my hand in hers, first to study my indigo-blue nail polish, but then to give my fingers a squeeze. "We should do that again. Soon."

"Deal."

She frowns at the back seat, filled with shopping bags of winter clothes and boots for both of us. "Maybe in spring, when I'm earning a paycheck again."

Cassie is waiting at the passenger side door by the time I've stepped out. "They're playing hockey," she announces, a hot chocolate mustache lining her upper lip.

"I see that. How are your nails doing?"

She holds them up with a sheepish grin to show me the bits of silver polish left. "I picked them."

"Oh, Cassie." I shake my head but laugh and she joins in.

"Are you coming over to watch a movie with us tonight?"

"I ... uh ... I have plans?"

Her eyes grow curious. "What are you doing?"

"Uh ..." I don't want to lie to her, but I remember what happened the last time she found out we were going to a party. Upsetting her might be worse.

"Hey, AJ! You're coming to Mower's house tonight?" Zach bellows.

And I guess that makes my decision easy.

"Is there a party?" Cassie asks and, in the next breath, "Can I come?"

Shit. "I think we have to ask your brother?"

"Emmett!" she hollers, unbothered that there's a hockey

game in progress. "Can I come to the party?"

Emmett makes a time-out gesture with his hands and trots over, throwing Zach a dirty look. He stops next to me, out of breath, his forehead glistening with a sheen of sweat. "Hey."

"Hi."

His hand settles on the small of my back, but he doesn't lean in to kiss me and I can't decide if I'm disappointed or relieved.

His eyes roam the back seat. "Did your mom's card start smoking?"

I laugh. "Almost."

"Emmett, can I come with you and AJ to the party tonight?" Cassie pushes.

He sighs heavily. "You wouldn't like it ..."

"*Please?*" she pleads, and I can hear the raw emotion in her voice. "*Please*, can I go? I *never* get to go."

His throat bobs with a hard swallow, his brown eyes darting to mine, begging for a way out of his guilt.

I can't help him much, because I'm feeling guilty now, too. "It's within walking distance ..." I say low, more to him. "It'd be easy enough to walk her back if she wanted to come home. She could stick with us."

He nods slowly, as if deciding something. "Okay, fine. *If Mom* is okay with it, then—"

"Mom!" Cassie's already gone, galloping up the path toward the house.

Emmett groans. "She's going to kill me for putting that on her."

"I don't see what the big deal is. We'll keep an eye on her. It's one night and you can't keep her in a bubble forever. It's not fair to her."

"I know. It's just ..."

"How much trouble can she really get into? She's, like, the most predictable person I've ever met in my life."

"Until she's not." He shakes his head. "I don't know why I'm so worried."

"Because you're a good brother and you care about her? But she'll be with us and all your friends who know her and wouldn't let anything happen to her, *right*?"

"Yeah, of course." He leans down to kiss me.

"Ticktock!" Zach shouts. "And nice friend, by the way, moving in on the girl as soon as you find out *I* like her."

My cheeks burn as eyes all around the cul-du-sac—including Mark's—land on me.

Emmett snorts, stepping away with a grin. "You never had a chance, Farmer."

A KNOCK SOUNDS on the front door as I'm finishing up the last coat of mascara.

"Hey, guys!" I hear my mom say. "Cassie, I didn't know you were going, too."

"Yeah, my mom let me. She said I have to stay with AJ and Emmett."

"That sounds like a good idea. I'm sure they'll take good care of you."

I can hear it in her voice—the relief. If Heather and Mark are allowing Cassie to come out, they must feel comfortable with the people we'll be with, and that means my mom can relax a bit.

I pull my bedroom door shut behind me and ease down the stairs.

Mom nods with approval at the fitted black jeans and

periwinkle off-the-shoulder knit sweater we picked out today.

"Your hair is wavy," Cassie announces, her inquisitive blue eyes roaming my long locks as if memorizing each curve. She's wearing a pair of black leggings and a flattering striped shirt. It's a simple but more mature, coordinated outfit than she usually wears to school, with no animal prints or logos. Bracelets adorn her wrist and her hair has been straightened and styled. I'm guessing Heather helped her dress for tonight.

I shrug. "I felt like something different today." Something special, to ring in my sixteenth year.

Emmett stands beside her, wearing dark-wash jeans and a wool jacket, the collar flipped up, and looking more like a magazine cover model than a high school kid.

"And you're wearing more makeup." Cassie squints as I approach. "You have eyeliner ... mascara ... eyeshadow ..."

"Okay, enough analyzing her." Emmett chuckles and shakes his head. He leans in to whisper something to her.

"Yeah." Cassie nods, grinning. "You look pretty, AJ. For your birthday."

"Thank you." I bend to zip up my camel-colored boots, but also to hide my blush.

"You have your phone?" My mom hands me my jacket.

"Of course."

"Okay. Have fun. Remember, twelve o'clock or you're a pumpkin." It was easier to get her to agree to a later curfew than I'd expected.

Cassie laughs. "Hey! Just like Cinderella!"

"You're right, Cassie." My mom grins, the tension that normally floats around her missing. "And Aria?" Her eyes flicker to Emmett for the briefest second. "Make good choices."

CHAPTER
NINETEEN

Mower's family lives in a split-level house on a quiet street of older homes and large lots. We could hear the steady thrum of music all the way around the corner on our approach, and every time someone opens the front door, it blasts into the night.

"What are the chances someone's going to call the police on us?" I ask as we turn into the driveway.

"The police are coming?" Cassie's eyes widen with fear.

"No." I forget that she takes things so literally. "Only if a neighbor complains about the music being too loud. But we won't get in trouble. Don't worry. They'll just tell us to be quiet." By kicking us out and shutting down the party, but I don't need to get into those details.

Six people linger on the porch, laughing and puffing on cigarettes. A haze wafts up into the cool night air.

"They're smoking!" Cassie hisses.

"Just like they do outside at school," Emmett responds in a low, calm voice. "You're going to see people smoking and drinking and doing other things here tonight, Cass. As long as *you* don't do any of it and you act cool, you'll be fine."

"Yeah, I know." She stands taller, schooling her expression, her demeanor visibly shifting as if she's making a conscious effort to blend in. Meanwhile, there's a touch of wild panic flickering in her blue-gray eyes as they take in this new sight, unsure of where to land.

"As soon as you feel like leaving, let us know and we'll walk you home."

"*Okay!*" Her voice is full of irritation.

He sighs heavily, his hand settling on the small of my back.

The moment we step inside, I wonder if bringing Cassie here was a huge mistake. Maybe Mower's plan was to have "a few people over" but the entire house is crammed with bodies—many faces I recognize from school, some I don't.

And one—a beautiful face with a fake, sweet smile—that I'd prefer not to see tonight, or any other night.

At least Holly's across the room. She's leaning against the wall, fawning over Adam Levic, the guy Emmett punched out last year for being an asshole to Cassie, according to Jen.

I guess she's found a guy more like her. Maybe this means she'll move on from attacking me.

Heads turn toward us as we stand in the doorway. People watch Cassie curiously.

Cassie shrinks into herself, her shoulders curling inward, her eyes wide and unsure of where to look, the easily induced smile replaced by stony shock and discomfort.

She's fully aware they're looking at her.

I lean in. "Are you okay?"

She shakes her head and shouts, "It's loud!" She presses her hands against her ears. "It's too loud!"

I look to Emmett. He nods to the front door.

"Okay, let's go outside." I hook my arm through hers. She stiffens, but she lets me lead her out. In moments, we're back on the porch and Cassie is making a dramatic point of coughing and waving away the cloud of cigarette smoke that lingers, glowering at it.

"We'll walk you home, Cass," Emmett says softly.

"No. I don't want to leave." She shakes her head furtively, her jaw set with determination, even as wariness flickers in her eyes. "Where's Zach?"

"Probably in there." Emmett slips out his phone and sends a quick text. He watches his screen a moment. "Oh. Sweet. Okay, follow me." He leads us farther down the driveway, behind the house, to a separate garage at the back of the property. "Go up," he instructs, pointing for Cassie to lead us up a set of wooden stairs that end at a second-story door.

"Better?" Emmett asks as we step into the small apartment.

Cassie nods, her eyes zeroing in on Zach. She grins and Emmett's shoulders seem to sink with relief. Zach is sitting with four other guys on a sectional around the flat screen, battling it out in a game of hockey on the PS4.

"Who lives here?" I ask, taking in the beige walls and basic furniture. A simple, all-white kitchen runs along one side. A small hallway leads off the other side of the living room, I assume to a bedroom and bathroom.

"Mower's older brother, when he's not up in Fort McMurray working."

"Harty," Zach croons, dragging the ending, barely glancing over his shoulder to add, "Beer's in the fridge."

"Thanks, man." Emmett shrugs off his jacket and tosses it to a chair, then heads for the kitchen. "AJ?" His eyebrows raise in question.

I consider it a moment, my mother's "Make good choices" lingering in my mind. Having one or two beers and walking home versus five or six and driving is definitely a good choice. As was grabbing that extra-minty gum. I nod, slipping off my jacket and setting it on top of his.

"Hey. *Little* Harty's here, too!" Zach flashes a sloppy grin. He's already had a few beers. And possibly some weed, based on his lazy red eyes. "Come on over here, Cass." He shifts his big body, squishing the guys next to him, making room for her in the corner.

"Okay, *Farmer*." She laughs as she heads for the couch, shrugging off her coat, letting it land on the floor. She settles in, her eyes locking on Zach, studying him. In this unknown and unsettling arena, she has found her anchor.

Emmett snaps the caps off the bottles and hands me one as he takes in the scene before him—five hockey players and his little sister at a party—with a smirk.

"See? She's going to be fine," I assure him.

"You're right. I'm glad we brought her out. She deserves to do things like this. She's like everyone else. She just wants to have fun." He tips the neck of his bottle and clanks it against mine. "Cheers. Happy birthday."

"Not for another"—I check a clock on the wall—"three hours."

"Just practicing." He leans in to press his lips against mine in a teasing kiss and my knees weaken.

"Wait ... *what*?" Cassie exclaims, and we turn to see her staring at us. Her eyes flip from our faces to the bottles in our hands, and to our faces again—as if she's trying to decide if us kissing or us drinking beer is more bewildering.

Emmett's free hand curls around my waist, pulling my body against his.

"Oh, you didn't know about them yet?" Zach grits his teeth as his player loses the puck. "Your brother *stole* AJ from me."

"He did?"

"No."

Cassie grins. "You're joking."

"I *am* joking."

She considers us another moment and then mutters, "'Kay, whatever."

"Exactly, Cass. *Whatever.*" Zach jabs at his remote control with feverish thumbs. A loud chorus of curses explodes as his opponent—I think his name is Ben—throws his remote on the couch and climbs out of his seat, heading for the fridge, an empty beer can dangling from his fingers.

"Get over here so I can finally kick your ass at *something*, Harty."

With one last kiss that makes my legs wobble, Emmett joins the fold.

"No, no, no, no ... ah!" Emmett tosses his remote and sinks into the couch beside me with a groan, as a round of raucous cheers erupts. His hand slips over my knee to casually rest on my thigh.

"Time to give someone else a shot." Zach turns to Cassie. "Want to try and beat me?"

"No. It's okay." She shakes her head, her eyes flickering across the faces surrounding us. People have been trickling into the apartment over the past hour and, where it was once eight of us, there must be forty people milling in here now, everyone save for Cassie drinking. I'm guessing she doesn't want to bring attention to herself.

The door creaks open and Emmett curses under his breath, his jaw tensing. "You've got to be kidding me."

A quick glance and I see why. Holly's there, arm in arm with Adam.

"That guy is such a dick," he mutters.

"Jen told me you fought him?"

"He told Cassie that there was no such thing as Santa Claus last year. I know, she was fourteen and it was probably time someone told her, but he did it to hurt her." Emmett glares at the stocky guy. "We were friends for years. We played on the same team. Our families hung out a lot. But I got better and he didn't, and they cut him. He got pissed that I didn't drop down a division to keep playing with him." Emmett shakes his head. "I can't believe she'd go after him."

"Do you care that Holly's with someone else?" Jealousy flares inside me with the possibility.

He seems to consider that. "I'd be lying if I didn't say it's weird to see her with someone else, but no. She's not the person I thought she was. At least we've both moved on." He leans into me. He's downed three beers already and his body is relaxed against me. "Maybe she'll see us and leave."

If only ... "Is the bathroom down that hall?"

With Emmett's nod, I squeeze his knee and head for it, thankful it's available.

I take my time, checking my makeup and clothes, fluffing my waves, hoping Emmett's right and she's gone by the time I come back.

Something tells me that's not likely to happen, though.

I reemerge to find Emmett waiting in a casual pose, his back pressed against the wall, his hands in his pockets.

"All yours." I gesture behind me.

"I like the sound of that." With a grin, he herds me against the wall in the corner, his face dipping into my neck, the smell of his body wash and shampoo teasing my senses. His lips skate across my skin, sending my blood racing through my veins. "How much longer do I have to wait?" he whispers, his grip on my waist tightening.

"Uh ... I ...," I stammer as my body tenses. Is he asking what *I think* he's asking? "I'm not sure?"

"Two hours left till midnight?"

It dawns on me that he's talking about my birthday, and I release a nervous laugh. "*Oh.* Yeah. Just under." It's ten after ten now.

He pulls back. "Wait. What did you *think* I meant?" A moment later, as if replaying his words and realizing, his eyes widen. "Oh, shit. No. That's ... no. I'm not asking for *that*. I mean, it's not that I don't *want* to—"

"I do, too," I blurt out, but quickly add, "just not yet."

"Yeah. Not yet." He brushes a strand of hair from my face, swallowing hard, hesitating. "Is it because ... I mean, are you ..." His jaw tenses as he fumbles awkwardly around the personal question.

It's so endearing to see Emmett *not* confident about something for once that I can't help but laugh. I decide that I don't mind him knowing—I *want* him to know.

I nod.

A soft smile touches his lips as his fingers thread through my hair. "That's okay. There's no rush." He ropes his arms around my shoulders, the weight of them welcomed. Stooping to press his forehead against mine, he whispers, "You having a good time?"

"Yeah. But I'll have a good time anytime I'm with you."

That earns me a sweet, soft kiss on the lips.

"Are you crazy?" Zach's booming voice explodes over the hum of voices and music. "Why the hell did you give that to her?"

We peel away from each other and turn to find Zach squaring off against a smug-faced Adam.

"What?" He shrugs. "She wanted one."

"*Of course* she wanted it. She thought it was just a cookie!"

I know without a doubt who the "she" they're referring to is.

Cassie is on the couch, her face stony as her eyes flicker, surveying the situation and trying to read the sudden tension in the room.

Emmett has picked up on it, too. "What's going on?" His tone has taken on a razor-sharp edge.

Zach's normally carefree demeanor has been replaced by a stiff stance and a mixture of rage and apology on his face. "I went outside for a few minutes and this *shithead* thought it'd be a good idea to give your sister one of his cookies."

One of his ... oh God.

My stomach drops as I realize what's going on.

This is not happening.

"Are you ..." Emmett's eyebrows climb halfway up his forehead. "You're kidding, right? This is a joke. *Right?*"

Adam shrugs. "It's gonna be funny in about an hour."

He barely has time to get his hands up.

Emmett moves fast, lunging at the smug asshole, taking him and a table lamp down in the charge. And then his fists are flying with abandon, pummeling Adam's face over and over.

Shouts erupt and people circle.

My heart pounds like a jackhammer in my chest as I'm torn between wanting Emmett to hurt this guy and not wanting him to get himself into trouble.

Until I spy Cassie, in her spot, her face contorted with confusion and terror, her body trembling, fat tears streaming down her cheeks. Looking … traumatized.

"Zach!" I jerk at his arm. "You need to stop this now. Look at her!"

One glance at Cassie and he's diving for Emmett, his arms going around his chest.

Meanwhile, I'm shoving people out of my way to reach her.

"Did I do something wrong?" she asks.

"It's okay. It's not your fault."

"Is Emmett mad at me?" Cassie's mouth is shaped in a perfect pout.

"No. This *wasn't* your fault."

"Okay." She nods, but the tears keep flowing.

Zach and two guys are herding Emmett backward, away from Adam. A trickle of blood runs from one of Emmett's nostrils and down over his mouth, but otherwise he looks fine, save for his bloody knuckles and his torn shirt collar.

"Let's go," he barks, his tongue touching his upper lip. He lifts the hem of his shirt to wipe at his face. His torso is heaving from his rapid, heavy breaths.

I grab our jackets and help Cassie up as Adam hauls himself off the floor, staggering slightly, his left eye already swelling shut, his nose a mangled mess. He leans over to spit a mouthful of blood onto the floor. "It was only five grams, dickhead."

Emmett points at him in warning. "If I hear one word about hitting you from anyone, I'll be telling the cops that you're drugging fifteen-year-old special needs kids. We'll see if you think five grams is no big deal then."

"Did I do drugs?" Cassie's eyes widen as panic sets in. "I did drugs? What's going to happen to me?" Her bottom lip wobbles. "Am I going to die?"

"No." A laugh escapes me, though none of this is funny. "You're going to be *fine*." I put my hand on her shoulder as I lead her toward the door and, while she stiffens, she doesn't shrug away. "You might feel funny for a bit. You might even laugh a lot." God, I hope that's all that happens. What does marijuana do to a mind like Cassie's?

"I feel funny," she declares.

I smile softly. "It's going to take a while for you to feel anything." Glancing over my shoulder to see how far Emmett is behind us, I catch Adam and Holly in the corner. Holly's hand is smoothing over his bicep, as if consoling him. Meanwhile, he's snapping at her. Angry with her about something, it would seem.

She glances over, catches me watching her, and quickly averts her gaze to the floor.

And I can't help but think she's the one who put the idiotic idea in Adam's head. The person who knows how much Cassie loves sweets, how easily she'd be convinced to take it.

But is she *that* cruel? Or is she that drunk and caught up in the moment of revenge?

Either way, the fact that she's talking to the jerk now speaks volumes.

"Ready?" Emmett comes up behind me, still seething.

I hand him his jacket.

"Emmett?" Cassie stands at the top of the staircase.

"Here." Emmett shifts around me to take the steps

down, until he's directly in front of Cassie, ready to break her fall if need be.

"I'm feeling kind of funny now." Cassie ducks her head and wipes away her tears as we pass people. But their eyes are on Emmett—on his bloody fists, on his torn collar, on the silent rage emanating from him.

"No, you're fine. You won't feel funny yet," I assure her again.

"We need to tell Mom."

"No!" Emmett smooths his hand over his forehead. "Just let me think for a minute, Cassie. And next time, don't eat cookies that someone gives you at a party!"

"I'm sorry, Emmett." She sobs. "This is all my fault!"

He shakes his head. "No. It's not your fault. It's *mine*, for bringing you here."

And mine, since I'm the one who convinced him it was a good idea.

Is that what he's thinking right now? Is he angry with me?

Knots form in the pit of my stomach.

"I don't want to go to a party ever again," Cassie whispers, her shoulders hunched, her head bowed.

He sighs. "I don't blame you."

CHAPTER
TWENTY

Emmett sets the bowl of chips on the coffee table and then sinks into the couch beside me.

Tension radiates from every inch of his body.

"What did you tell them?" I dare ask.

"That we came home early and all three of us are watching a movie downstairs."

"And ...?"

He steals a glance at Cassie, who's curled up on the couch beneath a blanket, her attention locked on Spider-man's form as he swings between buildings on the TV screen. The ten-minute walk home felt like ten hours, a true test of patience, with Cassie stopping every twenty or so steps to announce with panic that she felt funny, and Emmett and I needing to convince her that she was fine. She retreated into her own world as soon as we came down here and has been quiet ever since, as if the walls and familiar setting have sedated her.

He shakes his head. "Not yet. I figured I'd let them have fun for a bit before I ruin their entire weekend. I'm still hoping there wasn't enough in it to do anything major.

Adam makes them himself and he's an idiot. I wouldn't be surprised if he screwed up the measurements."

That could go one of two ways—too little, or too much—but I don't bring that up. Still, it's been almost an hour and there's no droopy eyes or uncontrollable giggling fit, or paranoia. No sign of Cassie being stoned ... yet.

The first thing Emmett did when we got home was change his shirt and wash the blood from his face, and Adam's blood from his knuckles. I note the bruises forming. "Maybe you should put some ice on that."

"I'm fine." He stretches his fingers, setting his hand on his thigh. "My mom is going to lose it."

"I can't picture your mom losing it." Heather, with her soft smiles and her patient sighs. Then again, I have heard her sharp tone a few times. Still ...

"My mom is calm and level-headed until it comes to Cassie. She already wants nothing to do with the Levic family after what happened last year. And now, with this? I won't be surprised if she calls the cops. But then who knows what'll happen to me for beating the hell out of him."

What a mess.

"I'm so sorry, Emmett. I shouldn't have pushed you to let her come. You knew better." What could possibly go wrong? A lot, apparently.

He shakes his head. "No, this wasn't your fault. And it *was* a good idea. If I'd stuck by her like I was supposed to, none of this would've happened."

If he hadn't been making out with me by the bathroom. No matter what he says, I am partially to blame.

He looks from Cassie, to me, and then he finally reaches over to collect my hand in his, his thumb stroking my skin. "Maybe we'll be lucky and she'll fall asleep."

"I can hear you talking about me," Cassie mutters with annoyance, her eyes still glued to the TV.

Emmett smirks. "How are you feeling?"

"That cookie didn't taste good. I'm thirsty." It comes out in a long string, as if one cohesive sentence.

"Yeah, they usually don't. I brought you water. It's on the coffee table, by your head."

She sits up and reaches for it, downing half the glass in three gulps.

"Why couldn't you like beer instead of cookies, Cass? I could win money off your chugging skills." His lips curve slightly.

"Because I don't like beer." She sets the glass down again and flops back onto the couch, her attention on the TV. "*You* like beer. And AJ likes beer."

"And AJ would appreciate it if you don't mention that to *anyone* because I'll get in a lot of trouble with my mom," I say.

"I know."

"She's serious, Cassie. Debra won't let AJ out anymore if she finds out she was drinking. That's a secret between us, okay?"

"Yeah. *Okay.*" She's quiet for a long moment. "I don't want Mom to know that I ate the bad cookie."

"It wasn't your fault, though."

"No! She'll never let me go to a party again!" There's so much frustration in her voice. "I won't be able to go to prom."

"*Prom?* That's ..." Emmett's face twists up. "Since when do you care about *prom?*"

"It was in that movie we saw in the theater," I whisper. "And I explained it to her. She liked the idea of dressing up and going to a big party."

"That's not even ... you're only in grade *ten*."

"I guess she's planning ahead."

"I can *still* hear you talking about me," Cassie says. "Don't tell Mom. *Please*."

Emmett's jaw clenches. "We'll see how tonight goes, okay?"

"I think I'm fine." Her face pinches with exaggerated thought. "Yeah. I'm fine."

"Well, I'm not sure that *I'm* fine."

"Did you eat a bad cookie, too?"

"No."

"Then you're better than me."

Emmett rolls his eyes—she has a point—and slouches into the couch, as if the night has finally settled its full weight upon his shoulders.

WE HEAR the front door open at ten minutes to midnight, and a moment later Heather's heels click on the floor above our heads.

Emmett and I exchange a glance and then watch Cassie, who doesn't so much as twitch. She drifted off about twenty minutes ago—whether from the marijuana or exhaustion from overstimulation, I can't say, though it would seem that Adam's paltry skills with baking pot cookies might have saved us tonight.

"So?" I whisper, squeezing his fingers. "Are you going to tell them?"

His lips pucker as he considers his answer, and I so desperately want to lean in and kiss them, something we haven't done since before the incident at Mower's. "She's never asked me to keep a secret like that before. And she's right, my mom will never let her out again. Not that I have a problem with that after tonight."

The basement door creaks open and his chest rises with a deep breath. He worries his bottom lip between his teeth as soft footfalls land on the steps.

It's Mark that appears, though.

"Hey, guys, how was your night?" His voice is low and relaxed.

"Good," Emmett offers.

Mark bends over to peer at his sleeping daughter, his eyes dancing with amusement. "She must have had *a lot* of fun."

Emmett's eyes flicker to mine, ever so briefly. "How was the Coopers'?"

"Oh, you know. Lots of food." Mark pats his belly. "It took your mom a little while to get used to the idea of Cassie at a party, but she finally mellowed. The wine helped." He settles a hand on Cassie's shoulder, giving her a soft shake.

"What are you doing? Don't wake her up!" Emmett's whisper is harsh—panicked.

"I can't leave her in the basement all night. And she's too heavy to carry, even for you."

"I'll crash down here with her. I'm just gonna walk AJ home. She won't wake up alone."

Mark shrugs, eyeing his sleeping daughter. "Not sure how I'd wake her up anyway. She's out like a light. Too much stimulation?"

Emmett's gaze slides to the TV. "I guess."

"Well ... good night. 'Night, Aria. And, oh, happy birthday in," he checks his watch, "seven minutes."

I smile. "Thanks."

Mark is a soft-spoken man who works a lot, but when

he's here, he's *here,* popping allergy pills so his daughter can borrow a dog for a few hours. He's so different from *my* father, a loud man who can find the negative side to everything and missed my fourteenth birthday—didn't even call—because he was preoccupied by his "business trip" in Banff with his paralegal mistress.

I doubt he even remembers that it's my birthday tomorrow.

THE LIGHTS in the living room are off when we reach my front door.

Is Mom upstairs in bed already? Or hiding in the dark, watching for me?

"So, tonight was ... interesting." I dig the house keys from my pocket. At least it started out great.

"Yeah."

"How's your hand?" I'm aware it's the fourth time I've asked.

"It's fine. Don't worry about it, really," he dismisses, his attention drifting off, down the street, toward the direction of Mower's house. Is the party still going on?

"Okay, well ... I guess I'll see you tomorrow, at dinner?"

He nods, chewing the inside of his mouth in thought before leaning down to steal a quick, chaste kiss. "I should get back, in case Cassie wakes up high and freaks out."

"Yeah. Of course. Go." I force a smile to hide my disappointment and watch him trot down the steps.

He makes it maybe five feet before he stops abruptly, doubles back, and jogs back to pull me into his arms.

I sink into his warm body.

"My head is scattered." He leans down to kiss my lips softly. "Happy birthday."

"Thanks."

"I'm sorry tonight didn't go the way you probably wanted it to."

I smooth my hand over his chest, reveling in the warmth and the hard curves one last time before bed. "I was with you so it went exactly how I wanted it to go."

He clenches his jaw. "I just *hate* that Adam did that to her. It's one thing to do something like that to me or you, but to make *her* a target?" He shakes his head. "I wasn't paying attention to her like I should have been. I feel guilty."

"She's going to be okay."

He nods, and then presses a lingering kiss against my jawline, just below my ear, that sends shivers through my body. "See you tomorrow."

I watch him jog across the lawn before I step inside, locking the door behind me, finally feeling the exhaustion of tonight's drama weigh me down.

"Happy birthday!" Mom appears at her bedroom door in her pajamas as I reach the top of the landing, a rectangular box with silver wrapping in her hands. The soft hum of the TV carries from her bedroom. "Good night?"

A small voice in my head suggests that maybe I should tell her what happened. But then I'd have to confess to this growing rift between Holly and me, and that would only spark her fear and worry.

I shift my eyes to the gift in her hand and nod.

Dear Julia,

I'm not going to lie—sixteen doesn't feel any different than fifteen. Maybe it's because it's only been a few hours, so there hasn't been a chance for any big revelations, no time to take my driver's test yet. I'm still in bed. Waiting for Emmett to respond to my text about what happened last night with Cassie after he dropped me off.

I have this gut feeling that sixteen is going to be a good year for me, but nothing has happened yet. Here's hoping, right? I'll keep you posted, so you don't feel like you're missing out.

~AJ

"THE PIE CRUSTS are a little flakier than I'd like." My mom cringes with apology.

"Is dinner going to be at six? Because I need to eat at six," Uncle Merv reminds Heather as he climbs the front steps.

"Hi, Murphy!" Cassie beams at the old dog, ignoring everyone else.

I hang back, pumpkin pie in hand, watching as the chaos unfolds in the entryway ahead, until Heather's eyes land on me. "Come in, come in! It's cold outside! And happy birthday!"

The Hartford house is the epitome of Thanksgiving—the scent of roasted turkey and sage lingers in the air, the dining room table is decked out in fancy china and crystal wine glasses beneath the glowing chandelier, and the center is lined with oddly shaped gourds and short vases of white roses and cranberry sprigs.

"Wow, Heather. This looks ... you've outdone yourself." My mom's eyes twinkle as she takes in the sight.

Heather waves it off, collecting the pie from my hands. "It's my favorite holiday. Though, I'm taking it easy on the wine after last night." She chuckles. "But I have a bottle chilled and ready for you. Come in, please. Aria, Emmett's in his room, finishing up an essay. Go on up. Dinner should be ready in about twenty minutes." She adds with knowing eyes, "At six o'clock, *sharp*."

I smile. "Okay."

Mom glances warily upstairs before shifting to me, and I know what she's thinking—Aria and Emmett in his bedroom together, alone?

Really, Mom? With Cassie around? I even dip my head toward Cassie, who's currently enthralled with Murphy but won't be for long. Emmett said she slept through the night and when she woke up this morning, she seemed fine. Looking at her now, you'd never know about the drama that unfolded last night.

"Keep the door open," Mom mouths.

I can't resist rolling my eyes at her before making my way up. I knock once on the closed door, waiting for an answer. I don't hear one and assume there's too much noise carrying from downstairs to decipher his deep voice, so I turn the handle.

Emmett is sprawled out on his bed, his laptop pushed aside, his eyes closed, earbuds in his ears. His broad chest rises and falls slowly.

I push the door until it's open a crack and then ease my way over to study him in sleep—his impossibly long, thick eyelashes, his messy hair, his full, soft lips, the way his neck meets his collarbone, hard muscle carving the curves.

Is he more beautiful asleep or awake? I can't decide.

His hand—still bruised from last night's fight—rests atop his stomach, partially covering where his T-shirt has ridden up. I study the cut of his hips and the thin strip of dark hair that trails down below his belt buckle and elastic band of his underwear.

An overwhelming rush of nerves hits my gut at the thought of touching him there.

"Is it dinner already?" Emmett's deep voice cuts into the silence, startling me enough that I jump.

How long was he watching me gawk at him?

He grins as he tugs out his earphones, which makes me think, *Long enough.*

"Your mom said twenty minutes."

"Perfect."

I stifle my squeal as he grabs my hand and pulls me down to fall awkwardly on top of him. "Your laptop!"

With his free hand, Emmett pushes the screen shut and hoists it over his head to set it on his headboard's shelf, before rolling his body. I land on my back beside him, with my legs draped over his thighs.

"Hi." He leans in to press his warm lips against mine. The tension coursing through his body last night has vanished, replaced by languid touches and sleepy whispers. "Happy birthday. Again."

"Thanks. *Again.*" I smile against his mouth, acutely aware of the way his giant hand splays across my stomach, inches from wandering into dangerous territory in either direction—up or down—with a simple slide of his long fingers. I wish he would. Not that right now is the best time. "The door's open," I whisper.

"We'll hear the stairs creak. And Cassie's slow." With one more kiss, he leans back to rest his head on his biceps. "So, what'd you do today?"

"Nothing. Read." *Counted down the hours until now*. "Finish your essay?"

"About halfway there." He scowls. "I shouldn't have left it until the last minute. And I've got two midterms next week, too."

"That sucks. My math midterm is next week and I think I'm going to fail."

"You're *not* going to fail. But you know who you should ask to tutor you? Richard. There's something about the way he explains things. He's good."

"Maybe I'll ask him." I pause. "Cassie seems fine?"

"Yeah." The way he drags that one word out doesn't sound convincing. "I'm never sure with her. She may seem fine, but then do or say something a year from now that makes me wonder if she's been thinking about it all along. I played it off as no big deal this morning. That's what you have to do with her. But it'll be a miracle if she doesn't say something that tips off my parents and if *that* happens ..." He sighs. "Hopefully I'm in Minnesota by then."

My chest pangs with that reminder. "Let's hope she keeps her own secret, then."

"Oh, by the way, here." He rolls toward his bedside table and rummages in the top drawer.

I catch sight of an open box of condoms—my heart skips —before he pulls out a box wrapped in indigo-blue paper with silver stars. He grins as he settles in next to me again. "Open it now."

"Did you wrap this?" I peel back the delicate, neatly taped paper.

"What do *you* think?"

"Your mom?"

He chuckles. "I picked it out, though."

"Oh my God!" I burst out laughing as I uncover a Pennywise Funko Pop. "I love it!"

"It's nothing big ...," he says, his mouth against my neck.

"It'll remind me of that night at the fair." The first night I found myself in Emmett's arms. The almost-kiss. "It's perfect." I turn so our chests are pressed against each other. "I thought you promised no clowns for my birthday?"

"I lied." He smiles. "I didn't lie about the other thing, though."

I frown, searching my memories. "What other—ahh!" I shriek as Emmett's tongue slides across my cheek, leaving a wet trail.

"Shhh!" He chuckles as he holds my hands down to keep me from wiping his saliva off. "Or Cassie will hear you and be up here in a minute."

I press my lips together—I want some private time with Emmett, after all—and lean forward to wipe my cheek on his shirt, earning his laugh. And then his kiss.

"Thank you. For the gift. You didn't have to, but I love it."

"Yeah? How much."

"Like, I *really love* it." I tease the seam of his mouth with my tongue.

His sharp intake of breath tells me he likes that, so I do it again.

"The door's open," he whispers, echoing my earlier warning.

"We'll hear the stairs creak." I offer a shy grin a second before it's smothered by his lips.

Years from now, if anyone asks me what I did for my sixteenth birthday, I'll tell them I kissed Emmett Hartford. That's all I'll remember, and it will have been the best birthday of my life.

His thumb slips under the hem of my shirt to tease the small of my back as he deepens his kiss, pulling my body closer and closer until it's flush against his. And for the first time, I feel exactly how much Emmett wants me.

A small gasp escapes me.

The bed creaks as he shifts his weight, rolling with me until I'm on my back and he's on top of me. My body reacts beneath his weight, warmth coursing through my limbs as I shift, allowing my thighs to squeeze around his. I know it won't go *that* far—it can't, with our parents downstairs. But that limitation seems to embolden a burning frustration in my body. My fingers suddenly itch to peel off his shirt; my skin aches to feel his wandering hands and mouth.

I'm sixteen years old now.

And I trust Emmett completely.

A loud creak sounds from the staircase.

Emmett groans and rolls off, leaving me instantly cold. This ache only grows when I watch him stand and, as discreetly as possible, adjust himself.

I pull myself into a respectable sitting position on the edge of Emmett's bed, smoothing my hair, as the door swings open and Cassie barges in.

"Dinner's ready," she announces with a grin.

"Meet you guys down there." Emmett strolls to the bathroom across the hall.

"That was delicious, Heather." Uncle Merv wipes his mouth with the cloth napkin and then tosses it onto his dirty plate.

"Well, I hope you saved room for dessert," she says

through a glass of wine—I guess she didn't have *too* much last night, after all.

Leaning back in his chair, he rubs his protruding belly, his loose jowls lifting with his grin. "Oh, I suppose there might be some room left in here for *pie*."

"Or something *else*." Cassie grins, her eyes flittering to me before shifting to her mother. She waggles her eyebrows and nods her head, urging Heather. She's been giving her mother that look all night, and Heather has mouthed or whispered, "Not yet," over and over again.

I suspect it has to do with my birthday.

"Emmett? Why don't you help me clear." Mark collects dinner plates.

Emmett, who's sitting beside me, whose leg nudged against mine the entire dinner, stands.

I move to help.

Mark pats the air, winking at me. "Stay, relax. We've got this. Cassie?"

Her mouth makes an "oh" shape and, with a furious nod and her wide eyes flashing to me, she scrambles out of her seat.

I prepare myself for the ensuing embarrassment.

It comes five minutes later when the lights suddenly dim and Cassie's laughter sounds, and Heather aims a giant lens at me to take a picture. My cheeks burn as Emmett leads, carrying a homemade chocolate cake on a plate, sixteen pink candles blazing from the top. Everyone's voices meld together in song, including Uncle Merv's gruff baritone, and Heather snaps picture after picture.

"We made it yesterday. It took us *all day*! I helped decorate," Cassie declares as Emmett sets the cake down in front of me.

"Make a wish," he whispers, his eyes glimmering in the candlelight.

I smile up at him. *I've already got my wish,* I want to say. *All my wishes.*

Life is good again.

I take a deep breath and blow out the candles. Someone —Heather, I assume—has piped "Happy birthday, AJ" across the center in green icing. Messy, uneven squirts of pink and blue icing surround the tidy lettering, half of them with a Junior Mint embedded within. I'm guessing that's Cassie's contribution. Now the rattling sound in Cassie's pocket and her secretive behavior the other day make sense.

"There were supposed to be more mints on top—" Heather begins with a chuckle.

"But I accidentally ate them." Cassie smiles, as if she's proud of that fact and everyone, including Uncle Merv, can't help but laugh. Because Cassie makes people laugh, just by being herself—her innocent, curious, kindhearted self.

An unexpected wave of anger ripples through me. How could Holly be a part of something so cruel as what that asshole Adam did to Cassie last night? How could she allow something like that to happen?

I temper my anger and smile, pushing thoughts of Holly from my mind. "Thank you. This is a nice surprise."

"Yeah." Cassie shrugs, as if it's no big deal, her hungry eyes sizing up the cake. "So ... can you cut it now?"

CHAPTER
TWENTY-ONE

"MISS WEBBER ... YOU HAVE A MEETING WITH YOUR guidance counselor." Ms. McNair holds the slip of paper between her two fingers, hand-delivered by a mousy girl with thick glasses and a pale complexion.

"Oh! I totally forgot!" Holly croons.

Fake. Her voice grates on my nerves.

McNair glances at the clock. "Drop your essay on my desk on the way out, as I assume you won't be back before class end."

There's a rustling sound behind us as Holly gathers her things, and I steal a glance at Emmett, only to have him offer me that sexy smirk that makes me forget everything else.

The next thing I know, Holly is stumbling past me with a soft "oomph," her hand flying out to brace herself against my desk, knocking my pencil case off in the process. Pens and highlighters scatter across the classroom floor.

"Oh, I'm so sorry, Aria! I'm such a klutz!" She stoops and, in a rush, collects my things.

"It's fine," I mumble, stifling my eye roll.

"Here. I think I got everything. Oh, except this." Her upturned nose crinkles as she holds up a long tube and reads, loud enough for the entire class to hear, "*Herpes* cold sore cream."

My face explodes with flames as gasps and snickers and a few outright bursts of laughter sound around us. "That's not mine!"

"Sure. Okay, well ..." She tosses it onto my desk along with my pencil case and then holds her hands out as if she's touched something foul. Her blue eyes land on Emmett with her cringe. "Have fun with *that*."

"Oh my God, that's *not* mine," I mutter under my breath for only Emmett to hear, my eyes stinging with the threat of tears. It doesn't even say "herpes" on the tube!

"It's not a big deal. People get them," he whispers, clearing his throat.

"But *I* don't. She set that up!" I force through gritted teeth. Too loud, because McNair's gaze narrows at us in warning.

Her heels click on the classroom floor as she approaches. "Okay, Marshall, what can you tell me about ..." She directs everyone's attention to a guy across the room; meanwhile, her fingers slide over my desk to discreetly pick up the tube and carry it back to her desk.

It's too late, though—the damage has been done. How long before a cold sore turns into a high school-wide rumor of me giving Emmett an STD? It's the oldest trick in the book, and Holly played it beautifully.

I close my eyes and spend the last fifteen minutes of class keeping my tears at bay and my body from bolting from my chair, reminding myself how good it will feel when I crush her at regionals.

I *hate* her, I accept.

But I will not let her get the better of me.

I struggle to slow my pace as I head for what has become our usual table in the cafeteria, the dozens of eyes crawling on my skin, their whispered giggles like the menacing buzz of wasps nearby.

"Hey." I slide into my seat, my undivided attention on my ham-and-cheese sandwich, though my appetite was smothered hours ago by the fury and fear in the pit of my stomach. Maybe eating will help.

"Hey." Jen avoids making eye contact as she chews on a carrot stick.

"What have you heard so far?"

She and Josie exchange a glance and I suspect the rumor is already snowballing. By the time it reaches the end of the day, I'll have infected the entire hockey team with an incurable disease.

Rumors are just tall tales that fade with time, Dr. C. would always say.

But she was also quick to point out how cutting they can be while they're swirling around you. And in the bubble of high school—which is an entire ecosystem for a teenager— they can sometimes suck the air out of your lungs.

Swirling around a person who is already struggling for air, they can become lethal.

"She's out to get me because of Emmett." I tell them about the ambush at the mini-meet on Friday, and Saturday night's fiasco.

"Heard about Saturday night." Jen grimaces. "What a bitch."

"Karma will get her," Josie offers in her naturally soft voice.

And maybe dealing with Holly's nastiness is part of my punishment from karma. My intentions for sharing that video may have been honest. But they were also selfish.

"Speak of the devil ..." Josie's eyes narrow on the cafeteria entrance. Sure enough, Holly and Mandy are strolling in, Holly's head held high as she approaches, moving toward her usual table of friends.

She looks my way—she knows where I am—and offers me a smug smile.

My anger flares.

What would people around school think if they knew who she really was?

I could leak that video. That's my weapon. Nobody would be able to ignore how awful she really is. How fake those smiles and waves are. They'd start to question if she's talking about them like she did about us.

But if Cassie were to hear it, it would hurt her. And, in turn, it would hurt Emmett. Plus, it would draw attention to Jen and her weird clothing choices—today, it's a grossly overweight cat in a T-shirt with his belly hanging out and a bib with a turkey on it. An homage to post-Thanksgiving Day gluttony, I guess. Where does she even find these? And this one is clearly old, the print faded.

I'm not going to hurt any of them for the sake of getting revenge.

The right thing to do is ignore Holly.

But in this moment, seeing her grin and listening to her laugh, I find I can't be the bigger person. Not for her.

I wait for her to be out of earshot, and then I say, just loud enough for the nearby tables around us to catch, "Hey, did you guys hear about Holly's gross fetish?"

"Bye, AJ!"

I wave from the top of the stairs at Cassie, standing at the front door. "Have fun swimming."

"Okay. Bye, Emmett! See you guys in an hour!" She slams the door shut.

I venture into Emmett's room to find him sprawled out on his bed, his chemistry textbook within his grasp, deep concentration furrowing his brow. "Hey."

A lazy smile spreads across his lips, those deep dimples forming as he turns to watch me approach. "Hey." His voice has a sleepy rasp to it that I feel in my chest.

"Tired?"

"Nah. My legs are sore, though. My skating coach had me doing hard laps today."

"Skating coach?"

"Yeah. I've got my regular team practices and then a skating coach and a stick-handling coach, who also does shooting practice with me. That's why I'm on the ice every day." He shuts his chem textbook. "Ready to work on our project?"

"No." I laugh and toss my backpack onto the floor.

"Good." He grabs my hand and pulls me onto the bed, much the same way as on Thanksgiving weekend, on my back with my legs slung over his. He rolls onto his side to press up close to me, and lays a lingering kiss below my earlobe. I think it's his favorite spot to kiss me.

It's quickly becoming *my* favorite spot for him to kiss me, too.

"How was the rest of your day?"

"Horrible," I confess.

"You know ...," his fingertips trail over my cheekbones, my nose, the length of my bottom lip, "this guy in my chem class asked if the rumor about Holly was true."

I study his collarbone intently. "What rumor is that?"

"The one about how she used to beg me to let her suck on my *toes*. You know, because she has a weird foot fetish."

"*Wow.* That's kind of ... different?" I struggle to stifle my triumphant grin. That only took one period to spread through the school.

"It gets better. She used to ask me not to shower after practice, because she liked the taste of my sweat."

My cringe is genuine now. Someone's been embellishing. "What did you say?"

He chuckles. "I didn't know what to say, at first. I denied it, of course." His forehead wrinkles. "But it got me thinking about a certain girl who has a hatred for feet."

I feel the tips of my ears burning. "Yeah, that girl will definitely *not* suck on your sweaty toes, if that's the sort of thing you like." I cringe a second time at the thought.

Emmett laughs. At least if he suspects that I started the rumor—which he clearly does—he doesn't seem angry about it. "She might deserve that rumor floating around after what she did to you today."

Today, last Friday ...

"Yeah, that stunt of hers worked." Some jerk wearing an Eastmonte football jacket threw himself against a locker as I was walking by after school, as if I carried the plague.

"Don't worry, it'll blow over soon."

"I know." The question is, what will follow in its place?

Emmett trails a fingertip along my jawline. "Do you want me to say something to her?"

"No, it's okay. I'll deal with it. You've got enough going on."

He hesitates but then nods.

"You know what?" I shift my legs and roll onto my side to face him, smoothing my palm over his stubbled jaw. "I don't want to talk about Holly anymore."

"Me neither." He presses his lips against mine in the sweetest kiss. "Especially not when we have the house to ourselves for the next hour."

"What about your dad?" His car is in the driveway.

Emmett's hand smooths over the curve of my hip. "He's in Vancouver for a few days."

"Oh." *Oh.*

"Yeah." His hard swallow fills the growing tension in the room. And then he's kissing me again.

That surreal fog of "I can't believe this is happening!" that enveloped me every time Emmett was near is finally giving way to familiarity, to an urge to explore him.

An hour isn't much time at all.

We're shifting, rolling, until I'm on my back again and Emmett hovers over me, propped up on his elbows on either side of my head, his body pressing against mine. I let my hands wander, sliding up his shirt, memorizing the hard ridges of muscle over his back, the feel of his hot skin, as I venture all the way to his shoulder blades.

He breaks free from my mouth long enough to reach back with one arm to yank his shirt over his head. In another deft maneuver, he has it completely off and is launching it across the room, as if not planning on getting redressed anytime soon.

My nerves flutter in my stomach. It's the first time I've seen him shirtless and it is a sight. I sigh softly as I take in his bare chest, the pad of muscles begging to be touched. And I do, smoothing my palms over them, my fingertips drawing circles.

I feel a tug against the hem of my shirt, and when I meet Emmett's eyes, they're bright with earnest. "Can I?"

I simply nod, and lift my arms.

He slips my shirt off and his heated gaze drifts over my white lace bra. He makes no move to unfasten it, though. Not yet.

But if he asks, I'll let him.

I don't think there's anything I'd say no to right now, with Emmett.

Our lips find each other once again, this time in a heady dance of tangled tongues and bumping teeth, as his hot skin presses against mine, as his racing heart pounds against mine. "You drive me crazy," he whispers, and those are the last words exchanged between us.

I lose track of time, caught up in this intoxicating bubble that is Emmett—Emmett's lips on my mouth, on my neck, on my ears, along my collarbone. He doesn't venture further and seems to be making a concerted effort to keep his hands PG-13, which only builds my frustration, until I'm whispering his own words back to him, my fingers weaving tightly through his hair.

Car doors slam outside Emmett's window.

He peels away and rolls onto his back, exhaling slowly, his breathing ragged. "That was fun." His puffy, red lips stretch into a lazy smile as his eyes meet mine. "I guess we should do some homework now?"

I reach for my shirt with dismay.

DEAR JULIA,

I know it was wrong to start that rumor. But it was a

stupid, silly, immature rumor. Not a big one. Not one that would hurt Holly. And having people think you sucked your ex-boyfriend's sweaty toes is nothing compared to having the school think you have an untreatable, highly contagious STD. PLUS, I'm sure she had something to do with drugging Cassie.

And now I think Cassie may be scarred for life. Iris came by after school with her molasses cookies and Cassie asked her if there were drugs in them. You should've seen the look on Iris's wrinkled face. God knows how long it will be before that gets back to Heather or Mark. Holly has ruined cookies for Cassie for God knows how long.

AND don't forget what she did to me at the cross-country mini-meet.

I know Holly deserved it.

And yet, it's eating away at me.

~AJ

"Can I ask you something?" I peer at Jen over my tray of mac 'n' cheese. It's rainy and cold outside, and when I saw another student walk by with the cheesy, hot bowl, I quickly abandoned my bagel from home. "As your friend."

Her owlish eyes regard me a moment before she shrugs. "Sure."

How do I put this ... "You have an interesting wardrobe." I give her orange jack-o'-lantern sweatshirt a pointed look.

Jen grins. "I prefer to call it festive."

"It's definitely that." Yesterday's sweatshirt was all black with the word "Boo!" across the chest. "But what gives? I mean, why do you dress the way you do, which is ... not exactly like a nor—like *other* teenagers."

She stabs at her macaroni noodles with a fork. "They're my mom's shirts," she admits, biting her bottom lip. "Remember when I said we moved to Eastmonte when I was twelve? It was because she had cancer, so my parents decided it'd be a good idea to be closer to my grandparents while she was going through treatment. We moved in with them. It made things easier." She smiles at her plate of food. "She died two years ago, when I started tenth grade."

"Oh." I swallow. "I'm sorry. I had no idea." I've been so focused on my own life, I don't know much of anything about Jen at all, other than that Holly was her nemesis.

What would it have been like for Jen, to lose her mother at fifteen?

For years, my mother seemed absent—she was gone all day, and when she was home, her head was buried in work. But it's not the same. I knew she'd come back eventually.

For Jen, all she has left are memories.

And tacky shirts.

"So, you wear your mom's clothes?"

She rolls her eyes. "My mom had a thing for loud, fun shirts. She always used to say, 'I might not be the most handsome woman there ever was but I'll be the most fun.' And she was. She turned heads wherever she went. Not necessarily in a good way, mind you, but she didn't care what other people thought of her. It all slid off her shoulders, because she liked who she was." Jen smiles. "She told me that the sooner you figure out how to like yourself through your own eyes, the sooner you'll stop trying to see yourself through everyone else's." She shifts her pasta around with her spoon. "I miss her. A lot. After she died, I decided to wear one of her shirts to school. It was Valentine's Day and the shirt had a giant Be Mine heart across the front. It felt good. I felt like she was still with me. And so I started wearing more of her shirts. This was her favorite one for Halloween." She peers down at her chest and laughs. "I used to think it was so ugly but now all I see when I look at it is her."

"That's ..." I swallow against the lump in my throat. "She sounds like she would have been a fun mom to have." And suddenly the tacky shirts don't seem so tacky anymore.

"She was." Jen studies her lunch intently before shoveling in a mouthful. She nods behind me and a moment later, Josie slides into her chair, setting her red lunch bag on the table in front of her.

"Hi." Her eyes shift to me, partially hidden behind her heavy, dark bangs. She worries her thin lips, as if wanting to say something but holding herself back.

"What's going on?"

"I'm not sure if you want me to tell you this," she says in that near-whisper.

"Well, *now* you have to." Wariness slides down my spine. I already know this isn't going to be good.

Josie purses her mouth. "Okay, so I heard people talking in class about this Instagram account that someone started for Emmett Hartford's new girlfriend."

My stomach sinks like a rock in a lake.

"The handle is SWF Eats." Josie's cute face is apologetic. "And there are pictures—"

I leave my lunch where it is, barely touched—my appetite vanished—and, grabbing my purse, dash for the nearest girls' bathroom. Ducking into the last stall, I dig out my phone.

It doesn't take long to find the account.

My chest burns as I study the profile picture. It's a

zoomed-in candid shot of me—my face contorted as I open my mouth to take a bite from a sandwich. Holly must've taken it during lunch when the lunch monitors weren't watching.

There are five pictures loaded in the feed and they're of equally unflattering shots of me eating, three taken in the last week.

And two taken ... *today*.

I look down at my red shirt—a shirt we bought on the weekend shopping trip. Holly hasn't come to the cafeteria yet. Which means other people are taking pictures of me, and she's posting them right away. They heard about the account, thought it was funny, and joined in. That's how these things start: a funny joke at someone's expense. It might only last a few days or a few weeks, but the damage will be done.

How long before the whole school is in on it?

My eyes sting with angry tears as I read the profile description.

Stalker. Thief. S.T.D. Advocate. Bathroom Voyeur. DM face-stuffing pics. Anon guaranteed.

There's no doubt Holly started this, but good luck proving it. She posted the first picture last Friday night, after the mini-meet. She probably sat in her room—by herself, or with Mandy, who seems to be of like mind—and giggled as she opened a fake account using a fake email.

And there are already seventy-four followers.

I close my eyes as a wave of nausea floods me.

I don't know what to do. If I tell my mother, she'll storm in guns blazing and make things worse.

If I go to Mr. Keen ... who am I kidding? Holly won't admit to it. He'll probably make things worse too. *If* he does anything at all.

Maybe I brought this on myself. I did start that idiotic toe-sucking rumor, after all. And I did help break them up. If I hadn't, I wouldn't be a target. Maybe I deserve this.

That thought brings me no comfort.

But there's not much I can do. I take a screenshot of the IG account, for proof, and then report the account, knowing it's likely futile.

And then I hide out in the bathroom stall until the bell goes for the end of fourth period, because there's no way I'm going back to the caf today.

CHAPTER
TWENTY-TWO

Ms. Moretti cuts my path off as I'm on my way to joining the rest of the team in stretching. "How's the knee?" She peers down at my leg, hidden by my favorite loose track pants.

"Fine. Just bruised." I bend it as if to prove my words. In truth, my entire kneecap is an ugly and concerning mottle of purple and blue, but it doesn't hurt anymore.

"Okay. Do me a favor and take it easy for one more day. We have two weeks until regionals. You'll make your time back, if you let yourself heal. Pace yourself with Richard."

"Sure." My eyes flicker to the group, to where Holly sits on the grass, stretching her hamstrings, her ponytail swaying as she laughs hysterically with the girl beside her. About what, who knows, but I've come to assume it's nothing kind.

Tension instantly courses through my limbs.

"Is everything else okay, Aria?"

I meet Moretti's eyes, now wearing a coat of suspicion. "Yeah. Why?"

"Are you—" She stops midsentence, twisting her lips in thought. And then simply nods. "I know starting at a new school can be hard. You seem to be on the right track. But if you ever need an ear ..." Her brow pinches. "If things get *harder* than they should be at school, I'm here to listen. You know that, right?"

I force a smile, even as my insides tighten. *Did she dig into my past? Did she find records she was not supposed to see?*

"Yeah. I know." I sound like Cassie.

Her shrewd gaze wanders to Holly. "We're not as oblivious to what's going on as you guys seem to think we are. I *hate* it"—she holds a manicured hand up— "no, that's a terrible word. I *strongly dislike* it when my students think they can't come to me with a problem. Especially a problem with another student. I'm here to help, but I can't do that if you don't talk to me. Okay?"

I purse my lips, and nod. *That's what they all say.*

Though, Ms. Moretti seems different from other teachers I've had. Maybe she is the real deal; maybe she is different from all the rest of them.

If I gave her a list of Holly's indiscretions thus far, what would she do with it?

Her lips spread into a broad, beautiful smile. "Okay, everyone! Two more minutes and then we work off that turkey!"

I make my way over to Richard and begin stretching my legs. "Hey, Rich."

"My grandfather calls me that. Richie Rich. Except we're poor." He adjusts his yellow sweatband. "Good Thanksgiving?"

I consider that for a minute. "Yeah, it was." Despite all the drama. "You?"

"*I* went up against a gelatinous cube." He pauses for effect. "And *won*."

"I take it that's something from your little dragon game *thing*?"

"Uh ... it's not *little* and it's *only* a dungeon dweller who consumes living tissue." He stares at me like *I'm* the strange one.

I give him two thumbs up. "Good job, you."

"Yeah." He shrugs and then takes a moment to bend down and check his shoelaces. "Saw Adam Levic, by the way." He stands to flash me a wide-eyed exaggerated look. "How's Emmett's fist?"

I guess everyone has heard. "Better than that jerk's face, I'm sure."

Richard snorts. "Is it true what he did to Cassie?"

"Yup."

"Man ... who does that?"

An idiot with a big-boobed temptress whispering in his ear.

"So, what's Cassie like stoned?"

"She wasn't. She was *fine*. Thank God Adam doesn't know how to use a scale."

Richard barks out a laugh. "I'm not surprised. I tried tutoring that guy in Math 9." He shakes his head. "Lost cause."

"We have something in common, then, because I'm going to fail my math midterm tomorrow." It's always been my worst subject and with the way Lewis tests us, I'm doomed.

His face furrows in thought. "What lunch do you have?"

"Fourth."

"Same here. If you want to come to the library, I could try and explain some things to you."

"You'd do that?"

He shrugs. "Sure. It *will* cut into my dungeon battle planning, but I guess I can spare an hour. For you. Because you're nice to me."

"Yes. Okay?" This is doubly perfect. Help with math and a valid excuse for avoiding the cafeteria, because there's no way I'm eating lunch in public while that stupid Instagram account is still up. "Thanks, Rich." He holds his hands up in the air. "I mean, as long as Emmett is okay, you know ... with you and me ... together, *alone*."

I wait for his serious expression to crack, but it doesn't.

I plaster the most somber mask I can manage over my face. "I think he'll understand."

Ms. Moretti's whistle sounds. "Let's get started!" She claps her hands and backs up, waving us off like we're race cars and she's the flag carrier.

I take off in a light, slow jog.

"Moretti told you to run with me because I'm slow and your knee is messed up, didn't she?" Richard says.

"No," I lie.

"That's okay." He taps his head. "It's this *big* brain of mine. It weighs too much. I can't move as fast."

I smile. He's funny without meaning to be. No wonder Cassie likes him.

Feet pound the pavement from behind. "Be careful you don't trip again, *AJ*," Holly calls out as she jogs past, her blonde ponytail swishing, my nickname mocking on her lips.

The simmering anger that bubbles deep inside me rises. The urge to retaliate.

Just ignore her.

Just ignore her.

Just ignore her.

I repeat it over and over in my head as I watch her gain distance on us.

"She pretends to be nice, but she's not, is she?" Richard asks when she's safely out of earshot.

"No, she's not." I hesitate. "She tripped me on purpose at the meet last week."

Richard's eyes narrow as he scrutinizes Holly up ahead. "What a gelatinous cube."

Despite my dark mood, I burst with laughter.

"THIS IS PERFECT. There's nothing to take a picture of, except the back of your head." Jen chomps on a celery stick.

We've moved from our usual table to one in the corner where I can keep my back to everyone and, hopefully, eat my sandwich in peace. It's a flag of defeat, a sign that I'm bowing under Holly's game, and I hate that.

But the sooner I ride this out, the better.

At least my math midterm is over. Meeting Richard yesterday helped. I might walk away with a C thanks to him.

Jen frowns at something behind me. "I thought Emmett had class now?"

"He does." I look over my shoulder to see Emmett strolling across the cafeteria, his stride fast, his gaze steely, his target obvious.

Holly watches him approach, her eyes flittering toward me a moment.

"This doesn't look good," Josie says softly.

He stops in front of her and leans in, resting his hand on the back of her chair.

I can't hear him from here, but I can read his lips without problem. "Shut it down, now," he mouths, each word enunciated, his face hard and unfriendly.

Holly bats her eyelashes as her forehead pulls with concern. She shakes her head. "I don't know what you're talking about," I read from her lips.

People at surrounding tables have quieted and are watching the confrontation. The caf monitor, a tiny, dark-haired lady, weaves through the tables, approaching cautiously.

"You know exactly what I'm talking about, Holly," he says, his voice now carrying, "and if it's not down within the next ten minutes, I might have to share a few pictures of my own."

Her face blanches.

With that, he peels away, before the monitor can reach them.

He pauses to seek me out. Spotting me, he heads for our table. And *everyone's* watching.

"Hey, what are you doing out of—"

He cuts my question off with a kiss that most certainly breaks the school's PDA policy, one that makes Josie duck her head and Jen clear her throat and me blush.

"Just wanted to say hi." He smiles softly as he slides cool fingers beneath my hair to tickle my neck. "Better get back to class, before I get caught." He kisses me once more and then heads for the door at a quick pace.

"I'll bet that was about the Instagram account." Jen watches Holly's table. "She looks rattled."

"What kind of pictures does he have of her?" Josie asks.

My stomach turns. I don't want to think about that, or why he would still have them.

"Look." Jen nods.

I glance over my shoulder again.

Holly is rushing out of the caf with her things, head down, avoiding eye contact.

"This was a long day." Jen slams her locker shut and turns her combination lock.

"Agreed." I stuff the last of my textbooks into my backpack. My shoulders are always sore by the time I walk home, compounded by the fact that a fifteen-minute walk always takes double the time with Cassie.

"See you tomorrow?"

"Yeah. Call me later if you want." I can't believe it's taken us this long to exchange numbers.

Seconds later, a heavy arm lands on my shoulder. "Need a ride home?"

I spin to find Emmett smiling down at me. My spirits are instantly lifted. "Don't you have, like, puck practice tonight?"

"Look at you. Learning the lingo." He pinches my cheek playfully.

I swat his hand away but laugh.

"It's canceled tonight. Come on. Let's get Cass. I promised I'd take her to get ice cream."

I shut my locker and we head down the hall, his arm hooked over my shoulders. Several guys call his name or bump his shoulder as they pass by. I don't think there is anyone in this school who doesn't like Emmett. Besides Holly and Adam, that is.

"How was the rest of your day?"

"It was ... better. Thanks, for what you did at lunch." By

the time I ducked into the bathroom to check my phone, the SWF account had vanished, like it had never existed. I wish I could erase it from my memory just as easily.

His jaw tenses. "How long have you known about the account?"

"A few days."

"Next time, tell me right away." He gives a delayed chin-up greeting to someone. "You shouldn't deal with that alone."

"Whatever. It's over. She'll get bored and move on."

A vacant look passes through his eyes. "I can't believe I ever dated her. It makes me sick, thinking about it."

Ms. Moretti is striding down the hall toward us at a brisk clip, her heels clicking against the tile, her eyes narrowing on us. I brace myself, waiting for her to remind Emmett of the PDA policy, but she merely gives me a thumbs-up. "Training hard this weekend?"

"Always."

"I'll make sure to chase her around Miller's Park for ya," Emmett offers with a grin.

"I'll bet you will. And you know where to find me when you're ready to talk, Aria." She winks and keeps going.

"What's that about? Ready to talk about what?"

"Nothing." I wave it off. "Cross-country stuff."

"You ever get the feeling that Moretti has her tiny little finger on *everything* going on in the school?"

"I'm beginning to." I haven't decided yet if that's a good or a bad thing.

Cassie is ready to go, standing by her locker, her backpack sitting over her shoulders. Her curious eyes search passing faces to find the familiar ones so she can call out their names and wave. Some wave back at her, some smile and offer their goodbyes.

Some keep their heads down, though I doubt they missed her voice.

And with each one of those people, I see that bright light dim in Cassie's eyes for a second as she watches them pass, ignoring her. I feel an unexpected urge to slap those people across the head.

Is it really too much to acknowledge her? Just give her a nod?

We're maybe ten feet away when a cluster of three guys —young, I'm guessing ninth graders—stroll past, catching her residual smile. The brown-haired one on the left waves at her, earning her curious frown.

"I don't know you," she says out loud.

"Then why are you waving and smiling at me like that?" he throws back, his tone full of scorn. He follows it up with a rendition of her, only he adds a goofy laugh that is clearly meant to mock.

Her smile slips. Not entirely, but enough to make me think she's picked up on the teasing.

Emmett's arm disappears from my shoulder and he charges forward, grabbing hold of the guy's shoulder and yanking him around.

"You have a problem with someone waving at you?" Emmett's voice is low and even, and yet it sets the hair on the back of my neck on edge.

The guy's amusement vanishes as he peers up at Emmett's towering form. "Uh ... no, man," he stammers. "No."

"Because that's my sister back there."

The boy's eyes flash to us, fear in them growing by the second. Has he heard what Emmett did to Adam Levic's face? "I didn't know."

"It doesn't matter if you knew. Don't be a dickhead to

anyone who doesn't deserve it." He gives the guy a small shove, just hard enough to make the guy stumble a few steps before he takes off briskly down the hall.

Cassie giggles, but then scowls, as if catching herself. "Why did you push him, Emmett?"

"Because he's a—" Emmett cuts off abruptly, shaking his head. "It doesn't matter. You ready to go?" He begins walking toward the doors.

Her eyes trail after the guy. "That boy was being mean to me," she says after a beat, as if she needed to roll the last few moments over in her mind to decide that.

"Yeah, he was." I smile softly.

"Yeah ... sometimes kids are mean to me." She says it in an offhand way, but I notice the way her shoulders droop. "Is it because I have autism?"

An ache forms in my throat at the fact that she's made that connection, that she's not wrong. "It's because they don't know how awesome you are."

"Yeah." She frowns, her doubt lingering. "I don't think anyone's going to ask me to prom."

It takes me a second to jump onto her new train of thought and think of a suitable answer. "Lots of people go without a date. Friends go together."

"See you tomorrow, Cass!" a girl with long white-blonde hair and bright green eyes calls out as she strolls by.

"Oh, bye, Allie! See you tomorrow!" Cassie's blue-gray eyes follow the girl, her wide smile back in place. "She's nice to me."

"She is."

After a moment, Cassie adds in a deadpan voice, "She knows how awesome I am."

"I took ten, see, AJ ...? AJ ...? AJ ...?"

"*Hold on ...*" My eyes are glued to Emmett as he speeds and weaves with quick hands around first one player, and then another, before stopping and passing the puck to his teammate, who shoots.

The puck sails into the net as Cassie's elbow prods my side.

"*What?*" She is so impatient!

Unbothered by my sharp tone, Cassie holds her palm out to show me the Junior Mints cupped within. A ring of hot chocolate surrounds her lips. "I took ten. Is that okay?"

"Yeah, that's fine." I dismiss her, my attention back on Emmett, who's bumping gloved fists with his teammate.

"These are my favorite, too."

"Watch the game, Cass."

She shoves the entire handful of mints into her mouth, and then shifts her focus to picking at her fingernails for the rest of the game, not uttering a word until five minutes before the end of the last period, when she inhales sharply. "Holly!" She grins and waves.

I follow her gaze and find Holly sitting on the other side with a few girls. "What is she doing here?" I mutter.

"Watching hockey."

"Yeah, but why? This is Emmett's game."

Cassie shrugs. "She's his friend."

"No, she isn't," I say evenly. "They broke up and they're not friends anymore."

"So, they're enemies?"

I stifle my groan. Emmett wasn't kidding—everything is

black or white with Cassie. "They're just not friends anymore, okay?"

Cassie shrugs, the eager smile on her face falling with each moment she watches Holly and Holly ignores her.

"Didn't Emmett tell you not to talk to her anymore?"

Cassie goes back to picking her fingernails, mumbling, "But she's *my* friend."

"No. She isn't. Holly was pretending to be your friend so she could get close to Emmett."

Her fingers pause as she glowers at her hands. "She's not my friend."

"No. And she's not a nice person."

More picking.

I cringe as the sight of her nails, ripped off to the quick, her cuticles torn and bloody.

"Are *you* my friend?" she asks suddenly.

"Yeah. Of course."

"Will you still be my friend next year when Emmett is gone?"

When Emmett is a sixteen-and-a-half-hour drive away —I mapped it out of curiosity—at college, with college girls and college life. I can't help but hear another meaning behind her words: when Emmett and I break up, because I'd be a fool to think we'll last. My chest tightens with that thought.

But that's not even what she's asking. Cassie wants to know if I'll still walk home with her after school every day, if I'll watch movies with her that I miss half of because I'm answering her bizarre questions; if I'll still tolerate her mindless chatter and scattered conversations.

If I'll still be nice to her.

This girl who speaks slowly and runs awkwardly, who can only manage short spurts of eye contact and stiffens under anyone's touch, who struggles to match appropriate emotions with situations.

Who finds joy in the simplest things, who will never sit at a cafeteria table or in a bathroom and say mean things behind people's backs.

Who understands more than most people give her credit for.

Whose heart can't seem to hold animosity, even toward those who have been cruel to her.

Who has only ever wanted to be a friend to me since the moment she stepped out of her mom's car with a bag of cookies.

"Of course, I will," I promise.

"Yeah, okay." She finally looks up to offer me a wide grin and a nod. "Are you going to eat those Junior Mints?"

"Three more slides, and *then* you can have another kiss." I roll off Emmett's bed and plant myself on the floor, my lips still tingling.

"Are you make-out bartering with me now? Is that what this is?" he says, flashing a lazy smile, his voice laced with amusement.

"I just want to get this done." I pull his computer onto my lap. "And the sooner we finish, the sooner you can get back to explaining those hockey plays," using his fingers as players and the full canvas of my torso as the ice rink. Cassie and Heather are at swimming, and Mark is camped out in his office on another conference call with Vancouver, so, while our shirts have stayed on, our hands have wandered liberally.

He groans and rolls onto his side to rest on the edge of his bed, his fingertips toying with my hair. "Okay. I think we should focus the last three slides on why kids bully, why the victims don't report, and possible solutions."

"Okay ... Reasons." I start a fresh tab. "Need for attention, learned behavior, low self-esteem ..." All those sessions with Dr. C. are paying off in a way I never anticipated. "Desire to fit in. Jealousy." I feel Emmett's eyes on my profile but I keep my focus on the screen, wanting to be finished with this project so I can go back to happier things —namely, kissing Emmett.

"Next was a slide about victims, right?" Every time I hear that word, my body tenses.

"If you flip to that last tab in the browser, there's some good information in there," Emmett says.

I don't have to look, though. My fingers fly over the keyboard with each bullet point. "Number one, they're afraid no one will believe them. Two, they're embarrassed to talk about what's being said. Three, they're afraid of retaliation." I think of Cassie. "Four, they don't even realize that it's a form of bullying. Or ...," I swallow as I type out the last one, "they deserve it. They *think* they deserve it," I correct, flipping to the last slide.

"What happened in Calgary, Aria?" Emmett asks softly. I love when he calls me AJ, but hearing my real name come from his lips always sends shivers down my spine.

Unfortunately, the shivers are cold this time.

"I don't want to talk about it."

"I know you don't, but I'm asking you to, anyway." His index finger grazes my cheek. "You already kind of told me, right? Don't you trust me with the whole story?"

"I *do* trust you."

"Then why won't you tell me?"

"Because you won't understand."

"You really don't think so?"

My mouth has gone dry under the unexpected pressure. If I tell Emmett the whole truth, he'll look at me differently. Just like everyone else did. But ... what if he *does* understand? What if telling him helps me shed this weight that still lingers after all these months, no matter how far away we've driven, no matter how many productive sessions with Dr. C. I've had, no matter how many times I tell my mother that I'm fine, that I made a terrible mistake but I've learned from it?

How much of the truth can Emmett handle, though? And what does he *really* need to know?

"There was ... *this girl.*" *Yes. Impartiality. Separation.*

I stare at my socked feet as I force myself to continue. "There was this girl in my school. She took a candid video of another girl in the library—a girl she didn't like, who was flirting with the guy she was *in love* with. So, this girl took that video, dubbed a conversation over it that said all kinds of embarrassing things, and then shared it with a few people who shared it with a few people. Soon it was *all* over the school. The other girl found out and she was pissed. So, she retaliated by spreading all kinds of rumors—*horrible* rumors. The girl who pulled the video prank had made the wrong enemy, but it was too late. This went on and on."

"Did she try apologizing for making the video?" Emmett asked softly.

I shake my head. "She should have, but she didn't." *Would it have made a difference?*

I swallow the ache in my throat. "We had this fundraising program in school. It was called Rosegram. You could pay money to send a rose and a nice message to another student to brighten their day. So, one day, the girl who took the video was sitting in the caf when a Rosegram came for her. It came with this *huge* sign that *everyone* could read right away that said, 'Will you go to prom with me?' Signed by the guy she was in love with. Who was also in the caf that day. It had been planned out perfectly."

"Let me guess—he didn't send it," Emmett says with a heavy sigh.

I shake my head. "And he wasn't nice about making that clear in front of everyone. He was a huge jerk anyway. She just couldn't see it." I study my socks a long moment, thinking back to that day.

"That would have been humiliating for ... *the girl*," he offers gently.

"It was. She started to cry, right there, in the middle of the caf. And she already had a lot of things going on—family problems, confidence issues, she was failing some of her classes. Add in months of horrible rumors floating around the school about her and she finally snapped." I take a deep, calming breath. "About a week later, she swallowed a bunch of pills from her mother's medicine cabinet."

I'm going to puke.

I can't believe I told Emmett that story.

The silence in the room is deafening.

I can feel his concerned eyes on me. I just can't bring myself to meet them. Because I'll see pity, sorrow, worry—all the things I don't want to see. "I really don't want to talk about it again, Emmett, so please don't ask me to."

"Thank you for telling me. I won't ask again," he promises.

Clearing the lump from my throat, I open a fresh slide. "So ... things that society can do to combat bullying—"

"Do you want me to say something? To Mr. Keen or

whoever. Do you want me to report Holly for that stupid Instagram account?"

"No." I shake my head. "You did enough today." I force myself to look at him, to smile. "That was chivalrous."

He snorts. "I wouldn't call it that. I basically threatened to be an equally shitty person." His jaw tenses as he studies me. "*Everyone*'s capable of it."

I hesitate. "You mean by sharing pictures of her?" I haven't brought it up, though it's been on my mind.

"Yeah," he admits, reluctance in his voice. "She sent me a few a long time ago. *You* know the kind I mean. Anyway, I don't have them anymore and I'd *never* do it. Just like I would never have hit that little shithead ninth grader, even though he was being a dick. But sometimes it feels like the only way to make it stop is to play their game."

"I get it." *You have no idea how much I get it.*

Another heavy silence settles over Emmett's bedroom, his gaze lost beyond the ceiling, deep within his thoughts. "I worry about what's going to happen to Cassie next year, when I'm gone. And Zach is gone."

That hollow feeling in my chest swells with the reminder. I don't want to imagine the halls without Emmett in them.

I push aside the laptop and curl up against the bed's frame, resting my chin on the mattress as I stroke his forearm with my fingertips. "I'll still be there next year," I assure him.

He smiles, but it's sad. "And what about the four years after that? You know, when she's the twenty-year-old and there's a bunch of fourteen-year-olds in the hall, and no one to defend her because she doesn't know what's going on. Or she does, and it makes her cry. I see those news stories all the time, about bad things happening to kids like her, kids who have no one strong enough to defend them, no one brave enough to speak up. Every time I picture someone doing that to her and ..." His jaw clenches.

"She won't be in high school forever, though."

"Yeah, but then what? She'll be an adult with autism. I don't know if that's easier or harder. I mean, there are plenty of adults out there with ASD who have jobs and houses and kids. But I don't think that's going to be the case with Cassie. I could be wrong, she's still only fifteen, but ... to us, she's *always* going to be the way she is right now." He shakes his head. "She's probably gonna live with my parents forever."

"You never know."

He chuckles darkly. "Can you imagine Cassie living on her own? In her own apartment? Have you seen her *room?*"

"There was underwear dangling from her chandelier the other day when I walked in." She broke out in hysterical laughter, wondering how it got there.

He shakes his head. "She'll never be able to focus for long enough to drive a car. I can't even imagine her taking the subway or a bus on her own. She can barely make herself toast. She'd live off Nutella sandwiches and microwaveable TV dinners. And junk. Cheetos and candy. She'll end up with type 2 diabetes because of all the crap she'd eat, because no one's there to stop her."

"She has no self-control, does she," I ask.

"*None.*" He chuckles again, but then his smile fades. "I never used to think about this kind of stuff. She was just my sister with autism. I knew she was different and she needed a lot of extra help. But now I hear my parents talking about her every once in a while. About what she's going to be like in fifteen years, about saving money so she's set up to survive after they're gone, about how she's going to survive, who's going to help take care of her. My mom worries constantly about money." He sighs again, and in that sound, I feel the weight of the unspoken words—will responsibility for Cassie fall on his shoulders eventually?

"Well ... hopefully you'll end up making gazillions of dollars in the NFL and it won't be a big deal for you. Wait—did I get that right?"

"Close enough." He chuckles. "How did we get on this topic?"

"I can't remember." But my heart is swelling with adoration at the fact that he feels comfortable enough to open up to me.

And maybe he feels the same, now that I've opened up to him.

The nausea that threatened with divulging parts of my past has begun to subside.

Maybe, just maybe, it was the right move.

"Oh, yeah." His hand settles on my shoulder, rubbing it affectionately. "All I'm saying is, if Holly does something again, tell me. She shouldn't get away with it and you don't have to deal with it alone. Okay?"

I nod. "You know, you're a really good guy."

His eyes flitter over my mouth. "You're not so bad yourself."

I abandon the laptop and climb onto the bed, crawling toward him.

He watches me approach with a curious smile. "What happened to finishing the—"

I cut off his words with a hard kiss, followed by the slowest, deepest one I've ever given anyone, dragging it out as long as possible, hoping he somehow feels how hard I've fallen for him.

When I finally break away to see the tender look in his

eyes, I think I must have succeeded. His fingertips brush my hair off my face and then he pulls me down into a kiss with as much intensity. It escalates quickly, until we become a mess of frantic mouths and wandering fingers, the worry of Cassie coming home or Mark checking on us the farthest thing from my mind.

CHAPTER
TWENTY-THREE

Dear Julia,

I'm in love. I know I said I was before, but now I know for certain. I've waited the obligatory amount of time (it's been a month since the fair, and though we didn't get together that night, we got together that night). This is not teenaged infatuation. This is not raging hormones—well, there's definitely that, too. I finally got the nerve to put my hand down Emmett's pants and I nearly got caught by Mark. He moves a lot faster up the stairs than Cassie ...

But I know, without a doubt, this thing I'm feeling is love.

I told Emmett about the prom joke gone horribly wrong. Remember how I swore I'd never tell anyone? Well, Emmett knows now and he doesn't hate me. In fact, I think telling him has brought us that much closer.

Dr. C. said a day would eventually come when I felt like I could move on. I think I'm there.

~AJ

"See you later, Cass!" Emmett hollers.

"Yeah. Bye," she says dismissively, intensely focused on her locker combination.

Emmett slings his arm over my shoulders as we walk along the hall toward our lockers. "I'm *so* tired," he groans.

"Aww ... Was running with me too hard for you this morning?" I tease with a mock-pout. The sky was murky when we met on the driveway at seven, donning toques and vests. Hope for a mild fall is waning. Halloween is tomorrow and Uncle Merv was grumbling about snow flurries in the forecast.

I get a playful poke to the ribs in return, and then Emmett pulls me into his side with a smile.

I can't wait to kiss those lips with abandon again.

We're almost at my locker when Cassie calls out my name. "AJ!"

I turn to see her galloping down the hallway, a stuffed dog in one hand, a piece of paper in the other.

I frown. Cassie never leaves her locker like this. Her routine is clear—empty her bag, go to her community class.

"AJ! I'm going to prom!" she squeals, a wide smile plastered across her face.

"What are you talking about, Cassie?" Emmett asks carefully.

I feel her words as surely as a punch to my stomach.

She shoves the card into his hand. "Zach asked me to prom! And he gave me this! It looks just like Roger Dodger!"

Emmett's face turns to stone as he scans the card.

Meanwhile, I'm close to losing my breakfast on my shoes.

"Where did you get this, Cassie?"

"It was in my locker." Her eyes veer behind Emmett. "Oh, *hi*, Zach. I mean, *Farmer*." She giggles, oblivious to the tension radiating off her brother.

"Hey." He strolls up. "I heard my name. What's going on?"

Emmett's teeth are clenched as he shoves the card into his friend's hand.

Zach scowls as he reads it, whispering softly, "Who did this?"

Emmett's eyes dart to me, and all I can manage is a fast and furious headshake. I would *never* do that to her.

But it means someone at Eastmonte found out. It's too coincidental to be anything else. And I can guess who that person is.

The hallway is spinning as a crowd forms around us, watching the unfolding commotion.

Cassie's once-brilliant smile has taken on a guarded hue, as her eyes flicker from Emmett to Zach to me. "Cassie ...," Emmett says quietly, gently, though his eyes are brimming with rage. His throat bobs with a hard swallow. "This isn't from Zach. Someone played a joke on you."

"It's not?" She peers at Emmett's best friend, whose jaw is clenched. "Oh. Okay." She smiles and gives a little nod as it sinks in.

As she takes in the crowd of faces now watching intently, a range of amusement to pity to horror in their expressions.

As her face turns the deepest red I think I've ever seen someone's face turn.

"Okay." She keeps nodding and smiling.

As fat, silent tears stream down her cheeks in rivulets. Cassie's the only person I've ever seen cry like that— without making a sound. Somehow it's more disconcerting to witness than a sobbing mess.

"Well, it's a good thing I was going to see if you'd go with me, Little Harty." Zach clears his throat and strolls over to put his arm around her shoulders in a friendly, comforting way.

Cassie peers up at him. "You were?"

"Yeah! It's just a few months early. I was going to wait to ask, but now you know. Come on, let's get you back to your class. We've got tons of time to talk about it."

A smile slowly stretches across Cassie's face as she nods and wipes at her cheeks, her furtive gaze darting from face to face around us. "Yeah. Okay." She giggles.

And for Cassie, I breathe a small sigh of relief. Zach has truly swooped in to save the day.

Someone in the crowd cheers and then a round of applause quickly follows.

"Zach!" Emmett calls out. They share a long, hard look and then Zach nods once.

"I'll get her back to class." He leads Cassie away.

Emmett moves straight for me. "Does Keen or Moretti know what happened to you?"

I shake my head, my eyes darting around. The crowd is dispersing quickly, the excitement over.

"Look ... I know you don't want to talk about it, but we need to report this. It's obvious Holly found out and wanted to get under your skin."

"Whatever. It backfired." Maybe if I tell myself enough, it will be. I need time to think, to figure out a way to shut her up.

"I think I like Wiser better than Jones."

Blood rushes to my ears as I slowly turn to face Holly's smug face.

"Gee ... A girl named *Aria* from a school in Calgary with a *llama* for a school mascot? It took me, like, an hour to find a student who knew you. Bennett Ackerman says hi, by the way." There's a wicked gleam in her eye. "You have some *dirty* secrets, AJ. I was *not* expecting that."

"*Don't*, Holly. You're in enough shit already," Emmett warns in an icy tone.

"I don't know what you're talking about," she says sweetly. "I didn't do anything wrong."

"Uh, how about that prank you just pulled on Cassie? You know her combination lock, and the whole dog thing, and that she has a crush on Zach."

"Have fun trying to prove it." She glances around at the lingering students. I swear, they're like sharks charging for a drop of blood in the water when it comes to drama. "Maybe you should ask your girlfriend," she says loudly. "She's the one who likes to play cruel prom jokes on people."

Oh God. The nausea is back.

The first bell rings, but no one makes a move. Where are the teachers? Where is McNair? Why aren't they stopping this?

"What's wrong with you?" Emmett yells. "Are you seriously doing this just because we broke up and I'm dating her?"

She lifts her chin. "No, I'm doing this because you deserve to know the truth about the kind of person you're dating now," she parrots the words I once said to her, almost verbatim. I should've known that would come back to bite me in the ass.

"I already know what happened, Holly."

Holly's shapely eyebrows arch. "So, you're okay with the fact that your girlfriend drove a girl to kill herself?"

Oh God.

I squeeze my eyes shut for a long moment. When I open them, Emmett's deep brown eyes are on me.

"What is she talking about, Aria?" He asks slowly.

"I didn't lie," I whisper, silently pleading for him to believe me. *I just made you believe a different truth.*

Holly folds her arms across her chest. "I'd tell you to ask Julia Morrow for her side of the story, but she OD'd after Aria humiliated her in school."

"That's not *exactly* how it happened." My voice is nothing more than a hoarse whisper.

"But you said ..." Realization sparks in Emmett's eyes as he no doubt replays the story I told him the other night, only from another angle.

The one where I'm not the victim.

"I can't believe you." Emmett's expression is filled with disbelief and aversion. He spins on his heels and strolls down the hall with his backpack, past McNair, without saying a word.

Emmett's never going to talk to me again.

And that's probably what I deserve.

"And *you* wanted to make *me* look bad in front of Emmett. Well ..." Holly's face twists with bitter triumph.

Only then do I feel the steady stream of hot tears running down my cheeks. "How could you do that to Cassie? Me? Fine! I would have deserved it. But *Cassie?*" Who has only ever been kind to Holly.

A flash of something like pain—or guilt—flickers in her big blue eyes, but then it's gone and her eyes are cold and hard again. "Whatever. Zach is taking her like I knew he would. She'll be fine," Holly scoffs, dismissing Cassie's feelings as if they're trivial, as if she's incapable of having them.

I don't even realize that my fist is flying until it crashes into Holly's nose.

I PICK at a loose thread on the sleeve of my sweater. If I don't stop soon, I'll ruin it.

"Assaulting another student is an automatic suspension." Mr. Keen's squinty eyes narrow into tiny slits as he studies me intently. "What reason did you feel you had for hitting Holly Webber?"

Because she's the anti-Christ? I bite my tongue before that slips out.

Ms. Moretti sits beside him, her brow furrowed with worry as she waits for my answer.

We're in a small conference room beside Keen's office. There's nothing in here but a round table with four chairs, an oversized clock that ticks too loudly, and a framed School Conduct poster on the wall directly across from me. The room overlooks the visitor parking lot, which means I'll see exactly when my mother pulls in.

Out of everything, I'm dreading that part most of all.

"I believe there has been some ongoing tension between Holly and Aria," Moretti offers. "It likely has to do Emmett Hartford."

"So, this is over a *boy*." Keen may as well roll his eyes for the annoyance in his voice.

"No, it's about Holly being a jerk and a bully and getting away with it for too long."

They exchange glances and I can almost hear the unspoken words. *We're finally getting somewhere.*

"What did Holly do to you, Aria?" Moretti asks.

"It's not what she did to me. It's what she did to Cassie Hartford." I explain the joke prom invitation.

"And you know for a fact that Holly was behind that?"

"Yeah."

"How?"

I stretch the fingers of my right hand. Nothing feels broken but my knuckles are swelling. The school nurse said she'd be by with an ice pack but that was fifteen minutes ago. I guess a bruised hand is less critical than a nose gushing blood.

"Because I used to be like her."

I CHECK the wall clock as Moretti pushes the blinds apart with two fingers to squint at the parking lot. "She was in Toronto when I called. She should be here soon."

That's right. Mom and Mick were looking at something for the bathrooms. Vanities or something.

Mr. Keen left five minutes ago to meet with Holly and her parents, a notepad listing the chain of events that led to this morning under his arm and a deep scowl of disapproval on his face. It first appeared when I played them the video of Holly in the bathroom and deepened as each plot point of the rest of the story was revealed—the ensuing threat, the "accidental tripping," the cookie fiasco, the SWF Eats Instagram account, and the final straw: the prom joke.

I left nothing out.

"I told you that I like to know about my students." Ms.

Moretti settles into her chair again and clasps her hands in front of her. "I was curious about you, about why you quit cross-country after ninth grade, that sort of thing ... so I spoke to your old guidance counselor, Ms. Forester."

The stomach-clenching reaction I'd expect to feel hearing that doesn't come. Probably because I've already confessed to everything. "When?"

"About two weeks ago."

I was right that day she started asking questions. "What'd she say?"

Ms. Moretti pauses for a long moment. "Boy, that woman needs to retire, am I right?"

The answer is so unexpected—and so on point—I burst out laughing, the simple act lifting some of the weight from my shoulders. "She had these printed one-page calendars on the wall in her office, for each year until retirement—2022, I think? There had to be, like, six years on there and she X'd off each day with a red Sharpie."

"Probably not the best person to have in that role, then." Ms. Moretti sighs. "She told me all about Julia Morrow. The video that started it. The joke that ended it."

I nod, focusing intently on the ice pack against my knuckles. I'd much rather have a bag of frozen peas. "There were a bunch of us in on the prom joke. Not that that makes it okay." My best friend, Denise, and three other friends who didn't like Julia either. We'd all gone to the same small elementary school together, so naturally we clung to each other as we navigated this new, daunting world of high school—of unfamiliar faces and pecking orders. I can't even say if the dislike for Julia Morrow was already there before the dubbed video she made of me. All I do remember is my friends' fierce loyalty and desire to avenge me afterward.

The prom joke was actually Denise's idea but I readily

jumped. At the time, I thought I was so lucky to have such good friends. Only after did I see us for what we really were —a pack of rabid wolves, feeding off each other's innate ugliness.

"We didn't know her." We didn't know that she had a learning disability—not a serious one, but one that had fed the chip she wore on her shoulder and a steady cloud of depression. We didn't know that there was a thick folder from Children's Services attached to her address, thanks to years of alcoholism and verbal abuse from her family. We didn't know—but we suspected—that Julia didn't have a single person she could call a friend, that she could talk to.

Julia was just the sour-faced girl who lived in a ramshackle house by the train tracks in town, who came to school in cheap clothes and greasy hair. She was the one who went after me for talking to the guy she was crushing hard on, and in our eyes, she deserved all the rumors spinning, all the laughter, the rejection.

And then she killed herself.

"And she didn't know you, either." Ms. Moretti's face fills with sympathy. "Ms. Forester sent me the video that Julia made and let float around, of you talking to that boy."

I shouldn't be surprised that they'd kept a record of that. "It came out about a month after I found out that my dad had this *secret* family." I went from a semi-obscure ninth grader to a punch line overnight, while my family was falling apart.

"I'll bet those daddy-issue jokes she made hit you pretty hard."

"I assumed she somehow knew what was going on. It felt like an attack."

And so I struck back, again and again, with the help of my loyal friends. My home had splintered and I had no control over it. But making Julia pay for using it against me made me feel better.

Ironically, everything she dubbed into that video likely stemmed from her own family issues.

Things changed swiftly after Julia Morrow killed herself. Students who freely joined in on the ostracizing, on the "Julia Morrow has scabies, pass it on" type rumors—many that my friends and I hadn't even started—were suddenly weeping for this girl who had been bullied and killed herself. We were suspended for two days, for the prom-proposal joke, but that's as far as our official punishment went.

That's when the unofficial punishment began. It started with a private message in my filtered IG folder, telling me I'm a bitch. It quickly escalated to dozens of messages a day, calling me everything from ugly to skank to whore. Anonymous notes were stuffed into my locker, one of them giving me instructions on the best ways to kill myself. All little acts of retribution, from people who felt justified.

The final straw was the day someone gave me a shove as I was climbing the stairs. I tumbled. Fortunately, all I ended up with was a broken ankle.

Unfortunately, my scattered things—along with the note on how to kill myself—were picked up by a teacher, who then showed it to the principal, who then called my mother.

She had no idea what was going on. I hadn't told her.

"I still think about her a lot. Julia, I mean." About all the things I should have said and done. I wasn't fake like Holly is; I didn't pick on kids for the sake of picking on them. But that doesn't mean I was any better than her, the way I behaved, bolstered by my friends or not.

"You still feel guilty." It's not a question.

I nod, my eyes stinging with tears. "I would do *anything* to change to past. But I can't."

"No, you can't. You can only learn from your mistakes." Ms. Moretti sighs heavily. "The school suspension will likely be for two days. And I have no choice but to remove you from the cross-country team. Both you and Holly."

I nod, studying my hands. "I get it."

"I wish you had come to me right away, Aria. Maybe we could've avoided all of this."

"I went to Ms. Forester once." I grimace at the memory. "She wasn't much help." She told me to delete my social media accounts and reflect on why people might be doing this to me. In short, she told me I deserved it.

And I believed her.

I still believe her.

A knock sounds and the door creaks open.

I take a deep breath before I turn to face the shame and disappointment in my mother's eyes.

CHAPTER
TWENTY-FOUR

Dᴇᴀʀ Jᴜʟɪᴀ,

I lied to you before. You know, when I told you that Emmett knew what happened in Calgary. Well, technically I lied to ME, seeing as you can't read this. At least, I don't think you can, but maybe you are somewhere nearby. Maybe you're haunting me. I'd deserve that, wouldn't I?

Dr. C. warned me to not lie in here and I know why now— I actually fooled myself for a second there into thinking all would be okay. But the truth is, I'd rather be you than who I used to be, because that girl? I don't know her anymore. I don't want to know her anymore. I wish I could erase her. Julia, you have no idea how much I wish I could go back and change what I did to you. I may not have realized that until people started harassing me, but walk a mile in someone else's shoes and all that, right? Emmett asked if you ever apologized for making that shitty video of me talking to Jeff Humphrey. Did you ever wish you had? I don't know how much it would have helped, to be honest. I was in a dark place then. But now? Julia, if you apologized to me now, I would accept it and move on.

Another truth? I'd punch Holly all over again for what she did to Cassie, and not feel bad about it. So, does that mean I haven't really changed at all? Is new Aria just old Aria but with a shred of empathy and misfit friends?

Mom has taken away my phone, canceled plans for my driver's license test, and booked an appointment with Dr. Zanelli, my new therapist. Dr. Z. from here on in. Beyond that, she said she needed time to think, so she sent me to my room and told me not to come out until Murphy needs a walk. But I just watched her head down the sidewalk with him so ...

Maybe I can just hide in here forever.

~AJ

MY STOMACH IS a ball of nerves as I trek past Emmett's Santa Fe and up the walkway toward the Hartfords' front door, Murphy hobbling beside me.

Cassie is the first to the door. "Oh, hi, AJ!" she exclaims. It's as if the drama with Holly never happened. But I know better than to assume that.

"Hey, Cassie, how are you?"

"Good. Well ..." Her face scrunches up. "Not so good. My mom knows about the cookie with drugs that Adam gave me and that you punched Holly in the nose."

What must Heather and Mark think about me now?

"Was there a lot of blood?"

I nod. "There was."

"Is Holly okay?"

"I'm sure she'll be fine."

"Yeah. Hi, Murphy!" She turns her attention to him. Though, I note, I got a few minutes first. That's progress.

Footfalls pound down the stairs and a minute later Emmett appears, his jaw clenched as he takes me in.

I shrink into my jacket under that gaze. As much as I came to check on Cassie, he's the real reason I came. But now that I'm facing him, I want to go home and delay the inevitable. "Hey."

"Hey." He chews his bottom lip a moment. "Cass, go help Mom. I need to talk to AJ alone."

"About how much trouble you're in?"

He sighs heavily. "And other things."

"Bye, Murph! See you later!" She waves and then strolls off, her heels heavy against the floor.

"Give me a sec." Emmett disappears to the mud room for his coat and shoes.

I lead Murphy toward the row of shrubs at the edge of the Hartford property. Next to Uncle Merv's rosebush, this is his favorite pee spot.

Emmett meets me on the sidewalk, drawing his zipper closed against the night chill.

"How's your hand?"

I peer at the red knuckles. "Not broken, at least."

"Why'd you hit her?"

"For what she did to Cassie."

He nods. And then a tiny smirk curls his lips. "Wish I'd stayed long enough to see that."

I smile. At least he's making jokes.

The amusement evaporates just as quickly. "You lied to me. You let me think that you tried to kill yourself."

"I'm sorry." What more is there to say?

He smooths a hand over his face. "Maybe I shouldn't have pushed you to talk in the first place."

"You would've found out either way, thanks to Holly." Maybe knowing part of it, albeit skewed, helped soften the blow. "I hate the things I did, Emmett. I'm trying to get far away from that person. That's why we moved here." So I could start over. So I had a fair shot of becoming someone better.

His eyes wander from his shoes to the grass, to the street beyond, avoiding me at all costs, it would seem. "I looked up Julia Morrow."

I figured he would. So has half of Eastmonte Secondary, I'm sure.

"Pretty shit thing to happen to her."

Now it's my turn to avoid his gaze. Is he picturing Cassie in Julia's place right now? "She started it by making this horrible video of me around the time that my dad left us and ..." My voice drifts. I won't make excuses for what I did. Not to Emmett.

"So, when you said that you shut down your Instagram and all that because people were harassing you, was that even true?"

"Yeah. That happened. Because of what *I* did." *Which is why I never deserved your pity.*

Uncomfortable silence settles between us. It was only this morning that we went for a run, that he had his arms coiled around me. That things were good and we were perfect and happy.

It feels like so long ago now.

He clears his throat, and when he speaks again, his voice is a touch huskier. "I'll present the first five slides for our project and you can do the last five. We're pretty much already done so ... no need to get together again over it. And I'm sure Jen will be happy to swap desks with me."

A painful lump flares in my throat. "So ... that's it?" I

was expecting this but now that it's happening, I don't know that I can handle it.

He studies his shoes. "I'm gone next summer anyway, Aria. And this year is too important for me to screw it up by ..." His voice drifts.

By getting mixed up with someone like me. I duck my head to hide the rim of tears that are welling, but they quickly escape, rolling down my cheeks. "What about getting to school and back?"

"I'll still drive you. And if you still want to walk with Cassie, that's fine. Unless you were only doing it because of me—"

"No." I let him see my tears now, because he needs to see the sincerity in my eyes. "That's not why."

His jaw tightens. "Prove it. But it won't change us."

"I know." Emmett and I are finished.

"So ...," he begins backing away, "I guess I'll see you around. Good luck with regionals."

"I got kicked off the team."

He nods slowly. "That's too bad. You would have done well."

I watch Emmett disappear into his house.

And then I walk home, counting all the ways I screwed up.

"Well ... on the plus side, no one's going to mess with you." Jen slams her locker shut, adjusting her Day of the Dead shirt in honor of November 1. It was Halloween last night— and the two-year anniversary of discovering my father's secret family. I sat on my window ledge and watched the children stroll up our doorstep for trick or treat.

"Is that what all these weird looks are this morning?" Fear, because apparently I broke Holly's nose?

"No, those are likely because you came in with Emmett."

But not *with* him. He had the decency to not make a point of putting a twenty-foot gap between us when we walked down the hall. I felt the distance all the same.

I kept my head down as I strolled into school, after taking the back seat in Emmett's SUV. Cassie kept asking if I was okay, the sudden change in seating arrangements—in our routine—jarring to her. Otherwise, she was the same Cassie—greeting every staff member by name, and then marching to her locker to unload her things.

The first bell goes.

"I'm sitting with you again, if that's okay?"

"You mean, I don't get to listen to Sleepy Steve snore in my ear anymore?" Jen smiles and softly nods. "Yeah. Of course."

I take a deep breath and steal a glance at Emmett. He's alone by his locker, fumbling through his textbooks. My heart aches.

This is going to be a *long* semester.

CHAPTER
TWENTY-FIVE

"Grab that end, will ya?" Uncle Merv juts his wobbly skinned jaw toward the burlap, flapping in the cool breeze. "Shoulda done this weeks ago." He guides the winter wrap around Aunt Connie's prized rosebush to help protect it from the coming snow.

I don't have the heart to tell him that I'm afraid Murphy has killed it, if it had any hope of survival to begin with, and so I bite my tongue and quietly help feed the cloth.

"Hi, Uncle Merv! Hi, AJ!" Cassie shouts. She's about to climb into Heather's car.

Uncle Merv pauses in his task to offer her a smile and a wave, something he always has for her, no matter what mood he's in.

Heather waves back, and then ducks into her car quickly. She has cooled toward me, though she's cordial enough. But I sense her watchful eye through the curtains when Cassie and I are walking up the sidewalk after school, and when she drives us to the animal shelter for our volunteer hour.

I know what she's searching for—any reason why she shouldn't trust me around her daughter.

I can't blame her.

All I can do is prove her wrong.

"That girl could talk an ear off a goat." Uncle Merv chuckles and hands me the staple gun "You know how to use one of these?"

"I think I can figure it out."

"Just aim and point. Down there. Not at me."

I hide my eye roll and begin punching staples through the burlap to secure it.

"Yeah ... I still remember this boy named Buckey O'Donnell, back when I was in school. Gosh, that would have been"—he scratches his forehead—"sixty-five, almost seventy years ago. He was a strange kid. A giant. Six feet by the time he was twelve, could barely read, couldn't add pennies to make four cents for the longest time. But he was a gentle giant. Everyone had a good time pokin' fun at that kid, myself included. Even the teachers told him he was stupid."

I cringe. "That's *horrible*." Suddenly Ms. Forester doesn't sound so bad.

"People didn't understand 'different' back then. And Buckey, he was different." Uncle Merv tugs on a corner of the burlap and then points to where he wants me to secure it.

"What happened to him?"

"Don't know. But of all the people I've met in my life, Buckey O'Donnell is a name that sits heavy on my soul ever since Cassie came along. She's made me regret how I treated him. Not that she's like he was but, you know, she's different, too." His jowls lift with his smile. "She has a way of lighting up a room just by walking into it. I pity the person who doesn't see it."

"Yeah, I know. I see it." I can't help the tone of accusation. Why is he saying this? And why is Uncle Merv telling me stories about Buckey O'Donnell?

Cloudy eyes turn to me. "I know you do. Which is why I know you're going to be okay, Aria." He hobbles around to inspect my stapling job. "Now it's your job to help other people see it."

"How?"

"Probably by setting a good example and not breaking a girl's nose," he mutters, heading up the porch steps.

"Next is"—my heart pounds as McNair shifts her reading glasses to scan her list—"Aria and Emmett. Their topic is bullying." She gives me a small nod. I'm sure she's heard my story. Or at least one version of it. Who knows how many versions are floating around within these walls by now, weeks after Holly's vengeful stunt put me under the school's microscope.

Someone in the class coughs as I stand, and I catch the muffled "ironic" beneath it.

I ignore that taunt, much as I've ignored all the comments and looks I've caught in the hallways over the last few weeks, and make my way to the front of the class, suddenly lightheaded.

Emmett unfolds from his seat on the opposite side of the class, where he has taken to sitting since we broke up, and that now-constant ache in my chest swells. I feel it every time I think about him, every time I see him. I've tried my best to keep my head high, to smile at Cassie like nothing's wrong on our morning rides, to hide my flinches whenever she mentions his name.

Thank God he hasn't started dating anyone yet. The day I see him with his arms around another girl will be the day that finally breaks me.

Aside from a body shifting in a chair and a few low whispers, there isn't a sound in the room as we meet at the front of the class. Everyone knows what happened between us.

He peers down at me with those dark-brown eyes that I could stare into for hours. "You have the file, right?" he asks, for the second time since we left his driveway. Aside from our morning rides into school, we don't talk anymore.

We might as well be strangers.

A reality that hurts more, not less, with each passing day, as my regret bubbles every time I see him, every time my fingers itch to reach for him.

I hold the flash drive up by way of answer and then plug it in to the port, my stomach churning with nerves. I pull up the presentation I consolidated last night, after he emailed me his five slides.

Emmett turns to face the class. He takes a deep breath and rubs his hands down the sides of his jeans, and then says, "We're here to talk about causes and effects of bullying on today's teenagers. I'm gonna cover the first five slides, and then Aria will jump in to do hers."

He begins to speak, and his words and voice pull me back to those days in his bedroom, sprawled out on the floor, planning this very presentation that I dreaded—that he had no idea I was dreading because he didn't know me. He didn't know the girl I used to be.

I only let him know the one I've been so desperate to become.

"In this day and age, cyberbullying has become one of the most prevalent avenues for spreading gossip. Social media platforms like Instagram and Twitter and text-messaging apps allow people to target their victims from behind a screen, sometimes anonymously."

My eye catches Holly's at the same time that hers shift to mine.

She has the decency to avert her gaze to her desk.

If there is any good that came from the war between us, it's that Holly can't hide her vicious mean streak behind a sweet voice and fluttering lashes anymore. People know better now. She earned herself two days' suspension for the prom-date joke and was kicked off the cross-country team, too. Add that punishment to losing Emmett and my banged-up knee for her broken nose, and we're about even, I guess.

I still wonder, though, what made Holly the way she is. With Julia, it wasn't too hard to connect the dots afterward. But Holly's smart and beautiful, and I heard she has two parents who love her. I asked Dr. Z what she thought. The tall, willowy blonde therapist didn't have an answer for me, other than to say that having intelligence and beauty doesn't equate to having tolerance and empathy.

I've thought about that a lot since. I've wondered if the old Aria and her friends had had more tolerance and empathy to begin with, would she have made different choices, too?

"Okay, AJ's up next."

I take a deep breath and flip to the first of my slides.

Surprise flashes in Emmett's eyes and then he frowns at me in a "What are you doing?" way. A low murmur buzzes around the classroom.

I clear my throat. Aside from conversations with Dr. C., I've never actually talked about this out loud. I sure as hell have never stood in front of a classroom and divulged my deepest, darkest secrets, from beginning to end. "I'm going to talk about what happened to a fourteen-year-old girl named Julia Morrow, and how it could've been stopped." I make a point of meeting Holly's blue eyes, which are filled with a mix of wariness and curiosity.

"Before I became Aria Jones, I was Aria Wiser." I take a deep breath. "And somewhere along the line, Aria Wiser became a bully without even realizing it."

UNCLE MERV's snore is a deep, rhythmic rumble carrying through the quiet house when I come down at eight that night in my running gear.

My mom is stretched out on the couch with her law textbooks. Murphy, lying next to her slippers on the floor, merely lifts an eyelid.

"How can you study listening to that?"

"It's oddly soothing," she says, pulling the curtain back with a frown. "It's snowing, Aria."

"I know, but I just ... need to run." To clear my head. I haven't been motivated to drag myself out of bed in the mornings lately. It's cold and dark and going to Miller's Park without Emmett is too painful. But, come the quiet evenings, I find the urge to get out, to snake along the side streets, getting familiar with this town that has become my home, keeping myself busy. Last night I ran almost ten kilometers.

She nods slowly. "By the way, Ms. McNair phoned me earlier today, about your presentation."

"Did she say if she was going to knock marks for going over time?" The rules were specific and I went over by at least five minutes. I don't want Emmett punished for that.

Mom's lips curve into a tiny, amused smile. "No, she didn't mention anything about that. Actually, she said it was the most impactful presentation a student has ever given in her class. She said even the boy who can't keep awake through first period was listening."

I study my shoes. *Probably because I nearly cried.*

"She thought you were incredibly brave for standing up there like that, and she asked me if I could convince you to give the presentation again at the bullying awareness assembly on Thursday."

"In front of the whole school?" A wave of nausea floods me.

"I told her I'd mention it to you, but that it was your choice." Mom's shrewd gaze studies me a moment. "But I think you should do it, even if it's terrifying. I think you need to do it."

"I'll think about it." Maybe she's right. Walking back to my desk after giving my presentation, I felt lighter than when I'd stood up at the beginning. Perhaps each time I tell my cautionary tale to someone else—the real, ugly version—I'll find just a bit more peace in the process, knowing that it could help the Julias and the Cassies, and even the Buckey O'Donnells of the world.

"Be careful. It's slippery out there," my mom warns. "Take a hat. And stay on the sidewalk."

I make a point of pulling my knit toque on in front of her. Time is slowly repairing the damage I did to our relationship, but it's going to be a long time before Mom trusts me again. At least she gave me back my phone.

I shudder against the cold air, taking a few moments to admire the falling snow as I stretch my hamstrings on our front lawn. The flakes are fat and light, clinging to the bushes and trees, coating the ground in a thin white blanket. If this keeps up, everything will be white by morning.

I steal a glance next door as I always do every time I step out of our house. The porch lights are on and all three cars are in the driveway. The light in Emmett's room that over-looks the street glows bright. A pang stirs in my chest as I picture Emmett sprawled on his bed with his textbook. I quickly push it aside, tuck my earbuds in, and take off at a slow pace down the sidewalk. Those fond thoughts will only weigh me down with regret.

Is it normal for a sixteen-year-old to carry this much regret in her short life already?

I turn right at the end of our street and head toward Mower's street, admiring the houses already decorated for Christmas. It's almost December, so I guess it's time. Mom mentioned Mick offering to help us string lights this coming weekend.

They've been having a lot of "It's just pasta" dinners lately. Last weekend she tried to sneak back in at 5 a.m. after a date night. I think they're having more than "just pasta" now.

My lungs are burning with the cold by the time I've lapped the neighborhood, and the next one over, and am heading back. The snow is falling heavier now, and I slow my pace a touch to avoid slipping, but also to admire the beautiful, quiet white night. It reminds me of a snow globe, with a single set of headlights easing along the street, a canopy of trees, and a lone figure in the distance.

As I keep going, I realize it's another jogger, and they're heading my way. Not long after that, I recognize the tight form and the fitted white-and-blue toque hugging his head.

Dread builds as Emmett gets closer. Will he at least say hi on his way past? Will he do more than give me a fleeting glance? Is he wishing he turned right instead of left back there?

My eyes sting with those thoughts and, as much as I try to keep my tears from spilling, by the time the distance between us has closed, fat, hot tears streak down my frozen cheeks.

Emmett doesn't run past me with a hi or a glance. He comes to a stop in front of me and, without saying a word, pulls me into his body, his strong arms wrapping around my back like a cocoon.

I sink into his warmth as the first sob rattles my chest. The soft thrum of music pulses through my earbuds, and regret for all my bad decisions overwhelms my heart.

The front of his down jacket is smeared with frozen tears by the time I finally break free, wiping at my cheeks and thoroughly embarrassed for breaking down on him in the middle of the quiet street.

He gently slips one bud from my ear and holds it up to his for a moment. "Well, no wonder. That's depressing music."

I laugh, and even though it's weak, it feels good to laugh with Emmett again. "So, you run at night now, too?"

"No." He offers me a dimpled smile. "Your mom said you were out here."

He came out here for me?

I finally gather the courage to hold his gaze. His eyes are shining brighter than they have when they've touched me lately.

"I didn't have a chance to talk to you after class today, seeing as you bolted out of there."

I smile sheepishly. "Yeah. I needed a few minutes on my own." I hid in the bathroom stall and was five minutes late for math.

"I ... that took a lot of guts, what you did today."

"Can't really pretend it didn't happen anymore, right?" And being a better person doesn't mean hiding from or lying about who I used to be.

"So much of what you talked about is shit that happens in school every day, Aria. The gossip, the text messages, the comments. People do it *all the time.* Everyone does it. I've done it. Doesn't make it okay but ... I can see how it spiraled out of control like that."

I shrug. "I figured, if my story makes people stop and think about what their words could do to a person, then I should tell it, right?"

"Right." He nods slowly, his eyes roaming my face.

"I miss you." I don't mean to say it aloud, but it slips out anyway.

He offers me a sad smile. "I miss you, too, AJ."

But you screwed it all up.

I study my snow-covered running shoes as another prickly lump forms in my throat, a fresh wave of tears threatening.

"I don't think you're Aria Wiser anymore."

"And yet somehow I ended up at war with another girl, and it started over a boy, *again.*" I laugh, though it's not at all funny. "So, who am I, really?"

"Look at me." His jaw tenses as his thumb catches the single tear that falls. "You're the girl who charmed a crusty old carnival operator into giving my sister an extra try. You're the girl who couldn't leave an old, unwanted dog in the shelter so you brought him home without asking." A sly smile touches his lips. "You're the girl who will sit in the cafeteria with Jen Ricci no matter what's she's wearing."

"That green Grinch sweater yesterday almost broke me," I admit sheepishly.

He chuckles, and his thumb grazes my cheek again. "I like that girl. A lot." He takes a deep breath. "So, do you think we could start over, from the very beginning?"

My heart skips two beats. *What's he saying?* "Do you mean, like 'Hi, this is Aria with the green face who likes dogs and hates tomatoes' start over?"

His head tips back with his deep laughter.

EPILOGUE

"Aria! They're all waiting outside!"

I check myself one last time in the full-length mirror that Mick installed on the outside of the closet he built me, and then grab my clutch and my heels and head downstairs.

Mom beams up at me from the landing, her eyes watering as they drag the length of the A-line, floor-length silver gown we bought in April, after Emmett asked me to prom.

"You look beautiful, hon."

I can't help but twirl the moment my toes touch the landing.

"You sure you won't be cold? Your back is awfully ... *bare.*"

"I'll be fine."

She fusses with one of my shoulder straps. Everything about the dress is perfect—from the V neckline and the lace bodice to the satin material.

A sad smile touches her lips. "When did my little girl grow up ..."

"Don't worry, I'm sure I'll still do plenty of stupid, childish things."

She sighs with exasperation. "Come on. Heather's waiting outside with her fancy camera."

A nervous flutter stirs in my stomach as I step out into the warm June evening. The stretch SUV limo we ordered is waiting in the cul-de-sac for our group of twelve—mostly Emmett's hockey friends plus dates, but also Jen and Richard, who decided to go together as "friends"—currently milling on our front lawn. Heather tests the lighting of various angles with her camera.

I see Emmett before he sees me, and it gives me a few seconds to admire him without shame—his masculine profile, his stylish hair, how his tailored charcoal suit hugs his form—before he turns.

His lips part as his dark-brown eyes drift over my dress. I catch the hard swallow.

I love the way he looks at me.

Zach lets out a whistle. "Can't believe you stole her from me, man."

"Shut up," Emmett throws back, accentuating it with a playful shove.

"Okay, kids, I think we're ready!" Heather hollers, then frowns, searching behind her. "Where's Cassie? She was just here!"

"Hold on! Uncle Merv is just giving me something!"

I take the newly built and painted porch stairs down to the flagstone path that Mick installed last weekend to where Cassie stands next to Uncle Merv, grinning wide. The soft-pink tulle dress that we picked out is so Cassie—the floor-length skirt gives off a princess vibe, and the sleeveless lace top is fitted but modest. We spent the day together getting ready and so

328

far, she's managed to not rub off her eye makeup or muss her updo or pick off her nail polish, and she's on a strict water-only rule.

"Here." Uncle Merv passes Cassie a fuchsia rose bloom the size of my hand. "I cut the stem short because of all those damn thorns, but there's just enough there to hold for the pictures."

Cassie beams as she peers down at it in her grasp. "Aunt Connie would be happy."

"She sure would." Uncle Merv chuckles. "She would've loved to see you two dressed up tonight."

"Girls!" We look back in unison to find the lens aimed at us. Heather checks the digital screen, smiles with satisfaction, and then calls us over to the group.

"Here, you need one, too, Aria." Uncle Merv leans in to clip another bursting bloom. He weighed in forty pounds' lighter at his last doctor's appointment, according to my mom. While he has a ways to go, he's finally agreed to eat one plate of "rabbit food" for dinner every night.

"I can't believe the bush survived. Murphy must be watching over it." A sad smile touches my lips as I look at the stone marker beside it. We buried the old dog's ashes with the spring thaw. He died in his sleep one quiet day in January, lying on the floor next to Uncle Merv. Cassie wailed for about fifteen minutes—which I still prefer to her silent crying—and then asked Uncle Merv if she could bring him home another old dog.

"I'll admit, I was worried at first." Uncle Merv's wrinkled face furrows with concentration as he clips the few thorns on the short stem. I've never seen him handle something as gingerly as this bloom. "Any rose can succumb to rot, given the right conditions. But, with enough attention, it can come back better than before."

I get the feeling he's not really talking about the rosebush anymore.

I collect the flower with my thanks and pick my way over to Emmett, on tiptoes to keep from sinking into the grass.

"You look ..." He finishes the compliment with a kiss rather than a word.

A click sounds and we turn to find Heather taking a picture of us.

"Mom ..."

"You'll thank me," Heather says in a singsong voice, moving on to snap a picture of Cassie and Zach. I note the tear rolling down her cheek. Mark had a matching one, though he discreetly brushed it away.

I know *I'll* thank Heather for these pictures. I'll thank her while I'm plastering the ceiling above my bed with them, amongst the glow-in-the-dark stars that need to be replaced because they've lost their phosphors.

Emmett leaves in just over a month for college in Minnesota and I'm clinging to denial. I'm excited for him and sad for myself, and trying to be hopeful for *us*. We've said we're going to try the long-distance thing.

I don't know if we're just being fools.

What I do know is that I'm going to make the most of this last month together, which is why I've tucked a condom into my clutch for tonight.

"Okay, Aria, Cassie, both of you in front of our house," Heather instructs. "Arms around each other."

Cassie giggles and slides her arm around my waist, her body stiffening a touch even as she grins at me. Hope and excitement radiate off her and I find myself absorbing it. "We're best friends," she announces.

I return her smile. "Yeah, we are." And I wouldn't trade it for the world.

"Gosh, Merv, the blooms on that rosebush came back more beautiful than I've ever seen them," Heather says, peering at us through her camera lens.

"I think you're right." Uncle Merv catches my eye and winks at me.

Cassie bursts out in laughter. "That's because Murphy peed on it!"

ACKNOWLEDGMENTS

Our first daughter was supposed to be named Cassandra (Cassie for short.) We were set on the name until she was born. She didn't "look" like a Cassie, so we went with our second choice, one that suited her perfectly. But that name has never slipped my mind, and when I decided that I needed to write this story—about a girl with autism, a girl much like our daughter—I knew without a doubt that Cassie would come to life within these pages.

This was not an easy story for me to write and it likely wasn't an easy story for some of you to read. Maybe you've forgiven Aria. Maybe you're feeling conflicted and need time to warm up to her again. Maybe you outright hate her and think her past choices are unforgivable. Whatever your feelings may be, I hope you found reflective value in this tale of regret and redemption. While it is set in high school, I feel it's a story that everyone can relate to on some level, no matter what stage of your life you are in.

A special thanks to the following people:

Alison Renzetti, for tolerating my many texts about cross-country meets and chasing down the answers.

Sandra Cortez, for always giving me your honest, sound feedback, no matter what.

Amélie, Sarah, and Tami, for running my Facebook group and for being the best, most supportive readers a writer could ask for.

Hang Le, for turning my vague ideas into a stunning cover. You are a true talent.

Stacey Donaghy of Donaghy Literary Group, for always telling me that I'm a far better writer than I actually am. It's a good thing I'm far too critical of myself to ever develop a big head because of you. I feel like we've come full circle, with another indie novel about serious social issues.

Jennifer Sommersby, I always told myself I would work with you again. Thank you for polishing this manuscript with your expertise, your sharp eye, and your wit. Any lingering mistakes are my own (including any in these acknowledgments that I didn't send to you.)

Jennifer Armentrout, Karina Halle, Claire Contreras, Renee Carlino, Tarryn Fisher, Rebecca Donovan, Dina Silver, Rebecca Lilley, Anna Todd, Lauren Billings, Marissa Stapley, and Cora Carmack, for always being only a text or Skype call away, whether it be for a rant or a rave, or much needed advice.

Colleen Hoover, I'm in. #KeathandRaulforever

Paul, Lia, and Sadie, for living this life with me, with all its ups and downs, its joys and frustrations.

Lia ... thank you for being you, chocolate face and all.

ABOUT THE AUTHOR

K.A. Tucker writes captivating stories with an edge.

She is the internationally bestselling author of over thirty books, including Ten Tiny Breaths, The Simple Wild, and the Fate & Flame series, Until It Fades, Say You Still Love Me, and Keep Her Safe. Her books have been featured in national publications including USA Today, Globe & Mail, Suspense Magazine, Publisher's Weekly, Oprah Mag, and First for Women. Several books have been nominated for Goodreads Reader Choice awards.

K.A. Tucker lives outside of Toronto.

Learn more about K.A. Tucker and her books at katuckerbooks.com